Crocodile Girl

Crocodile Girl

Sam Omatseye

origami

Parrésia Publishers Ltd.

Origami Books is an imprint of Parresia Publishers Ltd

82, Allen Avenue, Ikeja, Lagos, Nigeria.
+2348154582178, +2348062392145
origami@parresia.com.ng
www.parresia.com.ng

ISBN: 978-978-54860-9-4

Printed in Nigeria by Parrésia Press

Prologue

When Jim Fallows arrived in Orogun village with Tara in search of Tim, he was haunted by the event that had happened a few years back, and he wondered if it accounted for his frenzy to investigate the Foresters. Maybe it was his projection of denial. Guilt, as he once told Tim, had its virtues. Tim did not hesitate to call him an interloper.

It happened in May 1975. Jim Fallows did not know how to say goodbye to his fellow passenger. He did not know how to look at him, or whether he should look at him. Rob Fallows's tale had shed an ambiguous light on dark regions of his memory.

"Okay Rob, it was nice meeting you," was Jim Fallows' polite way of telling Rob Fallows that he was glad the plane touched down right on time. Rob Fallows, on the other hand, was merely puzzled at a certain fidgety air around his fellow passenger. Jim unlocked the seat buckle while the plane was still taxiing. Then he made a false start at rising to his feet. His face betrayed a comedy of a half-smile and half-fear that might have been ominous if the plane was airborne and roiling in unruly clouds. Rob thought he was on a roll, reeling out ream after ream of the family tree, and waiting for Jim either to reinforce his story or unveil a new tree.

"Have a good one," Rob replied simply.

Jim was the first to express curiosity when, by a strange working of fate, Rob sat on the aisle seat and he on the window seat. It was a flight from Atlanta to Pensacola.

"I see that we share the same last name," Jim said, and Rob expressed superficial delight at the coincidence. Rob had met quite a few Fallows in his lifetime of about forty years, and he knew there was nothing to the name. Given the diversity of their history, quite a few American names were a corruption of their original. He had met a Fallows whose name had been chiselled out of a German name of about six syllables.

Barely ten minutes to landing, Jim wanted to know if his Fallows was related to a man he had met at college in Cincinnati. Rob said he did not know any Fallows in Cincinnati. He said all his Fallows resided in the south and California and he traced the name back to antebellum America.

"My parents told me our name was forced on us by a family that owned a big plantation near Savannah in Georgia," he began. He did not want to use the word slave in 1975 America. He went on to tell how the family, was once known as Ebulu, or Obulu – he was not sure which – had a baby girl with striking beauty. She bore a child for a master, and the boy was married into the family when he was barely twenty. He was so white he could pass for one.

Rob paused then and tried to impress his listener with a flourish of recollections, naming almost fifteen of the relatives in the family and explaining who they were and what they did during and after slavery. Those that received kindness. Those that were lashed to death. Those who shone as intellectuals in their own rights. Those that became pastors. One was an unsung inventor in the days of the cotton gin.

Rob was generous in his telling. As he spoke of the orator, so he revealed others like the fool, the sluggard, the trickster, the thief. A famously fat woman, in particular, was noted for the sonority of her insolence. Her name was Bev. Her treble tamed any choral rivalry in the church. She knew how to insult people, white or black, as though she sang. It at once disarmed and infuriated the plantation folks. But her womb was no less fecund. She birthed twelve children.

"I descended from her," Rob said. It was at this point that Jim's ears twitched.

"This woman…" said Jim

"Bev," cut in Rob.

"Did you say she had a dozen children?" asked Jim.

From his recollections of his family tree, Jim knew of a woman who had at least ten children and, true indeed, their plantation was near Savannah, and he also knew of a notorious female slave with a great voice. No one told him about her insults. He was not clear in his memory if the great voice and the at least ten children belonged to the same person. But he had heard enough.

Rob was one of those light-skinned Americans whose features were white enough to pass. Jim also knew that, in those days, his family married some fruits of interracial union to a cousin of the white Fallows to keep the race inviolate.

After disembarking from the plane, Jim walked far ahead of his fellow passenger and namesake. He thought he had been delivered from this tribulation of memory. But just before he stepped into the cab in Pensacola, Rob yelled out. "Not all of us bear Fallows now. Some bear Obulu and others Ebulu."

Jim smiled as he crumbled out of sight into the car.

chapter One

In the eyes of the villagers, Alero the juju girl cast her spell on Tim, the white visitor. She turned the bright young man into a *mumu*, her special fool.

At the snap of her fingers, so went the story, he would crawl blissfully into the jaws of a crocodile. Alero was the crocodile. She inherited those awful scales and ocean-ready glides of nightly omens from her mother. They knew the reptilian light in her eyes.

They heard her voice of an enchantress. By the same token, they knew she had baited the wrong person in the world.

If she wanted to fall in love, she should have cast her net else-where. Not with an American. Was it love or some sort of wiles and guiles of mischief? Prior to this, she had felled many quarries, big and small men, driven to the giddy wave of her witchcraft eyes. She had all the stealth and suggestions of a beast.

But you didn't joke around with those Americans, not when one of them was trapped in the obscure corner of the world – in the entrails of the African continent.

Very soon, the world would know, and his relatives would worry and trace their steps to the backwoods lair of Orogun village. How would they react once they found their son changed into a tanned and bemused romantic, in the dubious comfort of an African witch? What would all the venerated elders say? What wisdom would they latch on to?

The thing, though, was that the villagers did not know how to handle this. This juju girl had helped nurse this white man back to life after the episode of assaults from wild pigs. The beasts wanted to waste him and his friend, Itse, in the Forest of Silence, the lure of abomination. Itse was, as they were pleased to say, a son of the soil. It was Itse who steered him there from his American home. The only thing the villagers knew about him was that he followed their son over to Orogun village.

They did not go through the social rituals of interactions and minimal familiarities before the incident in the Forest of Silence. He was just a being, or a ghost, a mystery of flesh and face, as one of the villagers characterised him.

Only Itse knew Tim's purpose in the place. All they heard was that the man was doing research. That was a strange word even in translation. Chief Omona called it "resash". But once Itse broke it down and explained that he wanted to see the tomb of an *oyibo*, his ancestor, who was buried in the forest many generations back, it made sense.

But not immediately. Some of the Chiefs suspected mischief. When did an *oyibo* sneak into that forbidden fortress? The Chiefs were not altogether fair, and they knew it. They knew the forest was not always forbidden. They knew about the time, in the foggy past, when *oyibo* men came around with weapons and captured their folk and took them away through bush paths to sea shores, chained and hungry. They threw the human cargo on their boats and ferried them far away to their lands across the water. They knew, too, that some of their Chiefs could never claim innocence of the turbulent era when kin sold kin to greedy men in skins as light as walnut.

"If you have a different purpose let us know"? asked Chief Ti-etie in the Itsekiri language. They suspected at first that the *oyibo* was a man of medicine. They had heard that people from the *oyibo* land travelled to forests of the world to search for leaves to conquer death. But they had scored only smaller triumphs like cures for malaria and headaches.

The ancestor, claimed the *oyibo*, fulfilled his exploits in the giddy days of slavery and the slave trade. The elders then feigned understanding. This did not wipe out suspicion. It only mitigated anxiety. They would not tell the visitor that they were aware of the past when their fellow villagers became wares to powerful Chiefs and the foreigners who saw a meaty prize.

Itse was now in a coma, and only God knew if he would make it. Both of them were in a coma until they were rescued from the bowels of the forest where they took a hike in search of the ancient tomb.

The Forest of Silence was an enchanted swath of riddle, fear and history. It held the souls of the people in many curious ways.

The villagers could not thank the gods enough that the white man was up and about. When he was unconscious, all the elders and villagers thought that the end was near for the whole community.

The Americans, known for their fighter birds and love of their own, would know that the people of Orogun had killed their son. In retaliation, their birds would charge into the village skies, fly low in a pre-dawn sortie and raze the village to rubble. No one wanted that to happen. May the gods forbid, as the locals would say.

Only one voice mocked this mass hysteria over an American backlash. But who would listen to Ajuya? He was a hunter who always claimed to know a lot about the world. But the elders felt it was always better to discount his ideas. Was he not the one who regaled the young ones with meaningless yarns? He told tales of the exploits of the Americans in the battlefield? Didn't he tell them that they had their military nose in every battle on earth? At any rate, the man had gone senile. They knew better than to listen to a man who knew about the world from tales he must have read from his strange, fat books. Few elders believed his claim to Western education. Although he told them of his exploits in battle, they discounted the veracity of his personal example. The loss of his right hand did not persuade them. Neither did his army uniforms and epaulettes. Anyone could fake the army gear, they contended. And who knows where the rascal put his right hand that forced his nemesis to cut it off? Who gave him permission to fight beside the white man anyway?

"Your illiteracy prevents you from seeing beyond the fog" was Ajuya's response. "This is a paradise for blind people."

They never believed that he was a veteran, a man of valour who threw heart and limb into the Burma campaigns and other conflicts in World War II. He continued to throw bad weather into their quiet noon.

So, against their better conventional judgements, they contacted this witch, or so they thought her to be, who happened to be the only person in the village with the white man's education they could use, and she was a nurse. They would not go to the hunter. She was also Itse's friend, if of the platonic kind. They wanted her to nurse both men.

Meanwhile, everyone dreamed apocalypse. They saw bombs and apparitions of the white man's birds blackening the skies. They were not sure what to call the Jets. Hawks were puny. Eagles had no bullets or bombs. These birds spat balls of fire and had people inside. For flesh or bones, they had huge metal panels and parts. They were rude and noisy and startled the gods in the sky. They would pounce on the fragile swath of the village. Humans on earth heard the voices of the white man's travesty of birds loud enough to burst the ear.

One of the elders called the planes "witch birds who unleashed several nails hidden in their chests."

Many of the young ones did not share in this hysteria. They listened to Ajuya. In the open, however, they denied the meaning of his prowess and the truth of his courage.

He had also told them of a black man who was looking to be the American leader. For want of a better word, they said he would become the king of their country. That meant a black man would not send an army to obliterate his people no matter the wrong. After all, the only person in question was a white man. He would not take sides with a white person and unleash mayhem on his own people.

As they learned later, he actually hailed from the village of Aloma, which was about an hour's walk away.

When the new black king was crowned, he would understand that the good and benevolent Orogun villagers would not go out of their way to imperil an *oyibo* man. What wrong did the white man do? How could his own blood also disgrace him back home?

But subversive thinking remained under the eaves of Orogun village. Nobody who thought aloud like Ajuya could escape the tyranny of the elders. So, the popular view held its ground. The Americans were coming. They had done so recently to a nation that played havoc with them. Who could guess how far a small and puny village like Orogun could go with the looming bombardment?

The gods answered two prayers, though. That no newspaper man came around and spread the word abroad and that this white man recovered so they could persuade him to return immediately to his country. They did not want trouble. They did not invite the man. He invited himself. Who knew what trouble lay in that hair of his with waves like the ocean in its uproarious moments?

Not only was he bringing death to their precious son, his coming threatened oblivion to the village. Itse had been in America, for all they knew, and lived well and had acquired enough to build a decent home in the village. The home was bedecked with electric lamps and tasteful furniture. He had also been kind to the villagers. That was why they welcomed his friend, the *oyibo* man.

Itse had told them he had returned home for good. He was not going back to America. He did not say much about the white man except that he wanted to see the long-forgotten tomb of his ancestor. The request was granted reluctantly because the forest was shrouded in mystery and had not sniffed human flesh for many generations. If they calculated well, it would mean a century. The oldest man in the village said his great-grandfather was not alive when it happened. But they let Itse and his friend into that place, and see what they brought.

Imagine everyone's relief when the visitor came to. A few days after the village youth rescued them from the forest, the white man began to cough, and his body jerked back to life.

chapter Two

Relief to most people in the village meant that the *oyibo*, Tim Forester would thank his God, pack his belongings and leave. That was all they asked of the white man. The villagers reasoned that, if he wanted to seek his kind in the forest, the spirit of his ancestor in the tomb was not excited enough to return the favour.

If the ancestor had been enthused, he would have restrained the gods from unleashing the pigs at him and Itse. Everyone expected him to know how foolish it was to pursue the project. What was it with these white people and adventure anyway!

Again the chances of Itse's survival were far-fetched. The villages would have wanted to apply local wisdom, but this man had imbibed the *oyibo* man's belief. He would not bow to their gods or allow the local medicine man to fish out the cowries and decide what the young man did wrong. If he did not do that, how could he divine the right herbs and concoction for his healing? And the *oyibo* man had to rely on him.

The *oyibo* man had to leave, concluded the villagers. He had to go back to his people so the villagers could return to their adobe peacefully with bamboos and *banga* soup. If they lost Itse, they could at least lick their own wounds.

Alero was the issue. She was the only person most of the elders believed could make the white man go. She spoke his language and was close to him. Dede, a wrinkly old man with a disruptive stutter, doubted Alero's power with the white man's language. He said his son, Efe, who was just ten, had as much mastery as the woman. The villagers dismissed his claim. He had a child in his hoary years, and he was always happy for the chance to show off, to remind everyone that he was not going to die in the solitude of a childless old age.

A week after the good news of the *Oyibo* man's recovery broke, the elders led by Chief Tietie went to see Tim Forester. They had been bracing for that moment forever. The gods, they maintained, had done a good thing. These were the last days of agony. Tietie led the delegation because he was the only chief who spoke a smattering of English.

Chief Tietie was not the most modest person in the village. He was a short man who derided short people even when they were taller than he.

"Short man devil," he called Boyo, one of the meekest people in Orogun. "He always smells the earth." At another time, he described him as "a brief man."

His smile often had the quality of a smirk, a satirical sneer emphasising his place above all mortals. His laughter was a mystery to many. People preferred to hear him rather than see him laugh. His big, bold eyes shrank. His face looked like a baby's and his voice sounded like cymbals of joy.

That morning presented no evil portent. The wind held back its pangs for a mid-June weather, and so the sun touched the village with good humour. Women headed to the farms, with implements in their hands and pails on their heads and a spring in their feet. Children frisked about in their wake. The men set out to hunt or fish. The Itsekiri language draped the air as mother called to daughter and father to son and neighbour to a neighbour.

Those who woke up late were enveloped by an earlier ritual of cleaning the house, cooking breakfast and feeding the hens and goats whose familiar clucks and bleats battled with the Itsekiri language for the village ear. Jakpa's household was notorious. He was the first to go to bed and the last to rise. As Tietie and his men passed by his house to meet the white visitor, languid wisps of smoke rose above the fragile palm fronds of his kitchen. No one knew what he was cooking, but everyone knew that, to him, every meal was a feast.

He belonged to the high order of the village. His home was a one-floor house like the others, but bigger than most. A big yam barn fat with the farm's late yields propped-up his private paradise. He wore his prosperity on his feather that sat like a lone finger of cockiness on one side of his commodious hat.

In spite of the giddy activities of the morning, everyone glanced at the royal emissaries with hearts tender with prayers. They knew the story enough to understand that a negative outcome could extinguish the routine glories of their lives. Itse brought this to them. They would not blame their son. They had to accept what happened. Even the gods could not hold back the sun from yielding to the moon in its time. But they had the wisdom to heal the past by saving the future.

As they hunted for antelopes, planted cassava or harvested corn, their ears itched feverishly for only one thing, and Tietie knew that his pride was at stake because they expected him to succeed.

As they stepped on the stoop of Itse's house where both the white man and comatose Itse lived, Chief Tietie knew that he did not know enough English to negotiate with this white man. Only the witch possessed that weapon and, for once in their lives, they needed the resources of the evil woman to extricate their souls from the monster to come.

Chief Tietie wore a colourful white damask cloth embroidered with a turkey preening its feathers. He wielded a new fly-whisk. He looked every inch a royal façade, smiling loftily and his eyes rolling with an exaggerated hauteur. Yet his gait was chastened as he opened the door and entered the front room where Tim Forester and Alero sat waiting for the visitors.

Alero stood first, bowed and descended to her knees in respect. It was the tradition. As a woman, she was not even supposed to sit where elders held court and deliberated on matters of exigency. Even her shadow was forbidden. It was ironic that she, a virtual outcast, was needed to rescue the village from an embarrassment. The irony did not impress the Chiefs or Alero, who thought the band of elders were cowardly old men. They were frazzled by the harmless presence of a white man. If she could tell them the truth, they would yell at her. She was lucky; no one had accosted her since she returned from the lofty anti-climax of her escapade in the city. No one had poured local vials on her hair or thrust a surly knife through her back. In her quiet moments, she had sometimes wished it. If she was like her mother, she could have induced retribution by her acts of overt defiance, of open-lipped accusations of the Chiefs draped in hypocrisy.

Tim rose to his feet and shook hands with the Chiefs. If he were from the village, the Chiefs noted in their minds, Tim would have bowed. He was evidently a younger man, although they did not know how to read the age of white people by simply looking.

From the bounce around his face and the zip of his gestures, they knew he was a young man. Chief Tietie was around fifty years of age, but he himself did not know. At the time he was born, births were not registered but stored in memories by their association with momentous events such as the visit of a prominent king, or a local disaster like a windstorm or the birth of another royal child.

Tim's face did not show much emotion. He was not familiar with any of these Chiefs. He used to deal with them through Itse who was now near oblivion.

"*My name be Chief Tietie. I please to meet you,*" was Chief Tietie's first string of words. He drew confidence from this sentence and reckoned he could pull this mission through, encouraged by the smile that clothed the American's face. He did not understand the smile. From Tim, it was a gesture of courtesy, the kind his people gave off as an imperative of the friendly. Tietie and his men construed it as a mark of deference.

Look at this stupid man, Alero thought. Who taught him English? Why is he disgracing himself? Why did they not speak in Itsekiri and ask her to translate? She knew the answer, she told herself. Maybe they did not trust she would be faithful in translation.

There were only three sofas in the room, and the delegation of ten cramped into them. They were cushions made from cloth wide enough to sit two people. But people hardly sat on them.

So, they looked moist. This might have come from the effect of vagrant rain showers that strayed in through the door or window. So, they gave off a smell that both Alero and Tim recognised as odd. They could do nothing about it. The Chiefs did not have this luxury at home, so they did not recognise the hygienic shortcomings of where they lay their buttocks. Rather their buttocks thrilled quietly to the luxury, even if only one side of their buttocks enjoyed that privilege.

Alero also observed that the men brought a smell with them, as they walked into the room. It was a familiar smell, flavoured by camphor and the moistness of the bottom of their fashion boxes, where they kept their best clothes. Alero, once a celebrated beauty in the world outside, hid her contempt for them. They were bush men who saw themselves as the avatars of wisdom.

Itse had brought the furniture from the city. The floor had a rug carpet, another luxury. The Chiefs felt an easy comfort walking on the softness. When he had laid the red rug the children had spread the word that Itse had deployed a lion's mane for his personal comfort. He had brought it from America, so went the rumour. Itse did little to stem the lie.

The wall was still adobe, but he employed some of the builders to polish it, so it lacked the unhygienic cragginess of most homes in the place. Of course, Chief Japka's eye for material distinction did not miss this. So, he promptly replicated the splendour. Jakpa was not in the Tietie crowd of visitors. A radio sat on a ledge near the door. It was powered with a battery. No one had played it for many months now. A few pictures lit up the wall. Of particular importance was an old one with a cracked frame and covering. It bore Itse's father. It sat on the wall perpendicular to the visitors. Another picture was new, and it was Itse with some of his friends during their hiking trip in Colorado.

Tim sat, but Alero was forbidden to share a seat with anyone. She did not want to. The peculiar smell of these dirty old men would suffocate her. Rather, she stood beside the American, her face drooped and famished of cheer.

The room was dim with melancholy. The windows were shut, and the people relied only on the timid light that limped in through the door curtain. Alero thought of opening the windows. But she knew better. If anything went wrong, they would say it was part of her diabolical design to usher in her kindred spirits of darkness to doom their day.

Chief Tietie soon sat forward and bore the carriage of the royal emissary. He cleared his throat, as most Chiefs did before they spoke on special occasions. He also moved his buttocks around the sofa as though looking for the right posture for the words he was about to say. It did not matter that he made his other fellows uneasy. He was the king's chief messenger, and he had earned the right to displease others.

"We tank God dat tiy alife today and bad ting not happen in forest. It only God do dat."

Silence followed his statement. But, from the Chiefs' point of view, the American's face betrayed no feelings. Alero bent over so she could whisper to the man. Moments later, Tim's face lit up and looked in the direction of the Chiefs.

"Yeah," he said, "it's great to be alive, but the downside is that my buddy is in bad shape. I cannot claim to feel well until he recovers."

Some of the Chiefs confused the word buddy for body, and could not quite make out what the man said. They did not want to embarrass themselves, so they kept quiet. Chief Tietie however understood. Alero's translation confirmed what he thought.

It was clear, too, that the American could not pick up the accent and they would have to rely on the witch.

"Yah," replied Chief Tietie, *"God will do him work."* The chief turned quiet momentarily, poised to deliver the royal word. The silence made Alero aware of the shrunken space in the room.

"Our king send me here to say since the forest bring bad ting so we ready to help you anytime you ready to go back to your country."

The expression in the white man's face puzzled them. But this time they knew he understood what Chief Tietie said. Tim did not say a word. Rather he turned his head towards Alero and said, "Please explain to them."

Everyone turned their heads to the witch, wondering what the matter was that the man could not say himself. They also saw that the girl seemed as nervous as an ambushed squirrel.

Alero bowed her head as if she was talking to the floor and said: "the *oyibo* said he would not go yet." She tried not to sound petulant, but she was not sure her caution had not resulted in a rude and biting translation.

"Why?" chorused everyone in the room. The question was not only borne out of simple curiosity. It bristled with hostility.

Alero's face hardened into a ripple of furrows.

"He has forgotten his past. He does not even remember why he came here or the person whom he came to look for, or why."

There was a deep-forest silence. Chief Tietie twitched his nose, sat back and forward. Another chief tapped his thigh, another folded his arms and, quite often, a nervous eye looked into another nervous eye.

"If he has forgotten," asked Nikoro, one of the Chiefs, "then let him go back to his country, and meet his family and they will remind him." There was a 'yes' chorus to that.

"He insists," interrupted the witch, "that if that is why he came, he probably will need to go back to the forest to regain his memory. Again, he said he did not feel it right to his conscience to leave if Itse was sick. He says he owes it to him."

The leader of the delegation suddenly felt a huge burden drop on his shoulders. He could see a plague coming in the form of this ghost of an *oyibo* and, if persuasion did not work, he knew force was futile.

"Excuse me," he said to Tim Forester, "as for Itse we can take care of him, *but it good you go back for home and meet your family, and so dey help you remember.* Pity your family." Neither Tim nor Alero was amused by the man's peculiar grammar.

"I've thought this through," Tim said, raising his voice with a subtle rumble of defiance. "If I can't remember anything here, I can't leave here. I don't even know my way home."

"*Go your embassy and dem go help.*" It seemed to them Tim would not even consider that advice from Chief Tietie. Convinced that this American was not willing to yield to superior wisdom, the chief turned to the girl and issued a warning.

"We know what you have done to him. Is that the way you want to destroy this village. You have no shame stealing the brain of the poor boy for selfish reasons," said Chief Tietie who stole a glance at the white man whose face was puzzled again at what the chief had said in the Itsekiri language.

"It's all in your hands. If this man does not leave, our wrath and the wrath of the gods will come upon you."

He rose to his feet, and they all left in silence.

Chapter Three

Itse's planned return home to Nigeria came earlier than he anticipated. He craved the smell and sound of his home country. He craved the human chaos that marked sidewalks where shoulders brushed against shoulders on Upper Erejuwa Road in Warri. The smell of roasted corn contested with the stench from roadside sewers. The accents of market women collided in the fervour of curses and blessings. Dusk defined itself every weekend by a special disorder because daylight cringed when dust caught bulb lights. Lorries and cars clamoured, their horns blaring interminably. Children bustled with play in the village. His taste bud woke to kitchen favourites: *ogbono* soup, *banga*, pepper soup. The intrusive colours of fashion, the *ankaras*, George, blouses, and their admixture with Western idiosyncrasies; jeans, tee-shirts. The smell of Orogun fish and its river in tranquil lustre on hot afternoons. The divine repose of a village night. The rude welcome of a cock's early morning cry. The muscular frenzy of men in their morning work as goats bleated. The spontaneous temper of the people.

But he had no definite plan to return. He loved his days at the University of Colorado at Boulder. His memory lit up with its social amenity. He made enough good friends, savoured the parties, the opportunity to mingle with the children of America's upper crust. He witnessed their footloose habits with money. They had little qualms about unleashing wealth. Parents made the money. Children winked it into obedience. They were some of the children of the special order. They grew up around the swagger of politicians, hauteur of lobbyists, the top layers of the military and business brass. These were their parents and their world.

They did not appreciate the rigours of labour, the remorseless tedium lesser mortals invested in department stores, in the grind of kitchens and the fury of factories. But they knew how to make light of it. This was in the same America where most people, including Itse, scrambled feverishly for what he called the American eel, the dollar. He survived on scholarships. He had to soldier on narrowly between contentment and survival. Before his graduation, he was chained to bills forever. He understood the addiction of racking up bills and the pain of settling them. The credit system, another entrapment they warned him about, the seduction of loans. He fell for all this. He had to weed them gradually out of his life after school. But his friends did not have to bother much about these ritual burdens of society.

In the United States, he saw in flesh and blood what he read in the newspapers about the lifestyles of the rich in his own country. He had no access to them in Nigeria. When he left Orogun village for the bustle and greed of a city like Warri and Lagos, he saw the cars and mansions that partitioned the rich from the poor and struggling mass of the people. But he knew what the rich did when they travelled to Europe and the United States. They flew lean but returned with the nifty cargoes of the West, luxuries in sartorial varieties, cars and jewellery and furniture and perfumes. They boasted about world-renowned designers and their own indiscriminate appetites.

They had the capacity to retain excess in the big troughs of their mansions. He knew what they did with those big *Owambe* parties. He knew how much their shoes cost and how unwieldy their *agbadas* sat on their privileged bones.

These were the thieving politicians, the businessmen fattening on opportunities, not talent or ingenuity. He hoped to break into their circle in Nigeria. But how was he to attain that wild and sulphurous dream!

His father told him to read and make high grades, and maybe somehow, he could be lucky to make it through high school with high grades. If he did, he could get a job as a clerk in a good company, save money and sponsor himself through four heady years in a university in Nigeria. It was no mean task. But Itse was not a boy to faze. He wanted to be rich. He hated, at that time, the leash on rustic people. They did not see a world beyond the farm ridges and game in the world. Contentment chastened them like faith. He was one of them himself. But his thoughts bustled like his limbs. He saw himself in the high places of the world. He had to dream. He fretted in his dreams. Dreams were a buffer against the humiliation of environment. It was the illusion of conquests.

But Itse was lucky to discover the United States Information office in Warri as well as the British Council. That was after he started work in a fish company, called FilGate. It hauled fish from northern Europe and sold to cold rooms in Nigeria. It was a thriving business. Warri also was an oil town, and it attracted a lot of foreigners, Americans, British, French, Spanish, Italians.

Even though these Caucasians were in town, they lived separately from the rest of the people. They had their own clubs and restaurants and golf courses. But only the indigenous rich had access to those clubs and lived in the tony part of town with them. Even then, the racial walls were high and palpable.

Itse supervised the supplies to one of the cold rooms co-owned by Jack Horne, an American whose partner was a Nigerian, known as Mr. Ojevwe. But Jack called him Peter. He was the only one who called him by his first name. Ojevwe was a gangling man with a voice almost as low as a whisper. When he was not around, the workers called him 'Voiceless'. He was uptight and haughty to all the Warri people around him. He seemed to soar above everybody. He believed in his own stratospheric grace. He had a sports car, the Mustang, and a Mercedes 190E.

The Ford sports car was rare in the country. Jack arranged its importation. He acquired it not as a new car. The gangling fellow, however, boasted he bought it new and lied about the dollar amount he remitted across the ocean. No one could dispute it. The car looked sleek. When it glided under the sun, its sheen seemed to renew itself as though the sun polished it to retain its pride of shine.

That brand of Mercedes was a status symbol at the time. Only special people like Voiceless could conjure such a miracle onto the humble streets of Warri.

Voiceless was the closest Itse got to seeing Nigeria's rich. But the man was not really rich. He was a miserable wannabe, a pretender. He was thankful though for the experience. It was through Voiceless that Itse met Jack. He interacted with him to reconcile the books. Jack was an unspectacular vision to Itse when he saw him except that he was white and American. But he seemed not to fit into the image he saw in the movies or read in the books. He had nothing of the dramatic presence, the brash self-confidence and the kind but superior look. After about five months, he knew this was not untypical, except that Jack did not carry those attributes like a halo over his impressively shiny, bald head. Maybe it was because he had spent a great part of his life outside America. He looked like he was in his mid-forties. He had been in the fish business all his life and spent about a month a year in his country.

The children of the rich in Nigeria were not destined to sit in class with a boy like Itse. He could not afford that. They belonged to the heavens. He was somewhere remote, on the humbler rungs of this wretched earth.

But in America, it happened. His girlfriend Cindy was from Chicago, the daughter of a top real estate maven who benefited from the hydra head of fortunes. He gained not only from market up-swings but also when the cities reeled with foreclosures and price turbulence.

Cindy and Itse met on an afternoon in between classes at the University of Colorado at Boulder. They were in the lounge. He had not noticed her that afternoon but he had seen her around. He was struck not only by her tentative steps. Those steps fascinated him the most because they belied her aggressive visage and the sometimes regal fortitude of her carriage. But he noticed her the same way he noticed a few other girls. He never thought they could meet. He wanted a girlfriend fairly familiar with Tamika, an African American beauty, not one to whom he only said hello in the food court. He had not generated enough self-confidence to talk to her about "the next level". Itse was never shy with women but, in the United States, he wanted to be cautious. He followed his father's advice about the hen stepping through the door of a house for the first time. One foot on the floor, the other in the air.

But that afternoon, Itse went to the vending machine and, be-hind him, was the svelte vision. He acted as though he did not notice and tried to hurry up. But, as his Mr. Pibb can dropped out of the machine and he bent to pick it up, the shadow behind him congealed into a voice.

"You don't have Mr. Pibb in Nigeria." The accusatory quality of the voice yielded to the playfulness of his eyes. He knew at once that she might have listened to some of his conversations with friends and classmates in the lounge. How else would she know where he came from? Itse looked at her shyly, like one cornered. But instinctively, he countered.

"The taste is not much different from a local brew in my village. Yeah, we call it *burun*. What do you want? I can help you," he offered with a sense of chivalry.

Cindy declined, after introducing herself and saying that she was in the English department. She did not ask Itse to wait as she slid a dollar bill and coins into the machine and punched out a pretzel and a Sprite. But he waited, and they walked together to available seats on the northwest corner of the lounge. Later, Itse said he lied about the Mr. Pibb equivalent in Nigeria, and there was no such brew as *burun* in his village. He did not know how he made that name up. The only brews were palm wine and *burukutu*, a heavily alcoholic brew that could knock her out of her seat. He added he made up the *burun* story because he was caught off guard by her remark.

"How am I sure you are not making up the bu…" Cindy fascinated him with her attempts to say the word as her lips curled into a near tremulous purse.

"*Burukutu*. Another variant is called *apketeshi* or *push-me-I-push-you*."

She looked at Itse's eyes light up.

"That certainly could kick one off her horse," she said.

They met twice in the lounge over the next week, and she invited him to a hiking party around Estes Park. Itse told himself he could have amused her further by telling her about *ogogoro*, the other brew of giddy intoxication.

It was late October; the summer was beginning to yield its pride to autumnal forays. He enjoyed the company, but he could not quite relate with the conversations. They were twelve in all; most of the guys came with their girlfriends, and they were all white. From their conversations, they came from wealthy homes, most of them. He also observed that they spoke about football, the guys and the girls flowed into the conversation. He heard the words, Broncos, Bengals, 49ers, Chiefs. But Scott, who hailed from Boston, was still gung-ho about baseball whose season had just ended. His team, the Red Sox, had won the World Series for the first time, in close to a century. Not many of them caught Scott's triumphal joy. Later, Cindy said it was because most of the guys there were Yankee fans.

They also spoke about clubs and the latest rock bands in the country, especially the Dave Matthews's Band.

He had so much to absorb, and all he could do was listen and smile. Most of them looked forward to the ski season. Itse did not know what it was about. He recalled that, back in Nigeria, when Jack Horne learned he had secured admission to the University of Colorado, he spoke about the cold of Denver and the thrill of skiing. He missed those, he said with a certain abandon, as though he did not mean it. Maybe because it was such a long time ago. Itse did not understand how someone could love a cold sport, as he described it.

"It was part of the fables of my youth," he told Itse in his home in Warri. But Itse could not imagine a better sport for body and soul than soccer. In his thrill to leave for the University and his gratitude for opening the way for him, he acted the ski enthusiast.

The fellow students spoke about their new skis, and what areas of their skiing they wanted to work on in the winter. Cindy chipped in another puzzle for Itse.

"I didn't do enough paragliding this summer," she said, staring at a tuft of grass she had been struggling to unearth.

Before they asked him questions, Cindy had announced that Itse was from Nigeria; that he was on scholarship to study software engineering and that he was a genius. From their body language, they wanted to know if he was Cindy's boyfriend. They did not ask directly, but they kept skirting the real questions as to how they had met and if he loved Cindy's horse and whether he would go with her for cross country skiing in a few weeks around Loveland.

After they had left, Cindy looked at him in the car, her new Ford Explorer:

"They wanted to know if we were an item."

"Item?" That word usage was strange to Itse, but he quickly understood what it meant.

"Yes, aren't we?" she asked.

"Maybe."

"Maybe? Don't you like me?"

"You are wonderful." Itse did not know why he said that.

She said she wanted to be with him, and Itse did not have the chance to say no. He abided the tyranny. When he looked back, he described it as the glorious ambivalence of his life. Cindy denied it was ambivalence.

"You said yes, but you didn't know it," purred the tall, extroverted brunette with a pair of deceptive sad eyes. Anytime Itse recalled Cindy's words, a pang of doubt troubled him. Maybe he knew. Maybe he told himself that. Maybe he was too timid to accept a girl over whom all the boys drooled, white guys from her world of money and fame. He was barely three months in the country then, barely aware of his foot in the system, let alone his foothold.

The hiking was brief, about an hour. He was a little scared when they walked through the fat barks of the bushes, scaled the twigs and under-brush and his feet alternated between hard soil and carpets of wood chips. He heard the birds. But what struck him were the leaves. They were in their last stand without the will of colour. They had lost their tone and flourish. They were turning pale yellow and sagging and wrinkly. The air had lost its robust, summer tint; a certain pallor and hints of shadows now rent the view of things.

He tried to compare the place with the years in Orogun, he knew the boldness and wiles of the world. He knew how to plumb the depths of its bushes. He knew the animals, smelled their augury, he knew how to anticipate their menace and how to tackle them. Even at that, there was no guarantee of safety. He knew how to confront the audacity of reptiles like green snakes, or the pythons, or the alligators. He also knew about wild pigs. But he had no idea how to deal with a bear or a mountain lion. These animals often came on the news. They had wasted a few people in the past few months. He read in the Rocky Mountain News, a month earlier, about a boy mauled to death by a lion. The parents were about a quarter of a mile away from him when the beast attacked.

But Itse concealed his fear. He also steeled himself, believing he would deploy his residual skill, his resilience as a fighter in the wilds of Orogun.

He never expected to have a white girlfriend. He had heard stories of interracial relationships and how blacks had been lynched in the past. He knew that did not happen nowadays but did some white people still carry the prejudice and could they still do him harm in secret? Could the boys, who laughed with him in their uproarious parties, not catch him in a furtive hour one night and dispatch him? Maybe that was why he hesitated. But he knew he never consciously contemplated that. Maybe that was what Cindy meant by that phrase that he said yes, but he didn't know. She saw the yes coming, but she forced the spring.

Cindy and his other friend, Abe, opened him to the world of the rich and also the world of play in America. He was not only going to be a bookworm. He wanted to understand the American way, the beer and baseball, the bars and girls, the giddy nights and sober churches, soap box and box scores. For all the years he spent there, he had his thumb on all the pulse. He made many friends and, in time, he made quite a few Nigerian friends, close ones, too. But Cindy gave him the best window to America.

He was studying software and dreamed of one day developing a patent that would vault him to wealth. After graduation, he was lucky. He landed a job with Bridge Software as a software engineer. At that time, he had already decided that he was not going to work for any company for too long. He wanted to be on his own, to go on a tear of entrepreneurial daring. He hoped to introduce leading-edge products to virgin Africa, beginning from Nigeria. But he had to make money first, save enough. He would not return full-time to Nigeria, but he would have a base in both countries. He also hoped that he could become a link between the technology giants and markets in Africa.

He never succeeded in the search for patents, but he would not despair. Great ideas come when one is not looking, he told himself.

He had started his business before he met Tim Forester. He had made such trips for over three years. The gains were modest so far, but infinitely more fulfilling than working eight-hour shifts five or six days a week. He earned less on his business trips than he would have on a salary as a highly needed software engineer, especially for a person who topped his class. But he said he was in his seed season.

He dreamed that, in time, he would be the big name in African technology.

He succeeded with his modest earnings to build himself a small
bungalow in Lagos and the village home. Each time he went back, he
spent a week in Orogun. The Orogunians thought he was in Lagos
when he was not in the village. They thought he was buried in work
in the city and amassing wealth. He let the lie fester.

It was true, at times, when he brought his software engagements
to Africa. But that ran into a bump with Tim's project. After an initial
reluctance, he devoted himself to the project almost as though he
had abandoned his obligation to himself and his future.

chapter Four

From her bland and unfurrowed mien, Alero did not seem to take the threat seriously. For one thing, she was happy to be gradually rid of the old Chiefs' suffocating body odours. Until then, she had thought she was immune to their nasal distractions. She had been in the city for too long where men deployed roll-ons to freshen their armpits. These village men, on the other hand, were locked in their rustic bliss, far away from the scents of deodorants and they hardly shaved their armpits. Ever since her return, many stayed far from her, and her nostrils were grateful for the alienation.

"Why did they leave like that? What did they say?" Tim asked. Alero did not say a word at first. Her first relief was that the obnoxious smell they invaded the house with had started to disperse. The place would soon be back to its airy sanity.

Back to a more sombre truth, she worried that the village had just burdened her with this white man who did not know his way back home. Before that day, he was the whole village's concern. Now, the cross was hers to bear. The only person she knew she could bring to her side was Ajuya, the veteran, the World War Two soldier who was out of town. Although his support was always only moral, it was invaluable.

And for an outcast, that meant a lot. She hardly crossed to his house on the other side of town. If she did, she would be fair game to the judgemental eyes of the men and women, and the venom of hushed remarks. As for the children, they pelted her with loud, maniacal chants:

Crocodile pikin
Crocodile pikin,
Come o, come o,
Come swallow me!

"They think I bewitched you to stay," she said.

"What?"

"They call me crocodile girl. They believe I'm not really human."

A mock laughter spurted out of Tim's mouth, and Alero cackled in spite of herself. She wondered, for a moment, if the white man would be on their side.

"You mean voodoo?"

"Yes," replied Alero, with a grave visage

She observed Tim's change of countenance. He looked like one looking for a solution. She noticed that the American had a look of languor leavened every now and then by spasms of passion: surprise, anxiety, laughter, a nasal tweak, an elbow nudge. The face of tranquil water now, a bubble now. She found that fascinating. He looked like a little drama in a mystery.

"Please," she told him, "try to recall what happened in your past. There is no way I am not going to be reproached in this village again. Is this the only place I can stay in this country?" her voice cracked with terror.

"What are they going to do to you? Kill you?" Tim asked, looking at once flustered with a subdued hint of chivalry.

Given what happened, Alero knew she had to let him in on her story and her status in the village and the whole nation.

"I can't put it past them. They killed my mother."

"They can't do that to you. You see, one more reason I won't leave here," said Tim almost without reflection; the words seem to rewire the veins in his forehead.

"Don't step into my case, I beg you. No one does that. No one ever did."

After a brief pause, Tim turned to look at Alero who was now standing on her feet. Alero observed this was the first time he had looked at her at any length. He had spent most of the past week recuperating, and Alero had only come there to make his meals and administer his medication. Conversations pruned themselves to essentials, except when he gave speeches of gratitude to her for saving his life.

Alero had often discounted the speeches of gratitude because death was playing havoc with Itse, her best friend in the world. If he did not make it, she would have no one to talk with in the village, except the veteran, who was of another generation. And, of course, her aunt who was never home.

This was the first day, unknown to the elders that the white man would spend outside the bedroom. It was his first day of physical well-being. He took a good look at her and then looked away abruptly, like one who had been struck with sudden knowledge. But he said nothing. He paused. Alero sensed he wanted to say something and then didn't

"What?" asked Alero, who was a little nervous. In spite of her nervous state, she did not share the air of mystery and even trepidation with the rest of the villagers about the white man.

"Nothing," he replied, "I know you white people are not that superstitious. I hope you do not have any suspicion that I'm evil"?

Tim did not want to delve into the superstitious part of her remark?

"Evil?" he said looking her in the eye. "If you were evil, then I could use a lot of evil people. Helloo! Can't you see that you saved my life?"

"God saved your life."

Tim was quiet again. Alero had noticed that he was capable of mood swings and had a pair of eyes that alternatively sparkled and dulled.

"Now, who killed your mother? When did that happen?"

"Before I was eight."

"Who did it?"

"I don't know. I know it was a conspiracy."

The word conspiracy hung heavy on her lips.

"How did you know that?"

"They thought she knew too much. They believed she wanted to expose somebody. She wanted to announce to the village who my father was."

"You mean…"

"Yes, I don't know my father. He might be in this village as I talk to you."

"Why would your father want to keep mute?"

Alero smiled.

"He will be guilty of rape. And that's a minute charge. He will be guilty of sleeping with an outcast. And worse, having a child with a crocodile."

The white man said nothing. He wanted the girl, whom he kept looking at from intensity to intensity, to flesh out her story.

Tim's curiosity was not rewarded. Alero withdrew into her familiar silence and thought she might turn her attention to something else, and that was Itse, the comatose friend of the visitor.

"I need to check on him," she said with a lisp, her register of discomfort. She observed that the white man knew she was pursuing a detour from the topic. He seemed to take her abrupt change of mind well, she thought.

Both of them walked into the room, one of the two in the house. Itse lay on a bed, his pulse unnoticed like an immobile ant. He had a face of ghastly peace. Alero's heart skipped. She thought he was dead. She made straight to feel his pulse. Her dour look revived. This cycle of despair and relief had become a routine.

Alero could not imagine Itse sick before this incident. She never knew Itse, in all his burly, bouncing and ebullient glory, to have complained of a headache. She could not have imagined him sick. Now she was being compelled to contemplate his oblivion.

Now, his big, round face was pale, his cheeks drawn in; the skin had lost its dark lustre which had always been part of his large and optimistic personality. His eyes popped beneath shut lids and his chiselled nose now looked like a shrivelled bulb. His stomach was flattened, and his legs displayed calves that resembled tubers more than human flesh. A doctor who came in every other day from neighbouring Warri to see him asked them to keep their fingers crossed. There was a chance he would make it. But this was all a doctor's gimmick, according to the villagers. They never once sought Alero's opinion, although they needed her to monitor their son and keep in touch with the doctor.

"I believe in miracles," she said, her voice barely audible. She waited for a response from the American, but he did not say a word. He just gazed at the sick man on the bed. "Don't you?" she asked him.

"Of course," he said with casual aloofness.

"Are you a Christian or you belong to those groups of people I read about in the university who don't believe anything? Agnostics."

"No mistake about it. I'm a Christian. But even in the most ardent of believers, there comes the agnostic moment, the atheistic moment. Don't ask me what moment I'm in right now."

After Alero had left, he returned to the solitude of the dream he had the previous night. It was no comfort. It had the quality of an intrusive nightmare, and it spoke to him in a cruel whisper. It was not a long dream, and he could not recall everything, but he knew that he returned to the forest and he encountered black smoke billowing out of which a headless face materialised. The headless creature had a voice that bellowed what sounded like a warning. He could not recall what the words were. But they were sombre enough to rattle him. He backed a retreat, stumbled over under-brush even as the huge, white smoke followed him. Suddenly, the whiteness melted into one of the trees as into some bubble... Tim could not recall what followed. He wondered if that was merely the doubt in him floating in his dreams. Or was there a spiritual validity to it? Whatever it was, it had the power to nudge him out of a sense of peace. He never believed in dreams, but this one haunted him.

chapter Five

It was about Itse's fourth year after graduation. He had just returned to the United States after one of his business trips to Nigeria. This was an exploratory sojourn on behalf of Qualcomm, a company based in California. They wanted Itse to help explore the African market for their new software called BREW. He had great hopes. The African continent would soon open up for technology and unfurl its wings to meet America and the rest of Europe in the new skies of knowledge and wealth.

He also noticed the explosion of wireless technology on the continent. It was early in the summer. Cindy was now about to complete her Doctorate at the University of Chicago. He wanted to spend some time with her. He was contemplating moving to Chicago since his girlfriend preferred life in the Windy City. Cindy's mother, Tracy, was one of Itse's fans. And he wanted to see her too. The father was indifferent to him. But they shared a common love for baseball; a sport Itse had come to understand and enjoy. He learned it from Abe, a Red Sox fan, who suffered long through many years of the Bambino curse. Itse spoke confidently about the rules and the icons of the game from Babe Ruth to Willy May. He also was enamoured by the stars.

Itse's love of baseball puzzled his fellow Nigerians, whose sports' interests located in the thrills of soccer and basketball. Itse loved baseball, ice hockey, football and basketball. Ironically, he could not accommodate American soccer. It played beneath the layer of the world. Since he could not see the latest contests on American television, his fascination with soccer lapsed into the thrill of nostalgia. He had a large storehouse of memory.

Cindy had rented an apartment outside the campus, and Itse would stay with her there for two weeks before returning to Denver, where he not only had a town home but also his business warehouse and office. He explored the possibility of setting up a business in Chicago. His business did not have to be in Denver. His supplies were everywhere in the country. After all, Qualcomm was based in California.

Doing business close to Cindy underscored his seriousness with his love, and would also impress her mother. The night he arrived, Cindy was on hand to pick him at the O'Hare Airport, and they drove right to her apartment. She always impressed him with how freely she associated with him in public. Even in the America of the day, whites and blacks were still self-conscious about how they related to each other, about hugs and kisses and other demonstrations in public.

That night, while in bed, he was forced to make the point. He did not know that she was also impressed with his bravery in tackling her, with her background and her looks. He never acted as though he had to impress others from Africa or blanch when whites were around. She said her mother never had any hang-ups about interracial relationships and she hinted that Tracy had had a black boyfriend whom she could not marry because of the prejudice of her folks.

"She loves dad but sometimes when she speaks about the guy, you know she bowed to the circumstances. And dad understands that too."

They enjoyed their night together as always. She planned to accompany him on one of his trips to Nigeria, to see the entrails of the continent, the smell, the colour, the concourse of men and women.

Itse had cooked a variety of Nigerian food for her. She loved the pepper soup with fish, a spicy affair. She did not get into the *ogbono* soup so much but she liked the *jolof* rice with *dodo* or fried plantain slices. Itse told her it tasted a little differently back home. In the United States, the spices had interfered with its original quality.

She wanted to see the village, especially Orogun village and the Forest of Silence. It sounded like something she not only wanted to read about in a book but also to see in a movie.

They agreed they would go the following summer. Itse was worried Cindy had a romantic view of Africa, of the wildlife, and simple folk, the trees and dirty roads. He tried to disabuse her mind. Africa was also like anywhere else. Some of its cities had skyscrapers and tarred roads, and cars, if not as opulent or even as neat as cities in America or some other Western countries. After all, he was taking software there, and he was making money. It did not have the interminable malls and wide roads, but Africa could be as modern or as ancient, depending on what a visitor preferred, Itse explained.

"The media gives a one-dimensional view of our people," said Itse. Even when the President went there, the Western media scarcely showed us the city. They were enamoured by the Serengeti."

"Yeah, I noticed that she said.

A few days later, he had dinner with Cindy, her mother Tracy and her father, Jason. Tracy was vice president of a public relations firm. She was the older version of Cindy, the eyes, the height, the carriage, the self-confidence. Cindy's parents were much older. She was their only child, and they had had her late.

Anytime Itse was around them; he had a sense that Cindy was special to them, especially to her father. Jason always wanted to know what Itse was working on. He knew he had two ambitions in business. He wanted to develop a patent and, of course, to be the big technology enabler for Africa.

"I am trying to develop an application that will bring such services as quintessential African rhythms to ringtones around the world. I am also working on entertainment applications as well as software for governments. This will allow governments talk easily and seamlessly to other governments without losing their secrets or proprietary material," said Itse. "In fact, that is one of the deals I am about to firm up with Qualcomm."

When they first met, Jason had to listen and watch Itse's lips in order to catch his words. He was getting used to it now, Itse could see. But it was a work in progress for everybody, including Cindy. Cindy sometimes asked him to repeat what he said. When they first met, he got used to the phrase, "say that again" with her signal smile. Tracy did not say much, but she was always quietly glad to see him around.

When they drove home that night, Itse asked Cindy if she had noticed Jason asking him so many questions. She said that she had and he was not asking more questions than any father asked a man who wanted to marry his daughter.

Itse was quiet because he had never mentioned anything about marriage to her. Her answer disarmed him. He expected her to frame her response in a milder, more apologetic language. He expected her to say something like, "You know, honey, I am an only child, and dad loves his daughter. Just answer his questions for me. I'll talk to mom about it."

Itse resented her response and believed she made it instinctively. Cindy knew her words rattled her man but she was not ready to do anything about it. He said nothing but looked straight on as he drove. Cindy often wanted him to drive. Silence dropped between them like a block of ice. No word rippled the air in close to five minutes.

"I learn it's going to be a very cold winter," said Cindy, tearing through the chill.

"Colder than any you've experienced?"

"Maybe not," Cindy replied resentfully. When did he learn this sarcasm, this sharp-tongued aggression? She asked herself. Too much of America had endowed him with this snappiness of verbal contempt.

He did not want to turn this beauty into a wasp, her ruby lips lit into tantrums. He did not want her to misunderstand him, angry as he was. He had to manage Cindy. She rarely jumped into a temper but when she did it uprooted her for days.

In the apartment, he walked to her as she undressed, and put his arms around her.

"Please don't mind my comment. I didn't mean the words the way they came out," he said.

"That's okay", she said. But it was not okay. This guy was trying to use the language thing on her, she thought. He could have pulled that off a few years ago. Not anymore. Itse understood the English language as well as any American, including Americanisms.

Itse knew she was still edgy and dodgy about the matter. So, he decided to tackle the challenge. He never wanted to let it slide, after he had exhausted his diplomatic approaches.

"Now, you think your dad should ask me so many questions?" His pitch was high, almost adversarial. She quickly turned and looked him in the eye. Itse averted his face. But she had seen what she wanted.

She said nothing.

"If I were not different, do you suppose he would throw me so many barbs?"

"So, you're calling dad a racist?" Her eyes sparked.

"Why do you have to take it to the extreme? I only meant he did not have to be particular about me. I am a guy just like anyone else. You know that. Why is he so nice and yet makes me uneasy at times? I love his daughter. I love you. But I should be allowed to love in peace."

Cindy said nothing. She stood up and walked into the bathroom with those deceptively half-determined steps of hers. She was there for what felt like an eternity. He walked over. The door was cracked open. She was sitting on the toilet seat, staring. Itse had no regrets about what he said. He liked her father. They were comfortable with each other on matters like baseball. But he asked questions about little details such as whether he had a girlfriend in Warri before he came to the United States. He asked it cleverly. Cindy looked up to him as he reeled out his complaints, leaning on the door.

"How was dating like for you in Warri before you came over?" He never asked that question when either Cindy or her mother, Tracy, could hear. But it needled him to have to be polite when he could have replied, how's that your business?

But Cindy said she heard him ask questions about his ability to sustain his business over the long haul, and whether his ties with the African community were strong enough. Itse did not understand what he meant by enough. Cindy said he could have misunderstood her dad.

"He wanted to know if you missed home and if the African community helped you adjust to life in America," she said.

"But I told you several times that as much as they did, no one helped me more than you."

She agreed.

"You should have told him that," he said. Cindy was quiet again, but she stood up. She was in her lingerie. She moved over to Itse and put her arms around him and they kissed.

"Is my dad going to come between us?" she asked, her voice was a little cracked.

"Nobody will," he said.

"I like the way you talk. I mean your frankness." At the first half of the sentence, he thought she meant his accent. He said that to her hearing.

"Well, that too," she added, and they laughed as they moved to the bedroom.

chapter Six

Alero knew that she had to make good on her promise to reel off her story to Tim. She could not deny that the American wanted to know. His ears had hung on her every word. She had teased him with a prelude.

She too needed a stranger to tell her story. Someone who did not know her pedigree, who would not judge her. Someone who could even be partial to her point of view and her hopes. Someone who would enrich the storehouse of her prejudice.

With Itse's silence, he seemed the only person to whom she could talk. But it was all going to be a one-way communication, she told herself.

Tim must have his story, too. Loads of yarns probably rippled behind that face of easy languor. His coming to Orogun must be part of the unfolding of a story. But this riddle of amnesia must first be conquered.

As they stood in the half-light of the room gazing at their mutual friend, she wondered how this American was going to win his battles. He wanted his memory back. He needed it. He wanted to see the tomb as the pathway to memory. The real battle was how he was going to pull this off. Who would show him the path? And how would he dislodge the elders' fears and convince them that he could come out of it all unscathed.

"Can you even recall how you met Itse?" she asked him.

"I don't even remember him," he said with pain in his eyes. He paced about the small room and stood still. He leant on a clothes' rack. The rack gave way under the weight of his arm, and the clothes preceded him to the floor in an embarrassing thud. Alero shrieked, and moved quickly to his side.

"I'm all right. No problem," he said, sounding a little hurt.

"Are you sure?" she panted.

"I probably need jolts like this. They could help my memory," he said as he tried to pull himself back to his feet. That piece of humour did not rhyme with the young woman who promptly turned on the fluorescent light to grab a full view of the accident. She was relieved the wound was minimal, a grazed elbow. It was, however, bleeding, if slightly. She asked him to sit on a chair beside Itse's bed while she went to get a piece of cloth to wrap around the little wound. As she tried to step out of the bedroom to the front room, she felt a crunch under her left foot. She looked down wondering if her feet had damaged one of Tim's possessions.

"What's that?" she asked.

"It just came off the jacket I took to the forest. I must have picked it up during the hike. I can recall picking it only faintly. I've been reflecting on it in the past few days but, it was no help."

It was a locket with a cameo on it.

"The bleeding is getting worse." She seemed not to have heard the man. Her eyes waxed glassy like a baby doll dreaming.

Suddenly she tore out of her torpor, ran into the next room without uttering a word, and ran back into the first room with a nondescript rag. She adroitly applied cotton wool to the wound and wrapped the rag over it.

Her eyes turned moist and seemed to dilate by the moment.

"Are you sure you picked this up in the forest?"

"Why are you asking me this? Why are you crying? What does it mean to you? Yes, I saw it in the forest. Where else could I have picked it up? It's the only thing I can remember in the forest. But why are you crying?"

She sobbed, and her body quaked like one seized by high fever. Tim held and took her to the living room, sat her down and tried in vain to elicit an answer from her.

Her face looked both disconsolate and frightened. After about twenty minutes, she stopped sobbing out of exhaustion.

"That was the last thing my mother had worn before she disappeared," she announced. Alero could not have forgotten the locket with her mother's cameo on it. It bore layers of memory.

chapter Seven

In a sudden burst of tears, Alero asked Tim to rattle his memory, to unleash the moments in the forest in words of pictures. She wanted to see the replay of the drama, the clamour of the pigs, the onslaught, the play of colour in the woods, the sinuous paths, the texture of the earth, a picturesque sense of place and sequence. What happened at the time he picked up the locket with her mother's little face on it? She was not going to be patient with him. She had to know the facts, and he had to remember.

Tim thought she was getting out of hand. Any reference to the forest kept bringing back the creature in black, billowy smoke. It agitated his mind. He couldn't even share the experience.

Yet, he needed to know what the locket meant and why it was so important that he remember that moment. Why Tim asked the agitated woman, did she expect him to remember the story of the locket's recovery when he did not remember anything about his own life before that moment? He could not have recalled the locket if it was not in his pocket.

"It's still a surprise that I remembered it anyway," he said, with suppressed irritation.

"That locket has been missing since I was about eight years old.

Everybody claims that my mother disappeared in the Orogun River and returned to her life as a crocodile," she said, her voice alive with tremor. "This is my talisman against history."

"There is a huge difference between a forest and river," Tim said.

"They are not even close," Alero was making an effort to chasten her irritation with Tim. Her dour visage, however, still unmasked her lack of ease.

Tim looked at the African woman and said: "We seem to have something in common."

"We both have secrets in the forest. They call it the Forest Of Silence."

"Yeah," interjected the American. "The difference is that you know who you are looking for."

There was a pause. The room waxed darker as if in defiance of the light, and the two people never looked at each other and never heard each other for about five minutes except for their heaving breaths that blended with the clamorous sadness of birds perched on trees that dovetailed the village with the Forest of Silence. The house was close to the forest.

"And I don't know why," Tim's voice pierced the dirge of the birds.

"Why what?" Alero stirred in her chair.

"Why I want to see the person in the tomb. It must have been important. I don't have a clue."

"If I had been around before both of you embarked on the journey, Itse would have given me some details, and maybe I would have passed them on to you now."

"We don't know if he told the elders. If I go to them do you think they will tell me given what happened earlier today?"

"I'm sure they will want to tell you something to make you forget about the project."

"You mean they'll lie?"

"Lies. That's all they do in this village."

"It all boils down to the same thing. I have to go back to that damned forest", Tim said with resignation.

"And they'll all think this witch made you do it. Whether they like it or not I will go with you." Alero paused. "I have to prove that someone killed my mother."

Tim took the locket from her and tried to look at it closely by the timid light in the room. The cameo was much faded and cracked. He could hardly pick up the face of the woman. Two things seemed unmistakable, though: the eyes and the signature of her plaited hair. Alero plaited that style of hair, a special cornrow with the ridges shining with coconut oil.

"Why would they call her a crocodile?" asked Tim.

"Because she was beautiful," she replied.

Tim didn't get the correlation. A crocodile was a great creature with all the impressive jaws, a network of scales, mastery of water and the loud, subversive growl. But how could anyone mistake these for beauty?

"My mother was called crocodile in order to deny her claim to beauty. In other words, if she was so beautiful, she could not be human. She was a huge deception foisted on the world by the evil forces in the river. She was a strange version of the mermaid."

"Why did they pick on her? Why did they not want to accept her beauty?"

He paused, stared at Alero and quickly looked away, and his voice dropped into a more deliberate level.

"You're also incredibly beautiful. Is that why they are also picking on you?"

Alero did not betray a flicker of surprise at the compliment.

The words seemed to cast a shadow over her face.

"Beauty is just part of the tragedy," she said in a broken voice. "In fact, beauty is a symptom. The real tragedy is history."

Tim looked at her as if at some extremely exotic creature.

"This must be a place of strange things. Maybe that's why I came here… Darn it, I'll give anything to get my memory back. That tomb must mean something to me or to somebody. I could not have come here if it didn't," he said with a little note of awe and expectancy.

chapter Eight

Bimbo Bello was on hand to pick up Itse at the Denver International Airport. He taught African history at the University of Denver. He was older than Itse, who was only 26 years old. Bimbo was 33.

Bimbo was eager to show his friend his new Ford Explorer. His wife, Marian, an African American, had resisted the idea of buying a new car for over a year. She preferred a vacation first. The previous summer they had gone to Europe and Marian had never lived down the cruises, the nights on the deck under the splendour of the starry nights and the kaleidoscope of Europe. Each city and each country gave a different flavour. They had visited six countries. They relished the range of accents and languages, the landscapes and architecture, the fury of their soccer fans, the cuisines, and the weather. They saw the heights of the Eiffel Tower and the depths of the underground trains. They also learned first-hand the influences of America, Disneyworld, McDonalds, the jeans' obsession. They sometimes saw this evidence of a European love affair with America as undistinguished. They could not escape the subtle resentments against what some American analysts were calling the world's indispensable nation.

It was Marian's first trip outside the country. Bimbo had seen a lot of Europe before. He had lived in England and Germany in his heady, peripatetic days before he eventually secured a visa to the United States. It was through the grace of Marian that he secured his green card. Marian was beside him through his toils in graduate school. He was now a citizen.

But Marian was a "tough cookie", as Bimbo always said when his wife was not around. He had to defer to her in many areas in order to have his peace at home. They were now married for close to eight years.

"She is getting too hard on me these days," was Bimbo's relentless refrain.

"Take it easy," was Itse's usual response. Even if it cost them a fortune, Bimbo confessed the trip soothed their relationship for a while. They had two boys, Sola and Bidemi, and Itse believed that the two boys and the pressures of child support payments in the event of a divorce still held them together.

"That's a beautiful beast," commented Itse as they walked to Bimbo's new possession in the parking lot. He was tired of the Camry, and he wanted an SUV.

"She finally let me go," Bimbo said.

"But the vacation meant a lot to her," Itse cautioned. "We sometimes don't know what these vacations mean to Americans. Sometimes it is like going to heaven and back."

"What's the point going to heaven when you know hell is waiting for you," Bimbo said cynically. They had left DIA and were at the intersection of Pena Boulevard and Interstate 225.

"Don't mind my comments. I still love my wife. I don't know what I'd do without her."

"That's the nature of all relationships. It's about making it work.

That's the excitement. Even as guys, we have our own fights from time to time."

Itse was referring to the recent tiff between them when he called the Yoruba people servile and shifty. Bimbo was Yoruba. It took weeks before they could watch Bronco games together again. The comment tested their relationship. At the beginning of their friendship when he saw him with Cindy, Bimbo had suggested that he was suffering from inferiority complex. The friendship almost never blossomed. Bimbo returned with an effusive apology, and said that he was wrong and that he was alluding to the relationships involving some other Nigerian men who wanted to sleep with white girls, whether or not they found the girls attractive.

That episode crossed Itse's mind as they drove past two slow cars on the highway, and he recalled the argument with Cindy over her father's comments. But he was not going to excuse Cindy's father. He ought to judge Itse on his own merit.

"What are you thinking about?" asked Bimbo who saw the furrow on his friends' brow.

"I had a little argument with Cindy. It was not really her but her father."

He reeled out the drama in Chicago.

"You have to understand the man. She's his only daughter. *And you be Naija man. Maybe he don hear some story about Naija men,*" he said. They sometimes spoke pidgin English to defuse tension.

"*But me no be just any Naija man. I be responsible guy,*" he protested.

"*I know, but him never know you well well. Maybe, he dey test you.*"

They had almost reached Itse's home when he remembered Marian's message.

"Marian sent me to you. A few weeks ago, she contacted one of her friends online, who introduced her to a website. It was in one of those internet chats where strangers talk over different topics. This was an African site. A certain Caucasian guy kept asking for anybody who had ever heard of a village called Orogun in West Africa. She thought you told her you came from there. She said she remembers because it sounded much like Oregun. Is your village Orogun?" Bimbo was half-ashamed to ask because Itse knew he came from Ilesha in Osun State in Nigeria. He only knew that he came from Delta State and spoke Itsekiri language.

"Yes, I am from Orogun."

"Good. This Caucasian guy wants to meet anybody who comes from there. You can find out the details from Marian. It looked like the guy has been looking for information on the village for up to two years."

"Orogun is too small to make it to any map."

The next morning, just before Itse woke up, his phone rang. He thought it might be Cindy. She sometimes called early to laugh at him and say, "Hello sleepy head." Cindy was an early riser and she would wait till about 8am, so her "sleepy head" barb made more sense. But it was not even 7am yet.

"Hello Itse" said the voice. It was Marian. She was learning how to say his name. Itse, often explained to Americans that the "ts" in the name sounded like "sh" in English but he was never disappointed when Americans pronounced the name poorly because he had the same challenge with fellow Nigerians of other ethnic groups as well.

She told Itse that she met a certain guy called Tim Forester online who wanted to visit Africa, specifically a village called Orogun. She had researched in vain to find it on any map. He had it on the good authority of his family history records that the village once existed and one of his ancestors visited, lived and died there.

When Itse confirmed that he came from Orogun, she felt triumphant. But Itse was cautious.

"I am not sure if there is another Orogun in West Africa. I only know of mine. There is another place in Bimbo's part of Nigeria called Ila-Orogun. Maybe that is what he is searching for. Maybe, the name has been changed or corrupted over the years. Who knows? I know my Orogun has been around for centuries," he said.

"Can I give the guy your number," she asked.

"Of course. It is not often somebody in America is so gung-ho about my village. Even most Nigerians have hardly heard of my village."

Immediately after Marian hung up, Itse called Cindy.

"Why is sleepy head up early," she asked. She was driving her car and he could hear Rod Stewart wafting out of the car stereo. "Marian called me this morning. She woke me up," he said and he told her the story.

"Maybe you have a white cousin," she said gloatingly.

"Not likely. It could be Alero."

Cindy had quizzed him about his relationship with Alero, and had asked him if she was not a secret wife in Nigeria. It was a topic that recurred over months before she eventually believed him. Itse thought Cindy accepted his story.

After, she wondered if Itse was also afraid to date the girl because of the stigma. Even though he denied it, she was still not sure if it was a subconscious caution that stayed his hand romantically.

"A girl of such fabulous beauty must have tempted you," she wondered. She used to call her Alejo, like a Spanish word with the "j" sounding like h. Itse corrected her and told her the "j" sounded the same way as in the English language. Alejo, he continued, meant stranger or visitor in Itsekiri language.

"That might be true if she did not feel like a sister right from my childhood days of innocence," said Itse defending his integrity on the question of any romance with Alero.

"But boys will always be boys," she persisted.

"I admit to occasional thoughts like that but they never turned to anything. I saw her have her bath when she was about 12 and I confess I was taken. But that was it. Believe me. Nothing happened.

"I believe you," she said with a view to putting his anxiety to rest.

That conversation took place when they were in college. Back to the moment, Cindy wanted to know where the mystery man who wanted to visit Africa lived in the US and what his name was.

Itse did not know where he lived but said his name was Tim.

He was not sure if his last name was Forester or Forster.

"He'll call me and I will know the details."

He said he would email Alero once he had confirmed the information.

"She may be too busy with her life as a beauty queen," Cindy said.

"I hear she is dating a famous prince now," Itse said

"Good for her," she said.

"Yes, and I am glad she is a happy girl now, after all she and her family have gone through."

When Tim Forester eventually told him his story, Itse eagerly wanted to hear back from Alero after sending her an email.

"It looks like somebody here in the United States, a white man, wants to visit Orogun. The young man says his great-great grandfather or something like that had a link with the royal family in slavery times. I am sure this will interest you, although you wouldn't want to see him in Orogun. I am sure we can arrange for him to see you in the city."

Itse was not sure he could be much help to Tim after a few phone conversations.

"He seems a little impetuous," remarked Itse in a phone chat with Cindy. "On the other hand, he sounds like a guy I want to have a beer with."

He did not know the real Tim. That made him a little hesitant. Tim had told him only a little about himself. He was a graduate student at the University of North Carolina at Chapel Hill, and he was working on a final essay on George Orwell's novels. But he was studying political theory, not literature. He wanted to show how a novelistic narrative could provide settings, characters and language that made a lot of sense to a political philosopher.

He said he was not a fan of the Carolina Panthers but a Green Bay junkie. He did not think much of the Denver Broncos. He also thought the Colorado Rockies were a waste of money by the owners and the city would suffer like the Red Sox, only that the city's heartache may not last as long as the torments of Red Sox fans all over America.

"You guys will be so pissed off the team will be sold off," he promised.

Itse did not care much for a fevered debate with him. He just wanted him to talk on. He was looking to eliminate any doubts, he told himself.

Taking the young man with him to Orogun would be a lot of work.

"I don't know much about that sort of research," he told Tim. "I am a software engineer."

"That doesn't matter," Tim said. "I just need your goodwill and a sense of security. Obviously, I have never been to your country before. I have never been to Africa. I don't know much about Africans, but I presume you can understand a young man's search for his own roots."

After a pause in the conversation, he asked if Itse was legal. It was not just the question but also the superior inflexion in the voice. Itse paused before he said yes.

"Thank God you are not like a lot of the foreigners," continued Tim.

Itse knew he was technically a foreigner, but he did not like the use of the word. It dripped disdain. He wondered why he used the word in reference to a man who was as conversant as anyone in the country with the cultural swagger of the society. He knew about baseball more than Tim. Itse had the stats in his palms, whether it was the National League or the American League. He also knew his basketball and hockey. His bragging rights intimidated many around him.

He let Tim know he did not like his choice of words, to which Tim laughed at first. But once he sensed the earnestness of Itse's silence, he apologised.

He also offered to see Itse in Denver in a couple of weeks.

Itse agreed.

Tim fixed a Friday for them to meet. They would have lunch together and see the basketball game between the Denver Nuggets and the Los Angeles Lakers. Itse wanted to buy his own ticket. He thought the young man from Chapel Hill was trying to wring his hands by bribing him. Or, as Itse thought, maybe he was considered another indigent black man who could not afford anything other than what he cooked in his kitchen. But he had told him he was a software engineer. That should count for something. Or did he think Itse a liar?

However, Tim had already paid. So, Itse decided he would pay for the drinks and snacks at the Pepsi Center and the lunch at the 16th Street Mall.

Tim was true to his word, and he arrived the specific Friday in November as he promised. Itse offered to pick him up at the airport, but Tim turned down the offer. Rather they met at an Alfalfa's Restaurant at the 16th Street Mall. But they decided instead to eat at the Cheesecake Factory.

The first impression Itse came away with was the intensity of Tim's eyes. He also cut an athletic figure, his bold carriage and confident voice now redefined all the conversations they had on the phone.

But the eyes emerged as though from fire. They seemed to tell his body what to do.

"How have you adjusted to winter in America," he asked in his southern drawl as Itse tried to adjust his leather jacket to the cold snap holding the street hostage. They walked briskly, both with their hands in their pockets. They stooped as though it would enhance the spring in their feet. The street also bustled with lots of fast feet, hoods, sweaters and jackets playing foil to the unruly swagger of the wind.

Tim's question had both good humour and a superior air. His smile was charming, even if the voice carried a starchy superciliousness. If he heard those words over the phone, Itse would have been more than a little offended. Now, he took them in his stride in that blustery afternoon.

During their lunch, Tim unveiled his quest. In between bites of sandwiches and swigs of coke, he told his African friend that he wanted to confront a monster in his life. The use of the word monster had Itse's attention, for its suggestion of humility.

"You see, buddy, I have had a lot of hate in my life," he began. His voice was even and his eyes shone as he looked Itse in the eye. He seemed defiant. "I almost did time in my undergrad years for assault. I was put on probation. I hit a guy after my slur did not work. It was after a local game and our team lost. I mean my former high school in Charleston. Some black guys sat near me during the football game and they rooted for the visiting team."

He noticed that Itse was now biting his bread deliberately, almost tasteless on his palate.

"I pelted the N word at one of them. He was shouting and hollering and out of control during the game. He knew that I was unhappy with the way he carried himself. But after my slur, he looked at me and went his way. He looked scared. So, I walked towards him and shoved him aside. He was upset and yelled something at me and I hit him. I hit him pretty bad. The cops came and arrested me. The black guy did not press charges, but the law still had to punish me for something."

Itse was not one not to probe.

"Why do you think you were so angry," he asked.

"That's a good question. I don't really know. Let me introduce myself properly. My father was John Forester, Senator Forester who died two years ago."

Itse held his cup of coke in the air as though he was not sure whether to drink it or drop it on the table. He remembered the buzz in the media when the famous senator died. He was a unique senator, avuncular, a fiery conservative in his heyday of what used to be known as Jim Crow south. He lived an irony though. He had a son from a black woman, and he never associated with him in public. He secretly cared for the son, paying his fees through college and providing for his other needs. He also provided for the son's mother. The media knew this, but somehow not much was made of this until late in his career, in his hoary years.

"You belong to a famous father," he said.

Tim observed Itse and was a little relieved that the African understood the circumstances of his tale.

"I challenged him about the love-child, and he would not come clean for some time. When he came clean, I had lost my patience with him. But that was not the real problem. He had given me a belief he could not take from me. He had become a preacher who did not live according to his sermon. As a son, I felt I was cheated out of the truth, out of my life. My father was such a towering figure in the country, especially in the South. Imagine the sort of role model he was to me. Once my father lost his integrity in that matter, I lost mine too. I had to battle the prejudice inside me. But instead of getting better, I got angrier. It was also in that circumstance that the high school incident happened."

He paused and took a sip of coke.

"I have tried to read books, understand other people. I had a deep healing exercise when I attended a church during Martin Luther King Memorial Holiday early this year. It was not just a church, it was interfaith and interdenominational. Christians, Muslims, Buddhists and so on were there. People stood up to talk about a society of giving and helping. Some of the songs and staged plays moved me. I felt healed, even if partially. Not long ago – and that's what really concerns you – a writer said he wanted to write a book on my father and wanted to advance the view that Senator Forester's secret affair with a black woman was not an accident. The family, he claimed, had a strong black fascination dating back to slavery times. A major ancestor actually was a big slave dealer and married in Africa and died there after making a life for himself. In essence, he is trying to prove that we have black ancestors.

"I told him that the book should wait. I wanted to be the one to tell such a story if it was true. But it seems it is. We have some documents that attest to some of the facts. I think I should go there, even if the man tells the story. It will be a lot of therapy for my soul. That's why I want to. The impression of my aunt Tara is that I want to disprove it, that I hate the idea of a black relative in my history. But that's not true. Or so I think. Who knows? She may be right. I would rather live in my lily-white suburb in Charleston than in Queens in New York. That's the truth. Look I'm not perfect. I just want to know what happened. Don't get me wrong. I am not always at peace with it. I grew up to look at the world in black and white. So, this adventure is a leap in the dark. It won't guarantee anything. But I need to try."

When the lunch was over, Itse saw a different person from the one he had spoken to on the phone. There was an edge of resentment even in his surrender to this adventure. It was this courage that impressed Itse. He said as much to Cindy after the basketball game. The Lakers made mincemeat of the Nuggets, but the day's triumph was the tentative bonding of two people who had no idea of each other about a month earlier.

"So, are you going to help him?" Cindy asked.

"Wouldn't you!" remarked Itse.

Cindy let him know that folks like Tim were not predictable, and she urged caution.

"People like him can snap and do stuff you don't expect," she said.

"I know," replied Itse, after a long pause. "That is why I think it is interesting. Two worlds are at war inside him."

"I agree, and I am proud of you."

It was not hard for him to agree to travel together with Tim. It had to coincide with his next business trip to Nigeria. Tim agreed.

Chapter Nine

One morning the elders of the village had just begun deliberation over the curse the white man might bring to their innocent village when one of the palace hands walked into their midst. Oruku's head shrank with anxiety. He carried an omen of bad news.

"What's the matter?" asked the king with subdued impatience.

Oruku hated this part of his duty because he had to step into the gaze of people. He believed that eyes only jeered at him. Oruku was a fat man whose size embarrassed him either in a crowd or when he was a centre of attention. Height was not liberal with him. Fat teemed around his bones. And he was 'brief'.

"Your highness, the *oyibo*…" Oruku almost stuttered. And that seemed to frighten all the elders in the huge chamber. But no one spoke. All stirred.

The king sat forward in his huge throne.

"What happened to the *oyibo*," he asked. A slight edge in his voice almost, for a second, devalued the solemn dignity of his royal presence. He realised that and sat back on the throne.

"No, he is here. Outside. He says he wants to see the elders."

"Let him in," the king roared. A mixture of relief and fresh apprehension led the king to order in the white man.

Except the king who sank into the huge throne – his minuscule figure further dwarfed by the timorous light in his part of the chamber – all the Chiefs and elders sat up. Huge candles lit to audacious flares illuminated the chamber. The candles stood often groggily on perches. The Chiefs sat up not out of deference for the strange visitor but out of curiosity. What mission was he bringing to them? Was he ready to go home now? Was his memory back?

Or, as one or two of them might have imagined, was the witch now about to go to the altar? Her witchcraft did not work in the city against the prince. Was she trying it on an *oyibo*, who had no counterfoil to any African juju? That was a subliminal part of the elders' claims against the woman.

Rarely was anyone allowed to interrupt the meeting of the elders. This was a special case. They looked at him as he walked into the chamber. They observed him in full for the first time since the beginning of the forest fiasco. They thought he was a little frail but bouncy for one who had almost waved goodbye to this earth.

He was tall and agile and seemed like one who might explode into laughter or shatter the world with a temper. As they watched him stand in the middle of the chamber, no one was sure what to expect.

"Mister Forester," said Tietie, "how may we help you?"

A tincture of hostile levity could not be suppressed in his voice. The elders noticed that the *oyibo* man was not impressed with the tone of the question. He probably did not understand it. One of the elders pointed to a vacant chair and he sat on it.

Apart from his skin colour, the Chiefs cast their eyes on the *oyibo* man's dress sense. No wonder, Chief Nikoro observed silently, Itse was known to dress that way. Tim looked rugged in a deep blue, short-sleeved, buttoned-down cotton shirt over a brown pair of trousers. His feet hid inside a pair of runners. The Chiefs had no shoes on. Only two of the ten present wore western-style shirts. The rest were draped in colourful cloths with garish designs that seemed to hang precariously on their ageing bodies. Like Itse's, the *oyibo* man's clothes were wrinkle-free. They did not forget he had the advantage of a generator. After he left the palace, some of the Chiefs remarked that, at least, he was enjoying some of the comforts of his home country. It was proper for him to treat the villagers kindly.

The chamber was large. The most distinctive feature was the throne, a voluminous chair that could sit two people and with a backrest higher than any man alive; at least, higher than anyone in Orogun. And the king, a little man, often moved around as though he was in danger of disappearing into it. Tim wondered about the significance of clusters of cowries and feathers and blood stains on the wall. Framed pictures of past kings and coronation ceremonies were also on display.

The floor was concrete, if a little cracked, but clean. The whole palace was adobe with a hoary ambience about it, especially the wall and part of the roof. He thought the palace might have been built a hundred years ago. The palace had a peculiar smell, he observed. Not necessarily objectionable but different. He did not know what to compare it with. But he told himself that was the least of his problems. He recalled Alero telling him that Itse said America had a smell. Tim did not understand what his Nigerian friend could have meant.

He stole a side-glance at the king. The man was also looking at him. He was slight but seemed to betray a restless charisma, a bold, wild, piercing pair of eyes, which seemed to compensate for his slight body frame. His rakish brown hat, with a feather tucked on both sides, tended to obscure his face. But the eyes flared out like two lonely balls of fire in a starless night.

Tim looked straight into Tietie's eyes and said, "Last night I discussed the issue of my memory with Alero and I wondered if Itse ever told you why I wanted to see the tomb."

A pause. Tietie seemed puzzled. But many of them, while not understanding the accent with its American drawl, were impressed with the near-perfect way he called his friend's name. This must have endured practice. Even strangers from other ethnic groups nearby missed its phonetic nuance.

"I mean, did he give you details other than that the person was some important person?"

Tietie translated the words to the others. He took pride in his role as mediator. He showed this in his words and looks with all their imprimaturs of contempt for Tim. He made a point to let others in Orogun know he did not like "the ghostly little intruder", as he put it in the Itsekiri language. He also said he never blamed the *oyibo*, as he put it once. If Itse had not been a good son, he would not be in this unenviable position. He would not have had to negotiate with an insolent youth who could not hold a candle to him if he were African and nurtured in the deferential ways of the land.

A few saw through this phoney exterior, and Tietie resented them. His revenge was to show more impatience with Tim. He knew that most of them who resented him were also jealous. They did not even know a smattering of English. They hung on Tim's lips but had to rely on the irritant to know what came out of them. He often boasted, if with quiet satisfaction, by asking where were the others when he demonstrated humility to learn from his daughter, Boyowa, who learned good English the way they spoke it in England.

The one person he dreaded was Ajuya, the retired soldier who was now out of town. The retired soldier spoke impeccable English and had contempt for Tietie. But the contempt was all the more potent because he showed up the haughty chief. His nemesis was out of town, so the chief had his sway.

The king muttered some words and, after a brief silence, Tietie cleared his throat and said:

"*He only say to us dat you want see de grave and write book and book will help famous our village.*"

"That's all?"

"Yes." There was silence. Each side seemed to expect the other to say or do something. The elders knew that the American wanted some detail, but they didn't seem to have anything to tell him.

Tim rose to his feet and said thank you. As he walked out, he heard the king talk to Tietie and Tietie, as if passing on a message, told him to "be careful of Alero. *She be witch.*"

They expected him to say nothing, a poker face absorbing the tension. But the American turned back in a dramatic pirouette, his body shaking with indignation.

"You have no right to judge anybody," he proclaimed in a voice as hoarse as it was imperial, his finger pointing straight at Chief Tietie and sparks dropping out of his eyelids. His body shook as if he was undecided whether to move forward and pierce the judgemental demon out of the eyes of the old man or simply walk away. He did not walk out but remained, groggily erect.

"If you really care about who the witch is, why can't you first deal with the truth?"

The king and his men were quiet, stunned by the visceral display of the foreigner whose attitude was a clear contempt of one of the most hallowed places in the land.

Chief Tietie was riled and was held down by adjoining Chiefs as he tried to stand on his feet. At that gesture, Tim turned without uttering a word and left.

As the American strode out of the palace, he looked up, and it seemed the sky was caving in on him. Barely thirty minutes before, the weather had no distinction. The sky, a bland blue, looked benign on a windless village full of human chatter and bare feet. Now, it was a frenzy. A feisty wind raked up dust, the atmosphere toned by the brown of the earth. The wind swished and howled and flew into Tim's face, as he hurried to the house. That walk would take another twenty minutes.

All about him, men and women and children darted about in defensive excitement. Tubs of foodstuff were being hustled into barns, wet clothes were unhooked from clotheslines, raffia-made windows slammed shut, mother called to daughter.

As the wind picked up momentum under the baleful sky, Tim began to run. Within twelve minutes, he was home.

The house had been built a year before. It was the only house built with a cement exterior and with city architecture. It also had electricity at night, thanks to the generator that Itse had bought. It sputtered interminably but it was the signature tune of the night, for many people. As dust stole into his eyes and the wind pounded him, he wondered how he met this guy who lived in this remote part of the world.

Alero was at the doorstep waiting for him

"I've never seen this kind of weather come so suddenly in this village since I was born," were her first words.

"It's all chaos out there," Tim replied.

Alero observed that Tim spoke in a conciliatory tone, and she suspected that the mission to the palace had ended just the way she had predicted. She followed him inside the house and saw his mood change almost dramatically. He sat in the sofa and raised his head to Alero.

"I have to go to the forest in a couple of days."

"What did they say to you?" Alero sat, her face a little frazzled.

"The point exactly. They said nothing."

"Then ignore them. They think you are under my spell anyway. Whenever you are ready, I am."

"I gave them a piece of my mind," said Tim. "That Chief Tietie called you a witch, and I flared up at him."

The young woman was not entirely surprised by the news. She knew he was capable of mood swings. But she told herself that his actions would confirm their prejudices that she had the foreigner on her leash. She realised long ago that she had no power over what her fellow villagers thought about her.

However, Alero felt very good about how things were turning out. She felt she was on the verge of a discovery. She wanted to see the spot where the locket was found. If the locket was there, then other valuables lay there too. But what she actually wanted to see were the remains of her mother. She would dig up the bones and bring them to the light of the village and show not only the people of the village but also the whole world, that she did not have the strain of crocodiles or any reptile in her family. They would see the skulls, the dry bones, and all the contours and angles of humanity in her mother's skeleton. She could now tell the world in clear language the history of her family's ostracism.

Alero brought sandwiches and a pitcher of tea with pasteurised milk in a can to the breakfast table. Tim had not eaten before he set out to the palace. He had woken up upset and helpless about his memory loss. When Alero came from her house, she had tried to calm him down and assured him that, in time, his memory would come back to him. She had said that the elders knew more than they were ready to reveal. But they would not say anything because that was their way.

"If there is a tomb in that forest, they know who is in there and where it is," she said. "That is not just another forest. It's sacred."

"So why won't they tell me and get this over with?"

"I don't know."

That was the reply that riled him and set him on the path to the palace. Alero tried to persuade him not to look desperate because the elders were accustomed to keeping secrets.

As Tim settled down to the meal, Alero referred to the veteran.

"There is only one person who can stand behind us in all of this battle. His name is Ajuya. He fought in World War Two. He's still strong enough to take on battles."

"Where is he?"

"He is not around. I hear he'll be back in a couple of days. He left just before you regained consciousness. If he were around, Itse would have told him all about your mission. He came briefly co-inciding with when you guys went into the forest. He would have befriended you. He always talks about Americans, though not always words of praise. He is the only one who does not treat me like an outcast. He claims to be enlightened."

After the meal, Tim saw some pictures scattered on the coffee table and reached out to see them.

"You only just saw them?"

"Yeah," he said, "I guess I was too preoccupied with what happened in the palace to see what was around here."

"I brought out all the pictures to see my mother's face again and also all the times of my glory. I was only a little girl. I never knew much before my mother was killed."

She did not say the whole truth. She knew enough at the age of eight. She knew her mother had lost her mental balance. Alero used to call her Marmalade after she introduced her to the jelly, and her mother described herself as sweet as the jelly. Marmalade was rare in Orogun, it was poetic on their palate. She said it jokingly, but somehow the name stuck. It was not long after that her mother lost her senses. She never took care of Alero much anymore. The only thing she did was to fetch water in the morning from the river. It was her only act of clarity. She performed it with manic zeal, with the efficiency of a pious ritual. After that, she returned home and lay on the floor outside the front door until her daughter woke up. Alero would have her bath, wear her uniform and cook herself breakfast. Her mother never knew how to help her with those chores anymore. She just wandered about the house until Alero was ready to go to school. Then she would accompany her to the school gate and wander away picking things into a large cellophane bag. She ate some of them, including rotten fruits. She often chewed on wood-chips and spat them away. She never agreed to change her clothes since the madness struck. But Alero tried a clever way out of this sartorial bind. When she slept at night, Alero woke up and tried to slip the clothes off her body. It was not easy. Mother fought with daughter in her delirium. She kept struggling and yelling, "leave me alone, or you must kill me first. You got a baby out of this the first time. Now you want to do it again. You cannot do it. You must kill me first." Tears rolled down her cheeks.

Alero was stunned. She did not understand, and Alero replied, "Marmalade, it's me. What did I do?" The voice affected her like a human finger on the touch-me-not flower. She folded up, her head tucked in her bosom, and her two legs pulled up so that her chest separated both her legs and her head. She calmed down and lapsed back to sleep.

Alero tried to change the clothes again, and it was the same ritual all over. That night, Alero did not change the clothes. She wondered what her mother was talking about. In her naïve mind, it was all so senseless, so needlessly accusatory.

During the day, after school, she would look around for her mother. People mocked her mother, especially little children. They called her crocodile, and they said her evil had caught up with her. She had swallowed many people in the village, and now she could no longer function as a real human being.

They also mocked her smell. With hardly any baths, she could never be Marmalade. They said they could not say which smell was worse, her body or the debris in her bag. The real marmalade, they contended, did not offend the senses. It made people drool.

This Marmalade inspired a contagion of retching. They knew that her urine was a big part of the smell and she had returned to her childhood. No one knew, they said, who was now the child, Alero or her stinking marmalade.

Even if she was so sweet to Alero, how could Alero not see her colour? She was light-skinned all right, they mocked. But look at how the sun had darkened her skin to ruins and had turned the marmalade into coconut oil, cooked and ill smelling. So, some of the children would call her coconut oil each time they heard Alero call her Marmalade. It originally pained the girl until she realised she preferred that vegetarian slur to the reptilian curse. Eventually she whispered her name. The other children did not hear and so they did not unleash their contemptuous chants. She had drained the power off the mockers' tongues.

In between her school homework and meals, Alero would follow her mother from a distance. She just wanted to know she was safe. She was never ashamed of her mother. She accepted her mother's madness. She also did not want to force her into a home. She wanted to preserve the integrity of her insanity.

Through rain and relentless heat, she kept watch on her Marmalade from a safe distance. Alero thought she had developed the unerring instinct to locate her in the hostile world of Orogun. But she recalled when she became an adult that Orogun was not that vast place with furtive alleys. What she did not articulate in her young mind was that she was often happy to find her mother alive, unspoiled by the village predators.

Nobody was ready to help her. Nobody even offered. The veteran did not have the resources; he would have taken her to a psychiatric institution in the city. All he did was to provide for Alero. Because of him, Alero never lacked food and clothes. Itse was Alero's only friend. They called him the crocodile girl's husband. Itse was never worried by the insult. He empathised with the girl because he never knew his mother and his father quietly encouraged the friendship. So, he often gave Alero food during breaks. Itse, however, had to play soccer, which meant Alero was all alone.

If she could not change her mother's clothes, she could work on her hair. That was what fascinated the villagers. Once Alero moved within her mother's ken and called to her, she responded as though transported out of her reverie. Calm would resolve into her face, and the jumpiness about her disappeared. She looked at her daughter as though it was a daughter looking at the mother. She would pay attention to Alero's every word. The children would mass outside and watch in amazement as Alero walked to her mother, and both of them spoke and the mother followed her home. In about an hour, the mother would appear on the street again, resuming her acts of lucid abnormality. But they also marvelled at her looks. Sometimes, the hair glistened with cornrows. At other times, it stood in rows of a woven mass. At some other times, the hair was plaited. She responded to that hour once a week. They bonded, mother and daughter. That was the only time their hearts met.

The first picture Tim laid eyes on was Alero wearing a crown over a beautiful dress in a grand ceremony.

"What's this?" He was astonished.

"That's me when I was crowned the most beautiful girl in the country."

He was quiet. He examined the picture and, in a low tone, said, "How did you turn from Miss Republic to crocodile girl?"

Alero looked him in the face to ascertain no mockery lurked in his eyes.

"That's one way of asking the question. You could also ask how I had turned from crocodile girl into Miss Republic. My life has gone full cycle."

"Well, I had always thought there was something about you. You are beginning to make sense. You sure have an interesting story to tell me. I would really want to know that story and maybe that could jolt my memory and bring my life story back to me."

chapter Ten

As they heard the wind thrash about outside, Alero stood up and asked the American to come with her to the window. He did. He preceded her to the window, looked at her and tried to compare the Alero he saw in the beauty pageant picture with the one standing before him. He observed the tall and willowy woman, her stately rhythm of the catwalk and poise of royalty anybody might expect of a person with such a pedigree. Her long, dark hair smothered both her shoulders. Her catwalk came to her naturally, he thought.

Yet she was a queen in virtual rags. Her clothes were almost nondescript, a faded gown that reached down to her calves. Her poise was now regal and now subdued. Her eyes, always melancholy, rolled sweetly; a canary's eye, an owl's eye. Her laughter cooed like the blues while craving the uproarious hilarity of rock or soul.

Both stood there as she raised the curtain. The view outside had become chaotic. The weather was now out of joint. But they could still see a remnant of people running about as a pall overthrew the horizon. Some of them were children caught off guard by the insolent visit from the sky. A knot of five children flitted by. They were four boys and one girl. But suddenly the girl defied the anarchy. In her wetness, she stood and looked at Alero and Tim. Whipped about by the wind, she stared with a defiant stillness through the blustery rain, mist and flying dust, eddy of leaves and rage of wood chips. She stared as though it was not raining; the wind was not howling or uprooting shrubs or shaking homes. Her eyes met Alero's. Her light blue satin gown clung to her, revealing the svelte outlines of her body, her small sharp breasts and tiny waist. She folded her hands across her bosom. In spite of the flurry around her eyes, she looked at Alero with unblinking boldness. Squalls thickened the mist between them, but both saw enough of each other.

This embarrassed Alero. She feared for her but did not know what to do at the moment. This one was not looking to mock. Alero smiled at her and waved. The girl, apparently shocked by the gesture, lifted both hands from her bosom and waved back, both limbs shivering in the wind. Suddenly, she woke up to the tumult about her, her eyes lit to a cheer; she waved again and disappeared into the village.

"What was that?" Tim asked.

Alero turned back to look at him, and said, "I don't know."

"That was quite an impressive girl," said Tim.

"Girls don't look boldly into older people's eyes like that. I did that as a child, and I was warned against it. Only witches show such boldness."

"Is she a witch then?"

"She should be careful if she does it to others. They might brand her a witch. As for me, I think the girl likes me. She is not a witch. You know I don't believe such nonsense."

"She likes you," noted Tim. "But more than that, she looks like you."

"Really?" Alero did not put much value to his assertion. All blacks must look alike to him. She often found it hard to distinguish white people, although she improved when she saw a lot of movies.

There was silence between them.

"Thank God we can still see the river," she intoned, as they looked out of the window again.

"That's where the story begins, Alero said, pointing to the river. "At least, the part of the story I know as it affects my family from about two generations ago."

"So, what's the point of the river?" he inquired.

She started, "I'm familiar with the story dating back to my mother and the crocodile legend. My aunt knows the rest of the story, but she would not say anything. She does not say anything. She is the saddest person I know. They say it dates back to the days of slavery. That's all vague. The leaders know this story as well as the veteran. He also for some reason would not talk about it."

In spite of the fog, the window offered a good view of the village. The two main features of the village were the Orogun River and the Forest of Silence. And since the forest was off-limits, people related more to the river. There was also a minor forest though the people merely called it the bush. There they entrapped grass cutters and chased down antelopes and humbled wild pigs. There were also several farms in the bush: locales of cassava, pride of yam tubers, forte of rubber and fortitude of oil palms.

The farm and river defined the lives of the people. As they looked out the window, they could see, as imperfectly as it was possible through the fog, the outlines of the river lying prostrate like a rape victim of the exuberant wind. The wind arched over her with the cargoes of dust, leaves, grains, pollen, small plants and the conniving shadows of the sky. They also had a fair view of the row of houses, above all, and the inhabitants taking asylum from this storm. The houses seemed to be doing all right until the thatched roof of one of them was swept off its hinges to join the elemental fury. Alero shuddered as they heard shrieks of agony from within.

"They'll be all right," she said, as if answering a question in Tim's mind.

Tim only concentrated on the river. He had seen that earlier in the day. He observed the river as the reference point for work and leisure. To fish, to water and farms, to cook and to swim. For ritual baths, for legends.

"At one time many years ago, people never swam there. The river was a snare and swimmers were meat for a notorious crocodile," she said.

Tim sensed that she was in the raconteur's mood. Her tone was deliberate and voice at once cracked and even.

As far as she knew, they only wanted to be happy and offered their space in this life. A place to tread, some air to breathe, a farm to till, and a smile and laughter. As far as they knew, every step landed in the dark, courted a wound. Every shoulder jostled a foe, every eye had a woe, every tongue secreted poison and every shadow hung in the air, ominous.

The crocodile was bad news to all who knew the river well, she regaled Tim further. No one had known of the river in such a malevolent way as far as memory could go. All good flowed from and to it. Until one sunny afternoon, when a ten-year-old boy, known as the "Other Fish" because he swam so well, was caught and eaten up by the reptile. Everyone present saw the boy being dragged away. They saw the reptile's jaws take him by the torso. Amidst the roar of waves and many splashes, they heard the boy's cry drop into a plea, into silence. They saw his flesh choke, his blood gurgle furiously and float on the river, a trail in a red line, leading into the distance. The fine boy had gone to the water monster.

Tim looked on at her, fascinated by her story. She continued her narration.

No one would forget the Other Fish, she said. No one would go to the river with eyes shut anymore. Father followed son, uncle followed niece. No one person was allowed to be there alone. No one went far into the river. No one could avoid it, though. So long as water was important to humans, rivers like the Orogun River would draw people. Where else could they source their water? They all prayed that in time the reptile would go back to the Atlantic Ocean from where it came. But bad news could not be stopped. People got missing only to reappear hours later as remnant bones afloat.

"Did they have a description of it?" asked Tim. "Were they sure it was only one crocodile?"

Alero responded, "They probably did not pay much attention to that. Very quickly, it was named the evil violator, the enemy of the gods. Ritual followed ritual to pacify it, to make peace. The water was sanctified; the village priest performed other nightly rites. Death and evil omen skulked the river. The villagers wondered: would they not go extinct someday? Was this some form of apocalypse, a brutal surrender to the gods!

"Even though people went in groups, mama went alone. She had nobody to keep her company, except on occasion when my aunt Mogha was around and she was hardly around."

"Is she the sad one?" asked Tim.

Alero replied, "Yes, the sad one."

Alero moved away from the window and went back to sit down. Tim came to join her. She then continued her storytelling.

"My mother was going to take the risk anyway. Or else who would provide us water. But the world had noticed. The outcast woman defied the great beast and fetched her water and survived night after night. The word began to go around that she actually swam and went deep into the river. They said they had a witness and that the woman must have some spell around her. Why did the crocodile not take her for dinner when all others who took precautions ended in its jaws? She told me she had to take the risk and I had to live with it. I was scared but helpless."

"She was a courageous woman. That was too much of a risk," said the American.

"It had nothing to do with courage, she told my little mind then," Alero said. "It was all about need. It was all about fending for a little daughter. It was all about dredging up the last ounce of energy to see the next daylight if it would come. She just had to do it. This went on for up to six months. But about two months later, something happened. My mother woke up one morning, and she could not coordinate things. She scratched her hair and she almost burned the house from what seemed like cooking. But there was nothing in the pot. It took me a while to note that my mother was losing her sanity. I had a mother with developing madness on my hands. But I did not know it that way until the veteran came. I had come from school and mother was already wandering in the streets. The veteran said I should remain in the house and be kind to my mother. She would be okay, he promised. She was only undergoing some worries. Once it was over, she would be fine. I prayed for the crocodile to die, or be caught and destroyed. I thought it was the worry. But since mother still went to fetch water for me, I was no longer sure. I allowed her because I thought that was the only thing she did for me. That was how I claimed her as mother again when I woke up and saw the pails of water filled and gleaming with water. The other one was when I plaited or matted her hair. The third one did not happen. I could not really bond. I wanted to change her clothing, but she would not."

Alero stood up and started to walk back and forth in the room, continuing her narration. "Before the madness bloomed, a shock came to me one day while at school where the usual taunt came from all the other children. I heard that my mother turned into a crocodile after swimming to some length in the river and transformed into a woman once she reached the shore. I could not wait to get home. 'Marmalade, they say you turn into a crocodile and come to eat everybody,' I said to my mother. She laughed as tears coursed relentlessly down her cheeks and she said, 'Don't mind the little devils. They say only what their parents say to entertain themselves.'"

"Did you believe your mother?" Tim asked.

Alero looked wistful and said, "I did and I didn't. Maybe she was not. The world hated her. She never ate much meat or fish. How could she have the appetite to eat all those dead people? That was the story behind the locket and the cameo. She wore it around her neck as a mark of defiance. She was the picture on the round-like encasement. Look at it, the big eyes and the massive hair and you know this was not a crocodile. Mama wore it everywhere, to the bathroom and sometimes she wandered onto other people's farms. People sneered and sniggered. She wore it almost as though oblivious to the world. A few days after that, she became another person, with incomprehensible words and gestures out of sync with who brought me into this world. The madness was in full flight."

Alero paused, her eyes looked moist. "One night she left and never returned. I made it a habit to wait for her. The headmaster did not view lateness with kindness. But I pretended to be asleep and waited to see the first flickers of light that heralded her return. But this night there was no light, no return. I waited endlessly and always thought that she would come. I waited until I drifted away into slumber. I woke up late. Predawn light wooed me. I told myself,

I missed her this time. She came and I did not see her. I rose up and left for her room. Maybe she went there. She did occasionally. I went there to greet her with good morning. The door was open. Nobody was there. She must have been tired, I thought. Or maybe she was out early that morning, so I checked the barn behind the house. She was not there. I called out to her. Marmalade, Marmalade. My voice shot through the shrill fog and rebounded in a thousand echoes."

Tim blinked as Alero's voice began to sound strained but he did not interrupt her as she continued her story.

"I began to notice the dryness of the ground in the hallway around the bathroom and kitchen. Wet ground was a constant marker of her trips to the river. Water often spilled from the pail. I did not see the pail around. No water meant no bath for me. Would I go to school without having my bath? I had no clue what to do. My mother did not answer my calls. She was not Aunt Mogha who left for the farm before the world opened its eyes. Mother made sure my water was ready before I made for school."

Some trickles of tears began to course down Alero's face. "I did not guess what had happened but my eyes dissolved into tears and my whole body convulsed. I muttered where's my mother, where's my mother? Over and over again. The morning was cold, or it felt cold, but I could not stay inside the house. I stood around the barn for a while sobbing and then something creaked inside and I remembered the veteran had warned me not to stay long in the barn because of snakes and other wild animals. It was empty but there was enough stuff inside like wood splinters, broken china, and lots of weeds. Snakes could hide there. I went inside and looked around the house but I remained restless and agitated. In spite of myself, I decided to head for the river not knowing what to expect."

"Did you think she was already taken by the croc?" asked Tim.

Alero did not directly respond to Tim's question but continued her narration.

"Like a wet cat along the lonely road to the river, I kept murmuring my mother's name. I knew no one could hear me, but I kept calling her name. I kept saying, Mama where is my water? I want to go to school. Marmalade I'm hungry where is my food? And I cried and hoped Marmalade would emerge from behind me and touch my shoulder and say 'I'm here, let's go home, it's cold outside.'" "What time was that in the morning?" Tim asked.

She said, "I don't know. Maybe four o'clock. No one seemed awake except me and the fog and pre-dawn glow that covered me like a funeral robe. My steps moved even if they were hesitant. I did not know what I was doing. I was hoping someone would come and say, 'I saw your mother. She is fine.' But if someone saw my mother, who would tell me except the veteran and his wife and Itse, who was my only friend in the world then?"

Alero stood up and went to look out of the window again. Tim stood and also went to the window. The rain was now falling evenly outside. Alero continued to tell her story.

"After what seemed like an eternity, I heard the swash and saw the subdued shimmer of the river. It was then I knew that I was in trouble. A whiplash, an electric shock. Where is Mama? 'Marmalade I want to go to school. Marmalade I am hungry,' I kept saying. Then I stood ramrod shocked. My eyes had seen something. The pail, a wide, deep bowl with my mother's imprint glowing around it, lay there, voiceless, unshaken, oblivious of me. The water had a timid wave. The air was still cool and shrill. I moved closer. I saw on the stream some of my clothes and Marmalade's clothes and a bar of soap and the river shuddered. The morning had lost its name. I felt a heat wave from inside me. Suddenly, I started shouting Marmalade, crocodile. I shouted into the still air. I cried convulsively. Marmalade, tell the crocodile to leave you. Mama, I want to go to school. Marmalade where are you? The village probably woke up. But two men came to the river suddenly and wondered what I was doing there alone in the morning."

"Who were they?" Tim asked.

"One of them is often called a prince up until today. His name is Aja. He is not royal in any way. The other person was his lackey. He was always sick."

"Is he still around?" he asked.

"Always around, especially during festivities," Alero said, "So, he asked me why I was there without my mother. 'Did I not know the rule? Didn't I know of the crocodile?' I told them I hadn't see my mother. By then more people had come around. I was weeping and shaking and had lost my voice. All of them gathered around me. Most of them said nothing. I was like an exotic animal in a sad affair or the little devil in the tale of the crocodile. Nobody said anything in a while. Nobody comforted me. Nobody touched me or asked me to stop sobbing. Until the warmth of a shadow cradled me, and the veteran's voice called my name. He touched me like a healer."

"*Do, do,*' he said to me."

"What does that mean?" Tim asked.

"Sorry," she explained.

"I've heard it around," he said.

Alero continued her story: "He took me to his house and told his wife to make me breakfast while he went to Warri to see Auntie Mogha and tell her that my mother was missing. I did not go to school for one week. I was bitter and angry with my Aunt for not being around. If she had, the crocodile would not have taken my mother. I did not want to eat her food and did not want her to take care of me. She took care of me anyway. One morning, about two weeks after, the veteran came to our house and said to my Auntie, 'If the crocodile had eaten her, they would have found something of her body parts or clothes.' I asked if that meant my mother was still alive. He said he was sure my mother was dead, but he could not figure out how it happened. What of the crocodile? I asked further. He said no one knows for sure if she was killed by the crocodile. I did not say anything. I was scared to ask the next question in my mind."

"What was it? That she might be the crocodile?" Tim asked.

"Yes, I learned that was the beginning of the veteran's fallout with the village authority."

"What did he do?" Tim asked.

"Nothing. He owed a lot to them, but they all respected. He was a bit bohemian and critical but never subversive. But he suggested to them quietly that they knew what had happened to my mother. Between him and the village elders lurked the omen; a secret. That was the character of the fallout," she explained. "My mother's case and the way I was treated that morning and the indifference to finding my mother pained him a lot. They didn't think well of my mother and we were discriminated against but he expected them to show a little compassion."

"He was close to your mother?" asked Tim.

"He was like her uncle. He was the only person who ate my mother's food, the only person who paid social visits. My Auntie was quiet a lot of the time, except when she wept. Once, she wept aloud in her room. She said things I had not heard. She said: 'I told her not to but she would not listen. I don't have a father. I don't care. But I told her not to. Let her father be. The world hugs its silence. The world prefers its silence. But she said she would say it out and let others know.' She kept sobbing and mumbling things I did not understand.

But somehow I didn't believe mother was going to say anything. Her mental faculties were not balanced. But her sister seemed to see clearly once she spoke on this matter. I think my aunt knows the person. She would not say it. She would go to her grave with sealed lips." "What silence was she talking about? Whose father? Yours?" Tim asked.

"Yes, my mother said she was planning to confess who my father was because they alleged that my mother was impregnated by an evil spirit, not human. She was not married or associated with any man. The incident of the crocodile made the matter worse. They said she was impregnated by a crocodile just like her. When I returned to school, Itse came to me and asked me not to believe what the other students would tell me during break. He found it hard to tell me what the students were planning to do. He said to ignore them. But a few moments after I sat on my stool, one student came to me and asked me when I planned to join my mother in the river. Another said my mother was a murderer. One teeny, tiny girl asked what body parts of the crocodile's victims did my mother give me and were they delicious? I burst into tears. Itse hit one of the girls and it was then that the teacher, who had acted as though it was not happening, intervened and asked her to kneel in front of the class for five minutes. The teacher also asked me to stop crying and do my work."

"He didn't ask you why you wept?" asked Tim.

"He knew, he knew the entire story, even if he did not live there. I learned later that he needed to keep his job, so he had to do the right things to stay out of the ire of the elders. I reached home that day and found the veteran with my aunt. He looked indignant and helpless. He said he learned that the crocodile had been killed two days before the disappearance of my mother. They had set a trap for it, killed it and buried it in an undisclosed place. But they kept it a secret because they needed to link my mother with the reptile. My mother's disappearance would coincide with that of the crocodile and confirm to all that my mother was not the warm-blooded mammal in angelic form."

"The croc, my dear, is in that forest," said Tim emphatically.

"That's what I think," Alero said.

chapter Eleven

I f the elders of Orogun knew anything, it was caution. They despised dithering. So, they gathered one morning and decided to send high-powered emissaries to the village of Aloma to enlist the support of Chief Oluku. Chief Oluku was the uncle of Lance Oluku, the man most people expected to become the president of the United States. The Orogun Chiefs saw him as a king, even though the larger country operated a democracy. One of them called him the king of the world.

"His father married an *oyibo* woman, and she thought he did not acquit himself well during their marriage," said Chief Otubu a few days before the journey. It was their first real meeting to tackle how to pre-empt any military incursion into their village. The king was not present at this little summit. They convened in a smaller room in the palace, a rotunda of thatched roof, spare space and small, round windows. It enjoyed a niggardly draft for ventilation and smelled of camphor. To stave off perspiration, each chief had his hand fan woven from raffia palm.

"How did you know that," asked Chief Ometie. "Were you there?"

"That is the story everyone is telling us, according to my daughter who can read and write," explained Chief Otubu.

"I mean what do you mean that he did not behave well during their marriage? Is behaving well not the woman's role?" asked Chief Orumatsoma.

"He told the *oyibo* that he wanted a second wife, and the woman said no. He got angry and decided to come back to Nigeria," Chief Otubu narrated.

All the Chiefs clung to his lips.

"These *oyibo* women can get angry very quickly. She drove the man out of the house. She was upset that the man could contemplate another woman. The poor man became helpless in a foreign land. He also wanted to come back with his son but the woman would not allow him."

"That's nonsense," Chief Ometie cut in. "These *oyibo* women are really crazy. I learn they control the men. The *oyibo* men don't know anything. They only know how to destroy and piss in their beds at home."

The Chiefs throbbed with laughter.

"You all just stand here and make up stories you know nothing about. Did you ever speak to the *oyibo* wife to hear her own side of the story?" railed Chief Boyo, one of the usually taciturn Chiefs, also known for his temper tantrums.

Chief Tietie did not like him but he found himself nodding his head. The other Chiefs were not ready to engage the irritable elder. They acted as though they did not hear Chief Boyo's throaty assertion.

"No wonder," Chief Otubu continued, "he left without his son. But when he came back, he married a proper woman and then another one. I think it pained him that he could not see his son; so, he got the court to allow him see his son. He visited the country about twice and he saw his son. The woman allowed him. That was because the court forced her."

"If the woman drove him out of the house, how come she allowed the son to bear the father's name," asked Ometie.

They all laughed again.

"Exactly," said Chief Otubu sarcastically. He was a little impatient with Ometie.

"The son did not know much about his father and where he came from. So he came back here many years later when he was a full man. But the father died in a motor accident in Warri. Some people said it was the will of the gods for marrying an *oyibo* woman. Others said it was the woman, the *oyibo* witch, who took vengeance because the man desired a second wife."

"Didn't he know?" asked Tietie, who was quiet with seething contempt. "Didn't he know that an *oyibo* woman would not brook a second wife when they married?"

"I think," remarked Orumatsoma. "Maybe he was desperate to sleep with an *oyibo*, so he lost his senses. By the time he realised it, he already had a son with her."

The journey to Aloma village gulped the whole day. If they had the resources for a car or an *okoala*, it would take barely two hours. If it were *okada*, then they would have to go in a convoy. Motorcycles would not take more than two people.

Ometie suggested that all six of them on the delegation could go in two *okadas*. Motorcycles had a seat for the rider and the passenger but somebody else could be squeezed in front, between the rider and the steering. The seats were no paragon of comfort. The leather wearied out of the way; the light-yellow cushions, browned from the depredations of sundry buttocks and the relentless lashings of sun and rain and dust.

"You don't know what you are saying," remarked Chief Tietie, who had been waiting for a moment to ridicule Chief Ometie. "You think we are little boys. Where is the room for all of us?"

Unknown to him, Chief Tietie succeeded in sniping at himself more than any of the other Chiefs. He carried the biggest paunch among the Chiefs. All of them had paunches. The protuberance heralded them wherever they appeared. But it was not necessarily comfort for all the Chiefs. The unintended raillery recreated in their memory of a few years back when they all followed the king in the same fashion to Igun village for a wedding. Two of the *okadas* broke down from the sheer weight of Chief Omonikanrin. He had paired with Chief Ometie, but barely thirty minutes into the journey had the motorcycle broken down. He had to pair with Chief Ololo.

The ride did not last twelve minutes. Only three motorcycles made it to the destination. Of course the *okadas* were old, sputtering and puffing ruthlessly. Sometimes a cloud of smoke enwrapped the rider and passenger so that the ride looked like a rocket exploding in slow motion. Coughing was routine for the riders. Some of the Chiefs had to endure the humiliation of walking the distance with their colourful clothes, the hats with wide felt brims and with the feathers hanging over the hats like ornate antennas tremulous in the wind. Chief Tietie had to rummage in a roadside bush for eternity to retrieve one of his feathers. It flew off his hat when he lost his guard while exchanging pleasantries with Chief Ololo.

The joke was on Chief Ometie's laboured breathing after only five minutes of walking. They all wore the traditional wrappers, made of thick cotton fabric in a variety of bright colours. But they tied the affair so that its top bunched up around their waists like a towel. Most of them did it artistically. It clung to them like trousers. They could walk and jump without the fear of it falling off their waists and unveiling their shorts underneath. But it did not always guarantee a nimble walk. The wrappers' hem often stretched to their ankles, which chastened their strides. Since this was a protracted exercise, they were going to subject themselves to the bully of a dirt road, most of it narrow.

The remarkable thing about their journey was that the atmosphere gradually lost the oppression of the fog. The air grew lighter. Ditto their vision. But the dreary thing was the mud. It had rained the previous night. Potholes slowed them down and thick clay clung to their bare feet, weighing them down as they trekked along. Sometimes they had to lift up their wrappers and leap over some puddles. Chief Boyo once slipped and careened all the way to the ground. The cries of "sorry" from his fellow Chiefs infuriated him further. Two of the Chiefs lifted him off the ground. The fallen chief looked as though ungrateful to his fellow travellers even though he would have soiled his white shirt further if he had tried to manoeuvre to his feet.

"No one can recognise your shirt again," said Chief Tietie. It was not clear if he said it regretfully or gloatingly. His voice was solemn. The silt had to be washed off. They went to one of the puddles nearby with opaque water. Chief Boyo pulled off the shirt, revealing his white singlet, which also did not escape the incursion of the stains.

Chief Boyo washed off the marks. The shirt and singlet did not return to their white sparkle but they were clean enough. They resumed their walk. The chief had to hold his shirt in one hand and singlet in the other, so they would get dry in time for him to slip them on. He looked ungainly with a bare torso over an ornate wrapper. The wrapper was a blend of red and yellow. They did not have to wash it, since its colours could conceal the damage of the fall. They plucked some banana leaves from the nearby bush to clean off the silt.

The others who travelled on motorcycles had to manoeuvre through and puddles and potholes. When they arrived, they reported no incident. The rider was very good, the Chiefs who trekked commented. The comment had the brew of envy more than goodwill.

They arrived at Chief Oluku's house in the evening. They were exhausted. Chief Boyo's clothes were dry enough, so he had them on. The Chiefs knew they had an important mission. They would not show their exhaustion. After all, they were the Orogun elite, the historic village of warriors and hefty yam tubers. The Forest of Silence was a marker of their redoubtable past.

Chief Oluku's home was much like Itse's. Ometie wondered aloud as they entered the sitting area from where he derived his resources. They saw a television set, a refrigerator, and an object, which they could not really understand. It did not have knobs like the radio or television but a lever at the side.

"These *oyibo* people with their many toys," said Orumatsoma.

But what struck them the most was the picture on the wall, just across from the entrance door. It was the first anyone saw while walking in through the door. It was Chief Oluku and Lance, his nephew. Lance wore a navy blue pair of jeans under a light blue tee-shirt. They were about the same height. Chief Oluku wore a suit, a brown jacket over a white shirt and a black bow tie. They had their arms around each other. Their smiles were more like half smiles as though each of them wanted to chasten their excitement. Chief Oluku's suit seemed to have been purchased ten years earlier.

The host walked in. He was tall and imposing but stooped a little. His huge frame made him walk ponderously at times. He moved to a special chair at the east end of the sitting room which obviously belonged to the man of the house. It was of a garish forest-green colour and it was separated from all the others. Unlike the others which had cloth seats, his was leather.

They were lucky they met him at home, he said. He had planned to travel earlier in the day to Warri, to negotiate with the regional examination board on how much he would be paid as one of the mathematics' examiners. He had a degree in mathematics from the University of Ibadan, the country's premier university.

His son had malaria and he had to stay behind. Chief Oluku smiled and shook hands with all the Chiefs. He held a big kola nut in his right hand, and he quickly swung into a traditional welcome ritual.

"I greet you my friends and elders of Orogun".

He placed the big kola nut, about half the size of an orange on a saucer on the centre table. The table's brown colour hid under a white lace cover cloth, which was beginning to fray. He took a pocketknife from a ledge. The pocketknife was at the ready for this sort of event. With effortless efficiency, the knife cut into the nut and diced it into many pieces. He picked one of the pieces.

He then chanted a prayer in the Itsekiri language.

"*Aghan do,*" he said when he was done.

He knew Chief Tietie well and when he spoke, he looked only at Tietie's face, although it was clear he was addressing everyone.

He asked one of his sons to serve the men drinks, and the son brought glasses and a bottle of Coca-Cola for each of them.

Chief Oluku said he was glad to see all of them. He also guessed that the matter that brought them to the village of Aloma in the evening must be serious indeed.

As expected, Chief Tietie cleared his throat and told the host why they came.

Chief Oluku smiled a rather affectionate smile. He understood their worries and the first question he asked was whether the American believed his country would invade.

"He won't tell us," cut in Chief Orumatsoma.

Chief Oluku smiled and looked away.

"Well, you know my son is not the US president yet. So, my position is not relevant in this matter. Maybe, in three months, he will win. No one knows. But you should not worry. They are too busy with elections right now."

"But if you talk to him, he will listen," remarked Chief Tietie.

"Of course, he will." Chief Oluku paused. "Look," he said, trying to disguise his true feeling and parry the questions, "you have had a long walk. I am sure you need a proper meal and a rest tonight. I will ask my son to arrange rooms for you."

Chief Oluku asked one of his wives to make a huge meal for all his visitors. He offered to take them all in his Toyota minivan to Orogun on his way to Warri.

The next day, after Chief Oluku dropped them off at Orogun, they felt the man had treated them with contempt.

"He does not want to help us," remarked Chief Tietie. He was too civil to them, remarked some of the others.

"He was secretly laughing at us," remarked Chief Otubu. "Did you observe he would not say a word during the ride back? He said he was developing a sore throat. A sore throat my foot."

The reticent Chief Boyo laughed. If Chief Oluku was laughing at them, why did they not turn down the offer of a free meal and bed and walk back that night? They ignored him again.

Chapter Twelve

The two still kept their eyes on the tumbling weather, at flying twigs and bowing trees and dust devils and remorseless wind and the river lying listless, like a deflowered maiden.

Alero was poised to go into her story, and Tim was ready to leave the window and grab a chair. But Alero saw a form in the opaque chaos of the horizon.

"Who is so unlucky to drive into town at this hour?" She asked.

Tim turned back and saw a Peugeot 504 wiggle uncertainly through the storm, the nervous wiper leading the charge against the dust and rain and splinters.

The driver must be used to this road, the visibility is almost zero, Tim commented.

It was an old car. Its engine puffed and coughed and its tyres, with threads limping out from lacerations, were in the last stages of resistance. The car was dented all over, but it had a resilient energy about it as it willed its way through the storm.

They could hardly see the outlines of the two people inside as the car boomed past the house. Cars were rare in the village and any time one wheeled into town, everyone gazed even if it was of the old and rickety variety like the one riding the storm.

Alero and Tim were fascinated by the tenacity of the car and passengers.

Look at where it stopped. Who might that be, she wondered.

The car stopped in front of a house about a hundred yards away. But the door was not opened for a while.

"What's going on?" asked Tim.

"I don't know, he's having problems coming out of the car."

Alero said the words in a tone of intimacy. So Tim asked, "Who's he?"

"The veteran," she said, a shadow cast over her face.

Moments after she spoke, the car door was flung open and an elderly man got out of the driver's seat. He looked weak and his movements feeble and hesitant.

"That's him huh?"

"No, that must be his friend. The veteran is older."

The driver walked to the other side of the front seat and as he tried to open the door, he tripped and fell to the ground.

"They need help," said Tim.

"Wait for me here," said Alero, "I will go there and offer some assistance."

She walked to the door and saw Tim following.

"You don't have to go," she said. "You know you're still recuperating. All I need to do is walk the veteran into his house."

"That's bullshit," he said.

Alero was astonished at the words but said nothing and yielded. The door opened to a burst of wind and rain that splashed into them and pushed them inside. But they regained their momentum and pushed back onto the street, denying the wild elements their victory. The driver was on the ground still trying to pull himself together. Within a minute, both Alero and Tim were drenched. Their strides were slowed as they lumbered along, the force of the wind tugging at them.

Within thirty yards to the car, Alero almost tripped.

"Walk slowly, we'll get there," Tim cautioned, his voice barely audible in the drone and clatter of the weather. He thought Alero didn't hear him. So he moved closer to her and held her arm. She flinched and withdrew and almost tripped again. A smile of easy languor spread on the American's face.

Tim held her hand this time, and they walked more deliberately. Before they reached the car, the driver had found his feet and was making for the front seat when Alero shouted into the weather.

"Wait, sir, we'll help you."

The man was astonished. He looked about seventy years old. He stood still, wet all over with caked mud on the rear end of his trousers and his feet.

The man did not know Alero. He was astonished at the sight of the white man in that part of the world. Tim observed.

"Take him into the house, while I get the veteran," Tim said.

The veteran was already looking at them from the car window. Alero held the driver's hand, and they walked gingerly over the stoop, and they opened the door, which was, like most others, never locked.

Tim opened the car door and extended his hand to the veteran.

"My name is Tim, I'm Alero's friend."

The veteran said nothing. He looked at the American with an eye you might call of contempt. In a flash, Tim thought the man's look flitted from something of an affectionate disdain to curiosity.

But he yielded to the hand of the young man who pulled him quietly out of the car and walked him into the house.

Tim observed the house was sparsely furnished, with a few, old, cane chairs, no carpets and it had the same peculiar smell he had inhaled in the palace chambers. He saw epaulettes on the wall and framed pictures of the veteran as a young man in uniform.

Without thanking Tim for his troubles, he made straight for his bedroom. Tim noticed that the man had only one hand, the left hand. By the time they entered the house, the driver was already in dry clothes and Alero busy was in the kitchen.

Tim was alone with the driver in the sitting room and all he heard the old man say was thank you, thank you very much. After a while, he asked how America?

"America is fine, thank you," said Tim.

The veteran walked in a few moments later and his eyes met Tim's. He gazed like one who never blinked. He was also energetic for a man over eighty years of age, and had vitality in his almost feminine voice and a pair of big eyes that suggested that he saw astonishment everywhere. He said nothing to Tim but asked for Alero in the Itsekiri language while his eyes still gazed at Tim yet the American knew he was not talking to him. The driver answered him and Tim knew that he was looking for Alero. The man strode toward the kitchen, buoyed by a walking stick he held in his left and only hand. He was short and slight but had an energy that belonged to another body.

Tim looked at him fixedly as he approached the kitchen but Alero materialised at the door and halted the veteran's choppy stride. Both of them spoke not in the Itsekiri language but pidgin English and Tim picked only a few words from the conversation, which were basically about him.

"*Who be that oyibo? Where you meet am?*"

"*Na for Orogun here,*" she said looking at Tim with a reassuring smile.

"*Who bring am come here?*"

"Itse."

"*Itse done come?*"

"*Yes, sa.*"

"*Where he dey now?*"

"*Sick.*"

"*Him bring sickness from America?*"

Alero then gave him the background story and told him about the forest fiasco and Tim's amnesia. The veteran had known about Tim before he left, although he never met him. He was hurrying out of town when they arrived. He only had a few debates with the elders and stirred them to discomfort. He knew he would come back to the histrionics of the village.

Alero knew the veteran knew about Tim and about Itse's condition and the *oyibo* man's unwillingness to return. But he wanted to make the drama in front of Tim just for the sheer fun of it. He feigned it all. Alero knew it and played along. She knew better than not to do so.

But she said nothing about the locket.

The veteran's seamed face lit up, and it was a brilliance of worry, not of joy. He said once the weather let up he would go to Itse's house. Tim knew from his visage that the sick young man must be special to him. He turned restless and his one hand fidgeted within his large blue robe.

Alero melted into tears and sobs and, at the same time, offered words of encouragement to the old man, saying that the doctor was hopeful.

The veteran wondered, in a return to the feigned dramatics, why the elders wouldn't take the child to a proper hospital. Alero explained that the elders were afraid the word would go abroad and reach the ears of a newspaperman.

"So what?" He asked with clear-eyed indignation.

"They feel the Americans will invade the village."

The veteran paused and walked to the American.

"Do you think America will invade this village?" He sounded comical to Tim, although his face was serious.

Tim didn't say a word.

The man walked back to Alero and said, "You see the American here knows it's all foolish thinking. These Chiefs can't make my boy a sacrifice."

Tim was impressed with his English, but he was not sure what to make of a man who would grimace rather than say thank you to his rescuer. Just as this thought crossed his mind, the veteran turned to him and said, "You are the first American I have seen since I left Asia during World War Two. I lost my right hand there and almost lost my life."

"So, what did you think of the American soldiers?"

"I don't think anything about them. They fought hard as I fought hard. But I remember Gabriel Wright. Nice man. Wasn't racist. Many of them were. They did not want to talk to me. Gabriel died five years ago. We kept in touch. He said your country did not take good care of the soldiers. But he was a proud American. Always loved his country. You Americans love your country more than other people I've seen."

Alero wiped her face and returned to the kitchen while the veteran continued.

"I hear you lost your memory. I am sure you will get it back.

When I returned from Asia, I lost the memory of the war. I still can't remember many things. I can't remember everything about how I lost my right hand and I don't want to. Memory is not always a good thing. But you need at least to know why you came here. Are you still interested in returning to the forest?"

"Sure, especially now that we have not only the tomb to look for but Alero's mother."

The veteran paused. The last time he discussed Alero's mother being in the Forest of Silence was over ten years ago.

"Who told you that she's there?"

It was a question that required no answer, so he called to Alero with an anxious voice and she ran into the sitting room. No acting this time, and Alero knew it.

"Did you discuss going into the forest with this young man?"

The veteran always spoke in formal English with Alero when the matter was very serious. This was one of those rare instances.

Tim felt embarrassed. He should have stayed silent on that matter.

Alero was a little flustered but recovered quickly and whispered in the old man's ears.

"What! Where is it?" inquired the veteran.

"I hid it," replied Alero.

"I will recognise it if I see it. Are you sure it's not a fake?"

The veteran asked this question, as though he wanted a reply from both Tim and Alero.

"How can't I know it?" said Alero.

The man retreated to one of his chairs and said nothing for over ten minutes, while Alero brought in bowls of pepper soup and yam. The soup was hot and spicy and the veteran and the driver fell to the meal. It was a clear antidote to the cold. She gave a bowl to Tim.

"This is the hot soup I told you about," she said.

As Tim tried his first sip, the veteran broke his silence.

"If that is the locket, then you have brought good luck to this village."

Tim coughed and choked a little. The spicy soup stabbed his throat as he contemplated the veteran's words.

Alero brought him a cup of water.

"Sir," said Tim, "that's the kindest word I've heard since my recovery."

The man was quiet again. And then he said, "That's why they want you to leave. A big fight is in the offing. You have nothing to lose and if we win, we will have changed a history of over a hundred years."

"What history is that?" asked Tim.

"You will know once it happens. I told you not all memory is useful. I will add that they are only useful when we are forced to confront them. They kill us if we are not prepared. All wars wrestle with memory. Memories define us. You are young and have no memory so you have nothing to lose. Alero has nothing to lose. That is when battles are useful, when bloodshed has value. You give us added advantage because no one will touch you. They fear Americans and if they will touch anybody it is Alero. They killed her mother and ruined her aunt and all of her family. Alero once escaped but here she is, the prettiest girl alive, with little in the world except her weary soul and that of her dead mother," said the veteran.

Tim's mind wandered to the dream, the creature in white smoke again and something skipped ominously inside him. Anytime his mind drifted to the dream, he looked distracted and overwhelmed. But it came and went and anyone who looked at him saw two people within two minutes.

As the veteran spoke the front door was flung open, a young woman strode in and she genuflected to the old man. She did not show much enthusiasm towards Alero although they exchanged greetings and she thanked her for taking care of her husband while she was away.

She said she had not expected her husband's return that day and she did not know he had returned because of the weather. Most people did not peep out because the wind could rip the windows if they kept them even a little open. They didn't have Itse's glass window.

"We can now leave, sir," said Alero who wanted to leave the veteran to the care of his wife.

Both Tim and Alero ploughed through the fog, and reached home as people began to open their doors and windows, mainly made of wood and raffia palm. As they entered the house, she made straight for Itse's room and was satisfied that his situation had not worsened.

"Is that his wife?"

"Yes," answered Alero.

Tim was quiet, and then he said, "How does he relate to a woman who is at least fifty years younger?"

They get along. I think she is a kind of price of silence.

"What does that mean?"

"They gave him the woman so he would not pursue my mother's case."

"You mean a bribe?"

"Yes. But he did not know at that time. They knew he needed a wife and wanted this girl but the parents would not let her go. He realised it was some bait only a few years later. He has not known how to take vengeance."

Chapter Thirteen

The next morning, Tim felt like one with an ulcer in his mind. In the past twelve hours, it seemed he was experiencing a semblance of recollections, the past on a rebound. But it was more like droplets of memory; of timorous fingers of light. There were patches here, a hint there. Hardly any assured illumination. He saw a face, heard a voice but all disembodied. He felt like one looking into a mist and seeing outlines teasing the eyes and suddenly retreating behind vapours.

The closest he recalled of Itse was when they were walking to the plane. He had no idea what airport or city it was. He only saw him walk clutching a bag and flashing a smile. He had no idea what it all meant. He could not recollect the demeanour of other passengers around him, the colour of the plane, the time of day.

He also could not picture Itse in the Forest of Silence, before the pig lunged at them. He recollected images of the wild pig within seconds of him and somebody in the wake of the animal. He knew a form was behind the animal and he could only guess it was Itse. But that was all. The rest dissolved in a disappointing haze.

He also recalled an obscure past, over fifteen years ago. He did not know why his memory selected that and even then he did not make much sense of it. A neighbour and a basketball playmate most afternoons would not come out and play. He recalled but only faintly that the boy was feisty.

Each time Tim bounced the ball under the hoop hanging over their garage door, the boy ran over to play. But this afternoon, his partner did not come and, when Tim tried to go over to his place, Tim's mother restrained him and asked him to play alone.

He also noticed that the boy was watching him through the window but promptly shut the curtain once their eyes met.

A few days later, both Tim and his father walked to their car outside simultaneously with the boy and his mother. Tim's father consciously did not talk to them for the first time since they were neighbours. He recalled asking his father why he couldn't play with his friend anymore. That was when the shutter fell on his memory. He could not remember the boy's name or what happened later with him and his family. He did not know how he looked. In his memory, he was smothered in a sort of rainbow dust, now blue, now red…

The last recollection was his presence in what looked like a funeral service with two caskets glistening in front of a church. A fleeting flashback. That was what pained him the most. It cracked his bone. Who did he lose? Were some of these recollections a mischief of memory?

When Alero walked into the sitting room that morning, she observed a mournful tint on his face. He looked weary on the couch as though he could not summon any strength to even look at the entrant. His face was distracted, lost in that rustic space.

"What's the matter? You look really sad."

Tim stirred out of his reverie but his eyes still held their anguish, while he tapped his left fingers on his lap.

"Let's have breakfast," she suggested, there was a glow on her cheeks.

"I'm not hungry. I want to go home. I'm an American. I don't know what brought me to this hell of a place. It's spring this time of year. I should be inhaling the fresh air and watching the blossoms arrive."

Tim's voice had a raspy edge, a muffled rage and the personality traits Alero had observed manifested again. He had swung from lifeless to mercurial.

"If you want to leave I won't stop you," Alero said and paused. "But I wish to know why you have taken this sudden decision. Was it what I did or was it the veteran? It will be some relief for me if you leave. Frankly, I mean it. The villagers will not hold me responsible for the troubles in the village."

Tim glanced at her briefly and rose to his feet with an athletic bounce of a body powered by a mixture of anger and anxiety.

"I just want to go. I must have a return ticket. I'll go ahead and check my stuff and get going immediately."

He walked into the bedroom, and his eyes fell on Itse whose body twitched at the light that flooded in from the sitting room. Alero, who had woken that morning with cheer, dropped into melancholy and confusion. She tried to recall what was responsible for this white man's sudden change of heart.

Tim had been in good spirits throughout the day and the only smudge on the day was when little children pelted their derisive chants at her and Tim.

Their chants at Tim:

"Oyibo pepper

If you eat pepper

You go yellow more, more."

Tim did not understand what they meant, but she explained it, and he did not consider it foul.

They believe the childish myth that white people derive their colours from eating a lot of pepper seeds, explained Alero.

Tim did not take offence then. He even sympathised when they pelted her with the crocodile chant. So where did the sudden change of mind come from?

Within an hour, the American walked out of the room all dressed for the mission to return home. He wore a clean pair of jeans, which cradled the hem of a black cotton tuck shirt. A blue denim jacket obscured the rumples on the shirt and imparted a half formal, half rugged personality. His most distinctive feature was his face, his eyes especially. He had the exhausted look of a daredevil, lacking the strength of blood or muscle but powered by the sense of a new purpose, the romance of the unknown.

His eyes were blood-shot, but flared quietly. His carriage was lofty buoyed by a strength that seemed to come from somewhere else.

By the time he had packed his all in the bedroom and walked into the front room, Alero and the veteran were out there waiting for him.

"Where are you going, that sort of thing?" asked the veteran. Tim was puzzled by the second half of his question. Alero wanted to explain, but she was too upset to stir her lips. "That sort of thing" was a speech mannerism with the veteran. It meant really nothing. He said it when he was excited.

Tim showed his contempt for that nebulous phrase by turning to Alero and asking her if she had made transport arrangements.

"It's not difficult, if you don't mind riding a motorcycle for seventy miles. That's the only way you can get to a motor park with a car that goes to the capital," explained Alero.

"The rider is warming it up," said the veteran in a half-mocking voice.

Tim heard the delirious cough of an engine trying to come to life.

"Is that the one?" Tim asked.

Alero nodded looking out of the window.

The veteran cleared his throat and said: "If you leave this village, you will be the first American coward I've ever met. I heard of cowards in the battlefield but the ones I met had rocks in their hearts. You have an opportunity to find something that brought you all the way to this country and, because of what I said yesterday, you have decided to back down. Look out into the forest, look at those trees and leaves, look inside and there lies salvation.

"When I went to the war, I did not know it had anything to do with me. I lived in the village and had no use for peace in the land of white people. I thought it was your war. But when I got there I saw real people suffer. I saw children without mothers, boys without legs, fathers without pride; I knew I was dealing with human beings; people who only wanted to be happy, to see the sun and sip water and dance their ugly dances and sleep the sleep of God."

Alero walked to the window as the man spoke. Tim kept a frozen visage all the while and, once the man was through, he walked back into the room and emerged with a large trunk.

"The motorcycle can't take that box," intoned Alero.

"Well," he replied, "I'll take my bare essentials."

The veteran had left. Tim sat on a chair and looked sullen.

"I hate to bother you, and I don't want you to take this the wrong way but I've got to go," he said.

"I hope the engine is ready in good time," was her reply.

"And I really thank you again for saving my life," he said.

"It wouldn't have been necessary if you had not been here," she said.

They did not look at each other. Alero still looked at the window while Tim faced down. No word dropped into that room for the next half hour, when the veteran materialised. In his wake were two elders. Tim recognised Tietie immediately. The squat man did not look half as colourful as he had in the last visit and in the palace chambers. He even had no hat on. His shirt was torn from wear around the left rib cage. Tim thought his voice still possessed that hollow hauteur; although his swagger was tentative this time. The other elder was not quite familiar to Tim. Once Tietie spoke, Tim thought he sounded like a beaten man, his lofty look notwithstanding.

The veteran said, "It doesn't make sense for you to leave, that sort of thing. The elders of the village have now come to talk to you on that."

Tim was not ready to hear the elders come there to congratulate themselves on his leaving.

"I've made up my mind. I don't have much time to talk. I want to know when I can leave.

"Mister Fosta," said Chief Tietie, "we don't want for you to leave any longer. Finish what you want first. That is wisdom word."

Tim was quiet and, as Alero heard those words, she walked into the room where Itse lay. She was mystified and full of disgust. She thought these people would be happy to let him go. What was their scheme this time? Did they want him to die now? Were they no longer afraid of the American bomb fighters?

Whatever the reason, Tim was not ready to listen. He wanted to leave. And he made it clear to all three men that the only thing they could do for him was to let him go and he was sure that was all they wanted. The barrier he erected between him and the villagers was impregnable. The two Chiefs left the room in a huff.

In less than ten minutes, the motorcycle was ready. It was an old affair; discoloured, with distressed tyres and broken rear view mirror and headlights. The seat covers were off while the foams had declined from their original yellow to a borderline between black and brown. But the engine, in spite of its erratic puffs and dense black smoke, seemed to have enough life for the journey ahead.

Tim looked out through the window and saw the rider already mounted on the machine and, about fifty yards away, many people were standing in clusters staring in the direction of the house. One thought had lurked in his subconscious ever since he decided to leave: The creature in black smoke. How much of him factored into his decision to leave, he could not determine. He wanted to push it away from his reasoning. It was probably because of his confused state of mind that he had had the dream. He did not consider himself a coward and although he could not remember much of his past, he did not feel like one with the heart of a mouse. His mind told him he wanted to return to America and that was what he was going to do. He belonged home.

It was an awkward moment when Alero handed a bag of his belongings to Tim. He could not go with all be brought, so she stuffed only the essentials in a small bag. All he could say was thank you. They barely looked each other in the eye. Silence consecrated the space between them and Tim stood still for an eternity until he turned and made straight out of the house to the quiet glare of the public. Alero looked through the window. The veteran had left to his house and was not part of the spectacle.

The village air was still overhung with fog. No one could explain why. Looking skyward, the sun glowed in full colour above the thick drapery but it could not throw any shaft through. A shimmer seeped through to provide a little light, like half dawn. The earth below crawled with potholes and mud.

Once Tim mounted the machine, the engine sputtered to life and roared out of the village into the dirt road, black clouds of smoke belching behind.

chapter Fourteen

The next morning offered no respite for the invisible horizon inflicted by the fog. No respite either to the villagers, who went to bed contemplating the ominous decision of the white man to leave. They knew they wanted him out of their ken but not this way. They wanted him out without ill will. Not with sullen silences, not with a grudge. They wanted him out on their own terms.

They had wanted to yield to him, and give him the opportunity to return to the forest and see his ancestor's grave if he could find it. No one cared about his ancestor. That was his history, not theirs. But if that was going to keep their humble village from the foul temper of world attention and the retribution of the white man's plane, so be it. Let him come, satisfy himself and leave the village in the halcyon quiet in which he had met it.

How could they not read the calculation of the witch in all of this? But the villagers were wiser. Her ploy was to send the *oyibo* man away to cancel the accusation that she forced him to stay, so if the man returned to his country and squealed and the bombs came, no one would point fingers. But a witch would always be a witch and her ploys would always lie naked like a madman beside a stream.

The other worry was the man's amnesia. Maybe the witch had

given him back his past. Didn't she take it away in the first place? So what did he know? With what weapon was he going to his country? That morning the elders were going to summon the crocodile girl and force her to confession. If the village was going to prepare for the Americans, they had to know what those white men knew.

Before dawn, Chief Tietie and two other Chiefs decided to walk to Alero's house. They knew she lived in a house that was like a sore thumb. They only went there to query, not to celebrate. It was like a haunted place in their imagination. They ploughed their way through the fog, aided by flashlights. It looked like a long walk. They wondered too if the girl had not disappeared but they knew how much she cared about Itse, so she would not leave the village just yet. And of course, they knew she came to the village for want of a better place to go. She had no refuge on earth. This was her home and her death chamber.

Chief Tietie knocked on the door with authority and his voice lacked the cymbal-of-joy resonance. It was imperious and shot through the pre-dawn fog.

"Open the door. The elders want to talk to you."

Within a minute, the door was flung open and Alero emerged wielding a kerosene lamp. She looked like one who had hurriedly put on a gown and tied a scarf over her head. By the light of the lamp, the elders saw her eyes and deduced that she had not had much sleep.

She back-stepped as she saw them and the elders stepped over the threshold with a proprietary attitude. As they entered the front room, they saw Alero's aunt, Mogha, who greeted them meekly and retreated into her bedroom.

Elder Tietie sat with the others and wasted no time before going straight to the heart of the matter.

"We did not lose our sleep early for nothing. The elders' council wants to know two things from you. One, did that boy gain back his memory before he left? Two, how much of your *juju* was responsible for his rudeness. I mean why did he change his mind about staying?"

Alero's head sank down to her bosom and she began to sob. Just then, a long shadow preceded a body walking into the front room.

It was easy to figure out the outlines of the white man. It made no sense to wait and even talk to him that night. Both elders rose to their feet and walked out wondering why they did not remain in bed and enjoy the languor of pre-dawn sleep.

Tim had returned only a few hours earlier and he decided to stop at Alero's. She was already asleep and it was her aunt, Mogha, who opened the door. Tim recognised her instantly.

"You came back?" asked the woman, as she raised her kerosene lamp up, so both of them could look into each the other's face. Tim noticed she was tall, slim and had some of Alero's facial distinctions.

"You must be Morgan."

She acknowledged with a smile that beamed wearily on her face. She excused cheerfully the mispronunciation of her name. She did not seem willing to talk, although her eyes flushed with wonder. Tim thought she looked like one who did talk a lot at one time. Her eyes looked tired, not from physical exertions but from traumas of the heart. But everything else about her belied her bruised eyes. She had a carriage just like Alero, a dignified walk and a nimbleness of one accustomed to overcoming the pitfalls of a treacherous world. She was about forty, but looked a little older.

As they walked into the front room, Alero emerged. But Tim was still curious at the glow of smile that lingered on Mogha's face, like old confetti. It looked sad one moment; happy the next. Alero sat down on one of the sofas and stared at the floor. Tim sat beside her. Mogha rustled out of sight.

"Did anyone see you come in," she asked.

"I guess not," he said.

Both of them did not feel like explaining anything, silence dominated the room and night around them again. Until once Alero wanted to break it and Tim pre-empted her and said, "No, I'm not hungry. I had something to eat and I could have my bath in the morning."

Silence again as the lamp flared in the middle of the room yielding and lapping up shadows. It was about 1:30am and both seemed tired. Alero cleaned up one of the rooms in the house and made the bed for Tim.

Neither was sure if the other slept through the night.

chapter Fifteen

In fog-bound Orogun, no one was sure what to make of what was going on, especially with the witch. What game was she playing with them? First, the white man did not want to go. When he wanted to go, she would not persuade him to stay and, suddenly, he was back. Tietie and company had no clue what to discuss with him, so they left. They acted as though they had seen a ghost.

The crocodile girl was desperate, they thought. She wanted to use this white man as her leverage, a revenge weapon to deploy as her ultimate blackmail. And it seemed to be working. She had everyone's attention in the village. Some of the villagers wondered, if she had not set up everything; from the accident in the Forest of Silence, to Itse's coma to the recovery of only Tim Forester. She must be in consort with her crocodile mother, crafting confusion and paving the path toward apocalypse for everyone. After all, she had nothing to lose. The elders must find a solution to all of this nonsense. They must find a way of casting out her spell,

If they wanted to be rid of her and send her back to the city, that would be a good thing. But she did not seem ready to leave. All by herself, she was impotent. Now, with Tim Forester, the *oyibo* man under her spell, she had all the blackmail spears and arrows that she could muster. What was her real agenda? It would do all a world of good just to have a whiff of her design; her crocodile schemes.

It was not for nothing that the whole place was enveloped in fog. Day was being shut out of their lives. The crocodile girl was darkness or, at least, the absence of light. The mother was the crocodile that gorged on the flesh of the unsuspecting. Goodness prevailed when the crocodile was killed and she disappeared from the face of their earth. Or so they thought. Now, she was back in another incarnation, more fell and dreary, with jaws that devoured, jaws with a shadowy menace, jaws no one could see or touch.

A few hours after Chief Tietie and company left, the veteran appeared in the house. Aunt Mogha also opened the door and she was on her way to the farm. But the veteran asked her to stay for a little while so she could contribute her ideas to the new development. He was one of the few people who could stand her foul breath. That was one of the reasons she hardly spoke and her mouth was always used to being shut. Once it opened, the whole room yawned for deodorant. She knew she could stay and discuss because she was in the presence of her people. Aunt Mogha knew who her people were. She had lived enough through the turbulence of the village, through the betrayals of youth. She knew the old men and their little schemes; they were not her people. There was no delusion about this. She knew who to count on. It seemed not odd in the least that she could count on Tim Forester, from a distant corner of the universe, as one of her own, while the majority of those wedded to a similar ancestry would rather maul her in a dungeon.

The veteran already knew that Tim was back and that was the

reason he came. Both Alero and Tim had finished their breakfast and were getting ready to move over to Itse's. The ex-soldier's eyes looked drained, like one who did not have much sleep.

Once Tim showed up in the front room, the veteran didn't show any astonishment. He only asked if the American had had enough sleep and if he had had breakfast. The previous day seemed to draw a blank for everybody. They all focused on the day's agenda.

"I just had a meeting with the elders about you," he said referring to Tim. "They woke me up early this morning and said they wanted to discuss you with me. I didn't have a clue what they were talking about and I thought you probably had an accident or something terrible had happened. The messenger didn't know much. But when I got there I was told that you had returned and they wondered what was going on. They wanted to know if I knew anything about your return and I said no. I was also stunned that you returned, that sort of thing. But what they wanted me to do was come here and tell you that they were prepared to let you return to the Forest of Silence and offer any assistance as you may wish to help you see the tomb of the ancestor you are looking for." Silence ensued.

"Did you get your memory back?" the veteran's brow furrowed as the words spurted out of his mouth.

"They want to know, huh"? asked Tim.

"Yes."

"He has not recovered his memory," cut in Alero. "But the elders must not know that. We need a weapon. We must intimidate them."

Tim rose to his feet abruptly and said he was headed for Itse's

"You know the doctor comes here this morning from Warri. It makes no sense for him to meet the sick guy alone," he said.

"We know they only know half the story," said the veteran, as if unaware of the man on his feet and what he just said. He was in no haste but applied himself wholly to what he was about to say. Tim walked two steps to the door and leaned on it, as a sort of compromise.

"They are concerned with your ancestor alone," he continued. "We have that and another agenda. The reason I'm saying this is that they are planning to offer you a map of the forest that they think will help you to the tomb."

"So they know where the tomb is?" Tim was aghast.

"They say they don't but if there was any tomb, it must be associated with the defunct empire of Ovwor which hugged the Atlantic Ocean, long before the forest came into full form."

At this point Mogha said she would leave and rose to her feet. It was getting too late in the morning and she was no longer at ease. No one baulked at her decision.

Tim and Alero were quiet and hung on the lips of the historian. But the man was not willing to say too much.

"A lot of that history has been lost in fables. One thing I can tell you is that the empire was crushed by Orogun during a war over two hundred years ago, and it was deserted and that's how the Forest of Silence grew. In the days of the Ovwor Empire, white people used to go there for business and religion. That's why they believe that, if your ancestor came to this region in those years, he must be in the Forest of Silence."

Tim's mind receded into a whirl after that speech. He wondered if he was not about to embark on a fiasco. As he saw it, if white people used to come to that kingdom, it meant that it was possible there was not just one tomb but several and, if there were several, how was he to sort out his target and zero in on the story that brought him there? He also recalled that, just before he left, Itse showed few, if perceptible, signs of life. That was no indication he would be fine very soon. But did it make sense to wait for him to recover first? What if he, too, had lost all memory?

"My plan," the veteran said, breaking Tim's flow of thought, "is to subvert their plan, that sort of thing. I don't expect Uvie's body to be where your man's tomb might be. If they hid it, it must be in the forest; in the heart of the forest."

"I assume that's where I found the locket and where the pig attacked us. We have to ignore the map and go through the heart of the forest," affirmed the American.

"Are they aware I'm going with him?" Alero was curious.

"I told them," said the veteran and did not oblige the appetite of his audience for a follow-up.

"So what did they say?" she asked, breaking the silence.

"Nothing. They just exchanged glances. I don't think they objected."

She said, "I'm curious. How did they become willing all of a sudden that I should go? Do they want me to die in that place now? Of course, they claim I know enough to cause a damn invasion. That can't explain everything. There must be a malicious purpose to all of this."

The veteran said, "Whatever that purpose is I will know in time."

The veteran was now done and rose to his feet and asked them to head for Itse's place.

Before they stepped into the fog-bound day, the veteran noticed that Tim was all of a sudden not in a hurry to walk out of the house. And it was because Alero went into her room to put on her head scarf. He wanted to utter some words, nudge him with a sarcastic smirk or ironic grimace, harrumph or simply shrug. But, just as he sorted through the options, Alero returned expecting him to be waiting as if she was entitled to expect it. Tim acted as though she had asked him to wait.

The veteran knew there was something sober in the moment. It might have been romantic and tragic, like moonshine at noon. The faces did not stare out of tenderness alone. He saw a pain wrinkle here, a fighter's defiance there. He was at a loss to hollow out what was binding them. They didn't seem like people who had had much conversation since Tim's about-face return.

All three walked through the village's main road and ploughed through the fog, watched by a crowd of children and women and a few men. Tim walked upright and fast, and Alero tried to keep pace with him. The veteran deliberately brought up the rear. The two young people expected the children to taunt but nothing happened. Alero chalked it up to deference for the old man, whose tardy, imperious swagger blended with his martial pedigree to shroud him with a good amount of aura.

Among the girls playing, somebody stood out. It was the girl from the other day of the storm, who had stared at Alero, in spite of the anarchy of weather. She looked mercurial with a hint of playful defiance. She held a half-eaten mango in her left hand and crunched out the words, "My name is Tuoyo." She said it in English. The duo were impressed that she spoke English with a tone of insistently haunting naivety.

"How are you, Tuoyo?" asked Tim.

"Fine, sir."

"I like your gown," she remarked rather shyly, her eyes inspecting Alero.

"Your skirt is colourful, too." Alero said. The girl's eyes cheered to the compliment. She might not have grasped the full import of the word colourful. She understood though that the meaning danced around the word colour.

"I just finished primary school. Can I go to college?" she asked.

"Of course. You look like a bright girl," assured Alero.

Suddenly, she said "bye" and ran away.

"That's a remarkable kid," said Tim.

It was a long walk for all three anyway, as they picked their way through waterlogged potholes and slippery spots and mud piles and rock outcroppings and plant splinters and tried to stay in the middle of the road, as far away as possible from the cynical faces and the venom of subdued chatter, which they knew was about them. Tuoyo, though, had been like an intimate whisper that afternoon.

Tim shut out the crowd from the intimacies of his heart. He focused on the matter in hand, on the forest, on the headless being, on the memory that teased him invidiously with little remembrance, but a lot of darkness and unresolved truths; on Alero.

He would not dwell on his aborted trip, on the conflicts that almost ravaged his mind as he tried to wipe out his only fresh and profound memories: the smell of Orogun, street urchins in frayed underwear chasing goats, the enchantment of a strange language, a Second World War veteran, with an ironic love for America; the Forest of Silence; a fog that shut out time; an unknown friend in a coma; his remarkable escape from death and a girl with flesh and eyes and a past as mysterious as a goddess.

He also wondered why no one was saying anything about the fog. It may be the beginning of a decisive storm, some sort of baleful wind or rain getting out of joint and smothering the little place. He thought that was the invasion they should be worried about and not the howitzers or the B-52s or the Apache helicopters. He may not recall much about his past but he did not consider himself that important to Americans to warrant a declaration of war. He, however, recalled making the point to the veteran, who pointed out that President Ronald Reagan once sent a force to Grenada ostensibly to save American lives, although Tim could not remember that incident.

He sensed his foul mood coming, a certain gloom of face and pain of heart and he instantly tried to battle it.

"What are you thinking about?" asked Alero and Tim knew the girl had sniffed the coming of the mood. She had a full smile on and Tim looked at her face and his face also filled up with a smile, as juice bubbles atop a squeezed orange.

About half a mile to their destination, Tim saw a man walk fast past them. His stride was leisurely until he observed the duo in front of him. He looked nervous. But it was not his instant briskness that caught Tim's eyes. It was the man's gaze. His eyes, in furtive disarray, looked at Alero. Alero greeted him without the customary deference of going down on her knees, and the man responded like one without a voice. Tim had to stop to let the girl catch up with him.

After the man had disappeared, Tim asked.

"Who was that?"

Alero was surprised at the question and turned to look at Tim who was also looking at her.

"Nobody."

"Nobody?" Tim asked incredulously.

"I'll tell you the story later," she replied to put the matter to rest.

They had reached the stoop of Itse's house. They heard the sound of life and they knew the doctor had arrived. As they opened the door, he stood on the threshold on his way out.

"Hi Tim," he said extending a hand and they shook hands.

"How is he doing today?" Tim asked.

"He is showing better signs today than I've seen. But it still calls for patience. I know he will make it. Just a matter of time."

When all three saw Itse, he looked straight at them. Alero broke into tears. She almost collapsed to the ground but the reflex of Tim's arms anticipated and held her and he said, "He'll be okay."

She thought he was dead. Itse stirred to reassure his friend. He could now see them, but his tongue was still tied. Everyone now understood what the doctor was talking about.

Chapter Sixteen

After the veteran and the doctor had left, Tim brought back up the issue of the mystery man Alero greeted on their way. Alero was eager to tell him about the chief. He was Chief Boyo.

"He is a dirty old man," remarked Alero. "But I feel sorry for him."

Since she arrived in Orogun, after the misadventure in the city, she had noticed the man's interest in her. He sometimes walked around her house, in the gathering shadows of the evening. Alero arrived from their farm around that time, and her eyes caught him.

"At first, I thought it was a coincidence. Of course, the man also had stuff to do in the bush."

But it became a pattern. She would greet him deferentially and he returned the greeting with the warmth that Alero craved in vain from the rest of the villagers. A few young people, especially the girls, greeted her with verve. Most did not want to hear her voice. Alero understood that and knew who wanted to exchange greetings with her and those who did not. That simplified her life.

After a while, Chief Boyo didn't only come around her house but stalked her to the farm. The man was careful not to be caught with her in any conversation that suggested he tolerated a witch.

Alero knew she could fall into the village peril if she walked alone. She had Marmalade's story to guide her. Her farm was close enough to those of the Ololos and the Ometies and she made sure that she was never out of the shouting distance of the people at anytime. Even at that, there were no guarantees.

But Chief Boyo, whose wife's farm was far away, would come to the bush path near Alero's. The bush sandwiched Alero's farm and Ololo's. He would walk to and fro that bush path stealthily with his full hunting gear, dane gun, spear, knife and charms around his neck.

Alero was also armed herself with a gun she obtained in the city before she came to the village. She anticipated the wiles and ferocity of the village. She knew her beauty was one of her handicaps. She did not want to be anybody's quarry. She obtained the gun from a retired police officer who learned of her story with her in-laws that never were. Mr. Faturoti was in charge of the palace security and took a quiet liking to Alero. He slipped the gun into her bag.

Alero had wondered aloud to him in her last days with Olu and his family, "How can I live with those dangerous men in the village? They might just destroy me." Faturoti said nothing, but mumbled something about God having the answers to everything. She never expected a gun from the man whose face was meeker than his trade. She never thought of holding a gun. She was too much of a shrinking violet for such an instrument of finality. In addition, it was against the law. The police officer knew only men like him were permitted to wield guns. But guns were common now and those unlicensed and jobless youths deployed them for robberies and other sundry acts. So, how did he think she would be at peace with it?

She had never had to use the gun since she arrived Orogun. Not even in the ominous solitude of the farm. She left the farm when she was sure to see traffic on the paths back to the village. It was because of the traffic that he did not accost her on the way back to the village. There would be too many eyes and too many ears. But on one after- noon, she returned a little earlier than usual. She had a subliminal fear of having not put out the kitchen stove. She wondered if it could flare out of control and raze the whole house. If it happened, no one would tell her. They would see the fire crackle. They would watch its tongues in their furious purpose. They would fold their arms and ogle. They could even gloat, while her only possession in the village succumbed forever. It would be another village fair.

The fear enlarged each passing hour.

"I decided I had to abandon the *okro* and the vegetables and ber- ries and tubers and head quickly for the village," she said, as she narrated her experience to Tim.

Chief Boyo had then accosted her.

"How are you, my young cousin," he said. Alero was scared, not only by the claim of family intimacy but also the inflexion and tone of the voice. He knew they were not cousins. The kindness rattled her. It was earnestly subversive.

Alero greeted him back but she did not look back. She was pet- rified. But rather than stand still, her steps quickened. He paced for- ward and overtook her, the old man.

"Don't be afraid of me, young girl. I mean no harm," he entreat- ed.

Alero saw his eyes for a quick second. He was at once bold and beggarly. Alero knew that kind of look and it scared her.

"I know the village has been wicked. Orogun people have de- stroyed your family. But don't blame all of us. Some of us can be good to you," he asserted.

"Thank you, sir," Alero said, not slackening her speed. She was so embarrassed she began to hope that somebody else would see them and make the man disappear. She also feared for him, wondering whether the man knew of the stigma that followed her about.

"I just want to let you know that you can always count on me," he said, after a long silence. He had a lot of energy. He was probably in his late fifties. He wore shorts, the type that most hunters put on as part of their hunting attire. The khaki was wrinkled and threadbare along the hems. On the left side, around the pocket, Alero saw signs of unremitting patching. A red thread used to patch the shorts rioted against the khaki colour and seemed ready to give in. She could see the hair on his lap tangle feebly with red and khaki threads. He was a thin, small man with wiry vitality. Veins and muscles burst out of his tight skin. His quick eyes and deft feet revealed a man accustomed to the ambience of hunting early in life. Village life had never pampered him.

"If you become comfortable with me I can arrange for some of your troubles to ease in this village. You don't deserve to suffer like this."

He was not coming down to the point. But Alero was frightened by his requests. It made her all the more uneasy. Suddenly, the man disappeared into the bush and that made Alero stumble over a creeper. She wondered what the man was up to. Out of fear, she stopped to look around for him. A squirrel just ran beside her.

"He thought somebody had seen you guys," suggested Tim.

"Probably."

He didn't have that sort of opportunity again for a long time until, one evening, when he saw her walking to Itse's house. He stopped her demurely. But he did not have much time to talk. He merely asked her to reconsider his proposal.

"I know they will not allow me to marry you in this town, but I will give all the kindness in my heart," the old chief offered Alero. He quickly disappeared into the night.

"Today is the third time we have spoken," said Alero.

Chapter Seventeen

"I want to show you something." That was the veteran. The voice was, at once, self-absorbed and vulnerable. He said it with the smile of a baby. To Tim, this was the most intimate moment he had ever seen of the old man.

"What's that," asked Tim.

"I want to take you outside and show you one of my great treasures." Tim thought he saw a sparkle of vanity on his face but his voice sank.

Tim thought it was the right moment to get away. Alero was a little weak and needed some rest and to be with Itse who seemed to have picked up a curious energy. No one knew how long it would last.

Tim rose from his chair and cast a glance in Alero's direction, which was sufficient to convey the message. She stared into space in return. The veteran understood the coast was clear and both men walked into the fog.

Few people were outside at this time and the crowd had melted into a straggle. The veteran knew the American was curious what the treasure was but he was not willing to reveal it, so he steered the conversation elsewhere.

"What would you really do if you knew everything?"

Tim knew that the man was playing a suspense game. That delayed his response to the question. But he was ready to indulge the old man.

"I've asked myself this question over and over. You know, I guess it may be relief and may not. I am both scared and excited about it. But I guess I am hooked on it. Nothing will ever happen in my life without it. If I returned to America, I probably would have had a doctor help me with it. But nothing is guaranteed."

The old man was silent as they ambled through the streets, amidst bleating goats, little boys building and frisking over mounds of sand, mud houses and huts, yielding smoke from their kitchens; all partly obscured by the fortitude of the fog.

"My experience during the Second World War taught me exactly that," said the veteran. He paused like one who had said the wrong thing and then regained his focus.

"I went to the war out of curiosity but returned without an arm."

Tim noticed the man blanch like a chastised little boy. He looked like one scared of something.

"That is the story of my life, that sort of thing," he said.

Their steps were slow; reflecting the gravity of their conversation. Tim understood that he was not trying to scare him. He merely wondered what was the matter with him. They were all committed to uncovering the transgression of ages, the root of the crocodile, the odyssey of the locket. No one was contemplating postponing the hike through the forest. It was too late. The village cabal could not win.

Tim diverted the discussion to Mogha.

"How is she coping with her breath?"

The veteran snapped out of his mood with a little boy's exuberance again.

"I was going to tell you her story." He paused as if revving up energy for a long talk.

"It was all about man and husband," he began. "It was all about taboo. It was all about a beauty that could not be. Many years ago, when she was in her prime, she was the most beautiful woman in the whole region. Like Alero's mother, she had a problem securing a spouse. She was believed to be under a curse. Everyone in the family was supposed to be cursed, so they were ostracised in the village. Some had the courage to stay. Most of them, especially the men, disappeared to the city and changed their names. Trust me, a village curse is nothing anyone in this country is ready to trifle with.

"In Mogha's case, she thought she had transcended it. She was like Alero's mother, a goddess in human flesh. She was bold and intelligent and even swore she would end the stigma. But the village always had something to say about any woman from the family, and their words were like an atomic bomb. It mushroomed out, over everything. In the past, some women had been called murderers and implicated in mysterious deaths. Some were dismissed as witches and a few others were poisoned or allowed to be killed by some wild animals.

"In Mogha's case, they alleged that the gods wanted no part of her with the civilised. So they afflicted her with bad breath no one could cure. They called her latrine beauty. Her self-esteem was quick to disappear. That was what drew me immediately to their family. I can't tell you the entire family story yet. You will discover it all in time. But I will unveil Mogha's to the extent that it teases you about the family and the worms reeking in the heart of this village.

"I could not understand why life could be so cruel. Why, in one breath, it had endowed you with all the favours and took them away in another breath. No suitor came from here but they abounded from outside. They heard of the beauty but discounted the breath until they met her and withdrew.

"The most spectacular of those suitors was a wealthy man of about fifty who had visited the village to explore the possibility of starting a rubber extraction business in Orogun. She was returning late from the farm one evening when he set eyes on her on a forest trail. The man was among a phalanx of village elders exploring some rubber trees.

"The man demanded to know the girl. Late that night, he defied contrary opinions from the village elders and showed up at Mogha's place. She knew the man adored her physical charms, but she never expected to see him again. The man was debonair and handsome, a quality oddly enhanced by a slight stoop. He had been married three times. He was single and needed a wife. He said his earlier marital failures liberated him into a hunger for romance for its own sake. And Mogha was all he wanted.

"Within ten minutes of conversion with her, he walked out and puked. No one knew of the puking part but me and Alero's mother. But this man did not give up on Mogha like the others. Mogha did not love him but he was all that she could get.

"Again, this suitor determined to heal her and intoxicate the world with his new bride. He took her away from Orogun and, for months, no one heard from her. Some said she was dead. Who gave doctors the effrontery to alter the finger of the gods? Another said that they had got married in some remote place after the doctors failed her and the man did not want to be seen by those who knew the girl's pedigree.

"One afternoon, she arrived at the village all gaunt, forlorn and reticent. She would not say what had happened for almost a year. That fuelled the speculation that the gods had afflicted her with madness in the course of the surgery. She revealed that the man was killed by a band of robbers in his house while she was in the hospital.

"She could not continue with the treatment because the man's former wives and children shut her out of his finances. But the Orogunians believed something else: the evil spells around her had killed the innocent man. They were also mad at her for ruining the only big business opportunity the village had attracted in years."

The veteran and Tim had walked out of the centre of Orogun, through a solitary trail, to a remote part of the village. Huts were sprinkled about and the sound of the village shrank into echoes. The trail thinned, broke, split and spliced. Right and left, the land was either green or bald, although no bush was in sight. The fog still overhung like a pestilence and the two of them walked to the end of the path, which bordered a pond. It was clear to Tim that few people came here.

"I made this pond long, long ago. There are many fishes here. But no one touches them. Neither do I."

A question rumbled in Tim's mind: "Why would you do that? Are you some sort of environmentalist?"

The pond was big and Tim saw the plenitude of fishes. The water was greenish and ferns and weeds of different kinds crept around the edges. A solitary creeper ran through the surface to the centre of the pond. The fishes tumbled merrily inside. The veteran picked a stem and dipped it inside. A rush, splashes and tumbles of water and the watery creatures capsized the tranquil afternoon. Tim saw the fishes, tilapia, cat fish and quite a few other species. They were robust and prosperous looking.

"No, I don't believe in that sort of environmentalist thing. Let me show you why?" The veteran said, held Tim's wrist and walked him to about twenty yards away. They stopped at a small house. It was at least forty years' old with a quaint design. It pretended to the grandeur of some European mansion. But, over the years, its pride had buckled under the cycle of rain and sunshine. The wall paints had faded or peeled off. It was untouched by the riot of vegetation around and it had a look of cleanliness without polish.

"What is this," asked Tim who saw it as some kind of museum. "This is my home," said the veteran, his voice sounding a little celebratory; even triumphal. "When I die, this is where I'll be."

He opened the door, as he warned the American to stoop, because of the low ceiling inside. He opened the window and a flood of light revealed a tombstone and a huge photograph of him in military uniform.

The tombstone was at one end of the room and beside it was what seemed to Tim like sufficient space for another grave.

"Is this for your wife," he asked the African.

"No, she has no place here. This is where my casket will be placed. I've saved for it. It will be here in a few months and then I will place it here and take naps here from time to time before my final resting day."

Tim then moved to the tombstone and saw an epitaph: 'Meet you later'.

"Who is that addressed to?" Tim wanted to know.

"It depends on your point of view," he analysed. "First, let me tell you that, inside the grave is my other hand, the one chopped off during the war. I preserved it and brought it here and organised an elaborate funeral for it. It was unusual. People thought I was mad when I arrived. They did not see the hand. Some of the village elders thought it was an elaborate hoax to show I fought in the war. Maybe they believe. They just did not want to reconcile themselves to my gallantry. But I had promised myself that I was going to come back home, all my body parts complete dead or alive. So, when the bomb put it off and I was unconscious for a while, others thought I was dead. But I came to, as well as one of my friends, who had come to accord me some befitting burial after the battle lamented. He saw the other hand beside me and you could understand he was not himself."

"But you were alive."

"Yes, I told him that. But something else was going on in his mind. He said nothing about it till we parted. And the hand was with me in our long journey on the ship. It was a prized possession. It is the story of my life. So, wherever your body part is, don't let it go. You will never be a complete man. Even if it rots and smells like my hand did. The soul is important; the symbolism of it too. I went after my hand. Your body part is in the forest. So is Alero's."

They walked out of the house back into the fog. But Tim noticed that the old man and World War Two veteran was a little proud of part of what he considered the treasures of this African village.

His eyes glowed with the certainty of destiny, with the light of one who already had the answers. In spite of his fragile age and tentative pace, the veteran had a little swagger about him, the force of a lifetime of many struggles and a few emphatic triumphs.

"I want to show you something else," he offered with a smile. "Just about half a mile from here."

"We are going to the house of one of the oldest and sweetest persons in the village. But no one talks to her. They say she is a witch. They say she killed her daughter who was much loved by everybody. In all my life, I have always been suspicious of easy rides. When life is full of opportunities for you as if God gave you only charms, be careful.

"That was the story with this girl's life. Her name was Boyowa, which means come with joy or prosperity. She had it all her life. Great in school. Great singer. Great beauty and no curses. The mother spent all her life's savings to give her an education. She finished from a school of pharmacy and went to law school and, just when she completed her programme, she died in front of their house. She was not sick, not shot or anything. She slipped on a treacherous little mud pile. Before they reached a doctor, she was gone.

"Everyone blamed the mother. Now that's an irony. When the girl was doing well, they credited the woman with being a good witch who used her special powers to elevate her daughter. But such was the regret over the death of this girl, that no one was willing to give the woman the benefit of the doubt…

"The witch, they claimed, had her meal."

"Her meal?" asked Tim

"When a witch kills a person, she is believed to have eaten the person even though their flesh is intact. They are believed to eat the heart of humans."

"How did they know that she was a witch?"

"Because of the owl?" the veteran paused, contemplating. Tim wondered why the man spoke to him as if he should know.

"O, I'm sorry. I just assumed you knew the story. It's common knowledge," he said.

Tim thought this man's mind was drifting away.

"An owl often perched on top of her house at night and sang weird songs. An owl is a bad omen. An owl is a witch who wants to commit something evil. If you see an owl at night and you can kill, don't spare it. If you can't, pray to God. Some people sighted the bird the night before her daughter died and they said the witch cried last night and the child died this morning, who does not know the connection."

"Do you think she loved her daughter?" asked Tim.

"Love is difficult to define. I have never understood that word. Love is like a contact sport."

"Do you believe she is a witch?" Tim asked.

"Today I don't. Maybe I did yesterday and maybe I will tomorrow," answered the veteran.

Tim noticed that they were approaching a lone hut but the fog blurred its true profile. The hut was separated from the next house by at least a hundred yards. In between it and the next hut lay rubble and debris and humps of razed homes. An isolated stoop, like a broken finger, stood limp a few yards away from a wall which was a relic of another house. But this woman's house was proud and quaint in the eternal fog.

"They call her white witch."

"What?"

"Yes, and I will explain to you later."

They were near the house and the veteran did not seem willing to elaborate. Within twenty yards, a person's head peeped out of the small and only window in the hut. Tim was amazed at the sight of the woman's eyes. They were bold like small moons in her small head. But she did not seem to see far. He eyes gazed constantly and rolled and twitched as she tried to recognise the people approaching her home. She was not excited or even scared. She was only curious.

"She's half-blind," said the veteran as he shouted something to her in the Itsekiri. And she yelled something back. Her skin wrinkled further but glowed with her eyes as she smiled. She promptly disappeared behind the window and materialised at the door front. She looked proud in a shabby kind of way with her broken skin and weary vitality and moon eyes and dishevelled clothes. Her voice was soft just like the veteran's but with a quiet thunder.

She looked at Tim with a mixture of joy and mystery, and said something to the veteran who replied with a smile but failed to translate. She said something else and the veteran said: "She says hello." Tim replied and she nodded her head even before the translation. She then motioned them to follow her into her hut.

The house had a dirt floor but the wall was full of papers. In the first few minutes, though, neither of the men could see until their pupils enlarged. Tim sat down on a chair beside the veteran who clearly was more familiar with the place. The woman walked into the bedroom and reappeared a few minutes later.

"As you can see, she doesn't have many visitors."

The woman wanted to serve them water to drink which both of them politely turned down. At this time, she was in a loftier mood than earlier and focused her gaze on the American. She began talking to the veteran while her eyes rested on him. The veteran was explaining Tim's story to her and she seemed excited by every word.

At one stage, she turned her whole fragile frame in Tim's direction and started talking to Tim and the veteran translated.

"My daughter loved your country," she said. "She always loved singing your songs and loved dancing like your people. She planned to go to America before she died. She always loved the actress…" She pointed to a picture on the wall. The room was a little too dark for him to see it. So, Tim stood up and walked to the wall and saw an old and rumpled picture of a white woman holding a microphone.

As Tim turned back to his seat, he said, "Marilyn Monroe."

Suddenly, the old woman burst into tears and her whole frail body seemed ready to crumble in seconds. Tim was nonplussed. He sat there and watched the woman as the veteran tried to console her. He spoke many words in Itsekiri until the tears subsided and she just sat still. After a long silence, the veteran announced that they were leaving. Tim was relieved to go. As they rose, the woman said thank you to the American and Tim thought it was a gratitude for the visit.

"The last time I heard that name was about forty years ago just before my daughter died," she said with aplomb.

As they walked in the fog, the veteran asked him if he figured out why they called her white witch. Tim guessed that it was because her daughter loved Marilyn Monroe.

"No, they think the mother is Marilyn Monroe."

"I don't get it."

"Listen. The daughter had just brought the picture from the city then and wanted to post it on the wall the day she died. But the mother posted it herself a day after she was buried. It was in her memory. But the villagers thought that was how she looked in the spirit world. They thought she posted the picture on the wall to mark her triumph. Witches are believed to travel nightly on broomsticks to faraway countries and it was believed that she was in America by night and here by day. When she was in America, she was that woman and it was with that power she killed her daughter."

"How many of them saw the picture?"

"Maybe one person saw her post it and no other person has seen it since, except us and they don't know who is in the picture."

chapter Eighteen

In epileptic flushes, the fog had begun to thicken in the village and the people began to worry more and more. At first, people could not see each other within a foot. Then accidents soured their daily grind. This spasm of invisibility imposed fresh burdens on the people and the air.

The Chiefs wanted the gods to intervene but the village priest still had no answer. What should they offer? Goats, hens, virgins? The gods kept mute. Divinity did not have to provide all the answers.

Gradually, they began to believe that it might be a good thing. It might be the gods' answer to the white man's malice. The gods had their counterfoil to the enemy, even if that enemy was the all-powerful *oyibo* with their agents in the beautiful demon of a young woman bred there in Orogun village.

Chief Nikoro summarised it for them in clear and pointed sentences. "If they want to attack us with their big and fat birds from the sky, they would not be able to identify the village," he boasted. "The gods are wiser than anything, any tricks human beings can devise."

They believed that the *oyibo* man's birds would hover over the swath of the village in vain. Who knew if the birds had not come and gone like a frustrated hawk, they wondered.

They recalled a story that Ajuya, the prickly veteran, once told them about the war. The planes, said the veteran, did not do well in bad weather. The pilots could lose control and the planes could crash and kill the pilot.

Anytime the veteran spoke about the war, he used the images the villagers understood.

He loved to patronise the Chiefs. The planes were birds, the bullets talons. In spite of this, the Chiefs felt superior. And Ajuya always marvelled at how the Chiefs often believed him in patches.

They said they did not doubt his knowledge, but they disbelieved his testimonies. They thought he was knowledgeable because he had read the *oyibo* man's books. So did some of their children now growing up. Many of them did not place much value on education until recently, and those whose children had the benefit of school had left the village and returned only occasionally for short visits inspired by nostalgia. Most of them did not go beyond the primary school level, so they proceeded to become artisans in the city. They did not know enough mathematics or English to do much for themselves. The standard of the village school was abysmal. Itse's father, who schooled outside the village, had the benefit of superior learning and so he paid special attention to his son. His father's superior learning was high school. He could not even complete it. But he showed a lot of fervour by reading lots of books and newspapers. They helped him to brush up his knowledge and basic skills of communicating in the English language.

It was now they began to know the value, thanks to the example of Itse. It was now they were trying to emphasise the value of education to the children they had in their hoary years.

But if the fog sheltered the village from any rampage from the skies, it could not stop the damage below. People stumbled and fell and sustained injuries. There were occasional collisions, especially in the bush paths, leading to the village. Those who fished sometimes relied on blind luck. There were stories of some fishermen who tripped into the river from the canoes. Hunters were more wary. They could not risk their lives with a cheetah or wild pig or alligator. However, because this fog lightened after a spasm of severe density, they managed to live with the volatile menace.

Sometimes, they had to carry candles and lanterns with them in the open. One of Omonikarin's sons suffered a snakebite. They did not know in time. The beast bit him in one of the nearby bushes in the outhouse. He flailed about. Then the boy fell to the ground in front of the home stoop. He writhed with pain and moaned for some time. When no help came, he began to cry. His father had to run his fingers to the spot before he recognised that it was the pattern of a snake's fangs.

He yelled. He quickly put his mouth to the spot and sucked out some venom. After that, he asked for someone to call his friend, Chief Nikoro, to help out with a concoction for his son to drink. Panic overcame his household. The wife brought the concoction, a dark, thick, slimy affair reputed to have healed many an ailment. The boy drank it, and threw up. All efforts to help failed. He lost consciousness.

The son eventually died. He was barely nine years old.

"That slithering idiot bit him long before he knew it, I think," Chief Nikoro said.

After he was buried, the people said that, if the *oyibo* man had not come to the village, they would not have witnessed all of this tragedy.

"This witch is more powerful than we know," commented one of the men who attended the funeral.

Chapter Nineteen

Alero seemed in a better mood when the two men returned. This was ironic because Itse's condition seemed to have relapsed. Tim was inclined to believe that Alero was hurting and deploying bravado to good effect. If her best friend caved in after a brief spell of hope, all you would expect is a beaten spirit, thought Tim. Not the candy joy of a six-year-old.

"I made some food for you two," she said.

"What is it," asked the veteran, a little weary from the long walk and putting aside his walking stick.

"Rice, *dodo* and fried chicken," replied Alero.

"That's not what I asked, that sort of thing," the veteran was a little impatient. "How is Itse?"

"He's not feeling too good again. He relapsed. But all will be well."

The veteran walked into the room to check on Itse. Tim had been in and out and had observed the deterioration of his friend's condition and contrasted it with what he regarded as the dubious sparkle in Alero's face.

"Why are you in a good mood?" Tim asked.

"I'm not in a good mood. I'm just not in a bad mood," she replied.

"Yeah. But before we left, you looked like a bereaved widow."

Tim sensed some cheerful resentment in Alero that kept her from pursuing the subject. So he kept quiet, not wanting to spoil anything. Moments later, the veteran reappeared and wanted to know when the doctor would return.

They settled to the meal, all quiet except Alero. At the table, her excitement rippled. She did not seem to overreach herself, though. Her words were more measured and her body language tamer.

After the meal, the veteran was tired and left for his home. His gait was tentative but he retained his brash, superior carriage and stare.

"Thank you for the meal. I would not need to bother my wife today," he remarked as he eased into the fog.

"Do they still have a marriage," asked Tim as the door shut.

"Did they ever have a marriage?" she replied like one who had had a lot that day.

"Their marriage ended not long after it started. As you know, he was given that woman to win his loyalty. But that done, the girl would not let him into her bed, and it was an embarrassment to him and everyone. No one spoke about it even though everyone knew. Each time he tried to consummate, she yelled and made a drama of her rejection. It became a routine distraction in the first few weeks of the marriage until he did not try anymore. He was not one to complain. So he bore his grief and rage with dignity for a long time; say three, four months.

"Until one night, when the weather went out of control and rain fell all night. He knew it was his time to strike. The squall deafened and persisted. He locked the door and put the keys away and forced himself on her. She yelled all through until she was conquered. That was the end of it all. We heard no more cries, and the veteran's aplomb paid off."

"How did the world know that it happened? Did he tell, or she did?"

"She did, but somehow everyone knew that it happened. They just knew. Maybe that's why she confessed."

"Did they have any child together?" A question Tim had been dying to ask.

"No, she got pregnant, and aborted the baby and even ruined the womb. She said it was her scheme of revenge for the man's unholy performance the night of the squall. They have been living together ever since. No love, no hate. It's still strange to him. He regards Itse as a son. That seems to help him since Itse calls him papa. Itse's parents are dead. They died in his teen years, and the veteran stepped into Itse's parents' role."

"So," broke in Tim, "Itse is his consolation for the aborted child."

"I would say, his revenge for the revenge," She concluded.

"Another question: why didn't he divorce her and marry someone else."

"Well," said Alero, "you will have to ask him that one."

"The white witch. What's with that?"

Alero was embarrassed by the question and her eyelids fluttered over a fluctuating light on her face. It was clear that Alero did not want to touch that subject.

"When I'm ready to talk I'll give you my take on it," she answered with a tremor in her voice.

A pause dropped between them. The meal was over, and Tim saw that it was time to ask her about Itse.

"Did you watch him relapse?"

"Yes," replied Alero with an even, contemplative voice. Her upbeat mood seemed curiously chastened. "He recognised me when he looked at me."

"What do you mean," he asked, trying to uncover the meaning of her words. Alero's feisty exterior was caving in to a sober joy, a joy with the burden of a secret knowledge.

"He recognised me and wanted to smile. He did not smile and then I lost him," she said, incapable of expressing herself better, although the knowledge was intact in her intuitive soul. She understood what she wanted to say. But once she knew she could not utter the words, tears lined her face, which also blossomed with a smile.

Tim held her trembling hands and looked into her eyes and saw what she was saying. She might have failed to conjure the words but he understood what she had said.

"I know what you mean. Don't give yourself pain over this."

She wanted to reply but her lips trembled and the words were limp in her throat. She swallowed and summoned some energy from inside and said, "I saw his face. We have to go to the forest. We have to go. His face is waiting for us there with my mother. We have to go and meet him."

Tim pulled her towards him and then she sobbed and her body quaked as the man held her in his bosom and felt her heartbeat and consoled her: "All will be well. It's just a few days. I have a stake in this as well."

chapter Twenty

Later that night, after Alero had gone, he started to think about the girl and how much she had meant to him since he came to the village. He was as sure as dead without her, he mused. And how lucky he was. It was he who seemed to survive and not their son. Maybe the selfish village elders' paranoia about American jet bombers played a role. That probably explained why they insisted that the girl take care of the American. They did not want to be burdened by the death of a vagrant white man.

But that hardly guaranteed anything. He could have died in spite of all efforts. Again, the insistence on partial treatment for him could not have worked with Alero who loved Itse, her only friend and ally through the delirium of the years.

Imagine her temperament earlier in the day. She was pure confusion. Excited to the point of nervous breakdown. Yet the two had no affair, she had told Tim. Was the guy also restrained by the shadow of the crocodile curse as well? If not, this must be a special relationship. Maybe he wanted to date her, to be intimate and maybe she didn't because she wanted to protect the guy from the eye and tongue of disgrace. The world would not let him sleep. But how did he manage to escape any tar brush in spite of his closeness?

It must be a real pain to be Alero, he thought. But what a beauty to inhabit a chasm of pain. To be alive must be pure courage. Tim's mind drifted to the moment earlier in the day of Alero's emotional collapse and recalled her heart beat. What was really going on, he asked himself. No, he told himself, fighting back the beginnings of a thought. It was all sympathy. She needed someone, just anyone.

And his mind drifted and drifted and he lost control of himself and wondered what her real story was. How did that powerful force of beauty end up in that part of the world? What was the nature of this curse? Was it really a curse or they had to believe? Where were the men of the family? If they survived why did the women not find a way in the world? They decided to roil in the trenches, to take hits and bullets and limp and bleed. But they had pride, he said. Maybe it was not pride. Maybe it was what had to be done. Maybe the pain was necessary. Maybe they loved the pain or needed it. Maybe they were sacrifices for an ignoble moment of history. Maybe…

Tim's mind drifted back to his condition. How was it that he had to come several thousands of miles to that backwoods of the world in search of piece of his history or whatever it was and, when he got close, he lost his memory? What was with that? Did his story factor into the grand tale of a village curse? He wondered why his memory teased him with flashes of half-images and truncated plots and a hodgepodge of events all of which made the enterprise of the forest hike all the more challenging.

What was the guarantee that the forest would yield anything? Maybe he shouldn't have returned and maybe he would have been in the United States and seeking medical help. What if he went to the United States and it was determined there that it all boiled down to this forest experience. Maybe it was none of all that, but a sympathy for this sick man, whom he could not retrieve from memory or maybe it was Alero, whose tale was now so compelling he was not sure he wanted to think of it. Thinking of her seemed to make no sense. Thinking of her seemed to make too much sense. Sure, why did he just walk straight to the house when he returned from his no-trip. Maybe it was because she spoke good English. Right! Maybe she spoke too clearly. Into his soul.

Was the girl using him as a replacement for Itse. But why him, a white man, who would leave anyway? Or was she using him as a buffer. Perish the thought, he said.

He needed to know the girl's story. She had not finished it. She had not even begun. He was tempted to ask the veteran, but the old man would think of it as a romantic gesture. Romantic? He asked himself, I can't believe I just thought that. Is this a confession? Is this romance or what's going on?

Tim paused. He felt restless and a whiplash of cold in that lonely room. He wanted to defuse the thought by trying to recall his romance back home. He must have a love there. But he drew a blank. He did not try to jog a sterile memory. If this girl is a curse to them, maybe she's a blessing elsewhere. But maybe she does not want anyone. If she is really a curse, what a marvel of flesh and mind. He wondered why he had no inhibitions about a black girl. Did he date one back home? Or was it because she was always in his face? But God! What an enchantment to be burdened with! What immaculate material of defiance and grace and suffering! What a way to clothe a curse!

He paused and tried to restrain himself again. He snapped out quickly, maybe he was fooling himself thinking of romance with a girl with so many issues. He lay awake for several hours. He wanted to figure out a lot of things. He also began to think about the huge risk of the project and how alone he was. What was the funeral he attended? Or was it a sleight of memory? Had he told members of his family where he was going and did he give them a time-line for his trip? Would they not come after him if time elapsed and there was no sign of him back in America? Did somebody back home not know what brought him out to this village? Did he not have a family? Was that why he had to accompany a black man to his village? He thought about Alero and her mother's locket and the way he was linked to all of this and told himself, maybe, God has a hand in all of this. I seem to have a hand in the resolution of a long mystery, he said to himself. Maybe God sent me here to end an abomination. Maybe I'm some kind of messiah. A messiah with a bad memory. God's heroes are always flawed.

That makes me feel better, he thought. Did he have a death wish? He had left the village long since and sighted a city with electricity and he chose to return. Maybe this is where God chose to martyr him, among a village of taboo-drenched people enslaving a family of beauties. Like Alero. A beauty degraded to desperation and near rags. Her skin dark and luscious and her eyes full of agony and seduction. One day a beauty queen, the next day a crocodile, a beast.

He wanted to know where, in all of this, was sympathy and love. Can you love someone you have sympathy for? Was that what was going on? He had to tell himself, he had transports of feelings that did not make sense. They came from regions of the soul his thought process could not say where. Now quiet, now wild, the feeling was a power unto itself. But Tim knew it would go away. Maybe he was feeling lonely, and this girl was merely filling a void.

But girls like Alero were not made to fill voids. She had too much intelligence and carriage and presence not to have a place in the scheme of things. She was either hated or loved. She was - in sorrow, a broken clock; in beauty, a tease; in failure, a funeral pyre; in victory, a parade torch.

Fate dared not toy with her; with this outcast - crocodile girl.

She wore a crown; yet she walked on feet of clay. She either collapsed or reigned. What had intrigued him so? The crown or the feet of clay? Suddenly, Tim knew that it was all too much to think about now and it was time to go to sleep and he sank back, vaguely remembering some line about 'fortune favours him who dares '.

When Alero walked the lonely path to her abominated home, she began to feel embarrassed by what she had done moments earlier. What was she doing in the arms of a total stranger and why had that happened in the first place. She was overwhelmed by the whole top-sy-turvy business of Itse's health, and the precarious hope that kept nudging her with the prospect of his mortality. And the only person she could lean on was this guy, this American.

Not long after she was on her bed she turned to the thought of her whole life and all the numerous false starts and abbreviated honours and episodes of grandeur. And she looked at herself and said it was no good thinking that her life would ever amount to any good.

So, it made sense if she quit contemplating Tim as a possible mate. That was absurd, she thought because, after all the activities in the forest and he came back to his memory and America beckoned, he would step onto the plane and return to his wife or lover in the United States. She had read of interracial romances in America and seen them in movies but, despite all that, she knew that there were no guarantees in matters of the heart.

She was wise enough to see the sparkle of interest in his eyes and body language. She had seen it all her life; from those who hated her and from those who loved her. If the world says you are beautiful, the wayward gazes of men will haunt you. But how wayward was Tim's gaze? she asked herself. He looks like one who might be nice. Maybe he has sympathy. And they say that's not love. But I have seen love without sympathy. Where then is my salvation? All I need is just one person who can love me. That's just what all women want.

Maybe I am really cursed. Maybe all my family is. Maybe there is no way out. Maybe I cursed this white man. My big curse drew him here and, when he was close to his target, I inflicted a curse on his memory. Maybe the villagers are right. I am the crocodile girl and Tim is one of my little victims. What if I charmed him not to return to his country? What if a terrible thing happened in the forest and he dies and also Itse dies. The villagers will find enough to say about me. Even if I die with him in the forest, they would say it was all my doing.

She paused and her eyes tried to penetrate the billowing darkness of her bedroom. The thickness of the night soothed her and unfurled her thought.

Maybe Tim is not bad news after all. Maybe there is good to all this. If he did not come here and did not go through the forest, how would she have known of the locket? And how then would all this wonderful revelation of history have appeared so near?

If there was any hope to win recognition of her humanity, this locket and trip to the forest were the only path to take, and the hero of this enterprise was Tim. So, who would reasonably say that he was bad news? Unless, of course, they went off to the forest and dug in vain for the one truth that would change the shape of all things.

I couldn't but be impressed with this man, she thought. He did not flinch from helping with finding the body of my mother. I could see the genuine interest to help. Yes, he claims that I saved his life. I don't know that I did, but not anyone would just ease into the problems of another person despised by the world, especially if that man is a foreigner.

When I was in his arms, I felt something strange. Something forbidden. No one had held me like that in a long time. The intensity almost burned me. I don't know how much I gave away and what impression was left in his mind. But I came out of his arms feeling like I just had a protector and lover and charmer.

What if all this was just a charade and there is a personality masked by this loss of memory, a maniacal, bumbling and irrational rascal. There are many out there. I have seen many of them and, on occasion, Tim has shown a capacity for unreasoned action and impulses of the wild. Was there something lurking behind the angelic façade? Or was this the real person, one untainted by experience? I don't know, but he has shown compassion and courage. My experience with men tells me that the kind of irrationality that he has displayed is not uncommon even in the most sensitive of men. So why am I defending him? Am I so desperate for love that I can't give myself the distance of objectivity, so I can look and judge? Don't I have enough distance? I know what I went through with Olu and his family in the city. These are our own people, and yet I could not fly with love. What of the white people? Would his family accept me, a black girl, an African? One rejected even by her own people? Maybe they have no such things as taboos? They don't see animals in humans? Would it mean I would go away from this country and live in America?

If this is the man that sets the stage for the end of a curse, then he is the beginning of a blessing. How simplistic. How can I love him? But if he does that for me, then I also owe him the task of getting his memory back. That much at least I should do.

chapter Twenty-One

Tim woke up the next morning with a mysterious appetite. He was hungry for something he could not place. His palate would know it if Tim could find the meal. In the misery of that longing, he told himself that his tongue probably had a better appetite than he.

Tim had not had an American meal since he came to and had just a vague idea of what the meals could be. But he knew it was something he longed for but could not access in that remote part of the world.

He was still lying on his bed that morning, and the first thing he heard was the song of a canary serenading him from a guava tree standing a few feet away from his window, which he had just flung open.

The burden of memory now mingled with the tug of appetite when he heard the front door creak open. It must be Alero, he thought. And suddenly, his mind raced back to the previous night's rumination. Something akin to a chill shot through his veins. Maybe not a chill. Some hot spasm in his veins, perhaps tingling. He wanted to see her right away and he did not want to see her at all. Within the span of a few hours, a thought had cracked open like an eggshell.

He heard Alero rustle into the bedroom next door to check on Itse. Normally, Tim often preceded her in that morning ritual, but he had slept rather late, so his excuse was genuine. He rose from the bed and walked out to join Alero in the next room.

She looked different that morning. So rather than comment on the sick man on the bed, he turned attention on the young woman. But he would not say what quivered on his tongue; he just kept looking. Alero noticed and was quiet for a while and rather than help the man out, she said, "He is just as he was yesterday."

"Well," replied Tim, gathering himself together, "thank God, he is not worse. As the doctor said, we can only keep our fingers crossed."

Alero, who was facing Itse, turned round and made for the door and Tim stepped out of her way. A little spring of female pride lifted her slow gait that morning, a certain bounce of spirit that Tim had not seen but only imagined.

"I'm sure you are hungry now," she said.

"Sure," he said. "I want to eat something American, but I have no clue what it is. I crave something different."

"That's a good sign. It's good to have an appetite and seek something new. I've been bombarding you with African and English meals. Well, that's all we can give. I guess if I were in your shoes, I would long for *fufu* and pepper soup."

"I would have said this appetite is good for my memory in that it means my organs are beginning to wake up to my past."

"Possibly," said Alero with an air of one who wanted to say something else. "I can see that you never saw me in jeans before." She said with a smile and subtle flirtation. But it surprised Tim who tried to cover his base by launching back a question.

"Why did you decide to wear them today?"

"Warming up for the forest," she said, an answer he least expected.

"What's the next step now? Are you sure they're going to let you make this trip?"

"Yeah, the elders want me to. They figure no other person would go with you. They think we are partners in the absurd. We are the only two in the village fascinated with sacrilege," she said.

"So," he said, "they figure out we are a team."

"Do you agree with them," he asked.

She paused and, seeing the many layers in the question, said:

"You are the only person they see me with."

"I think we're partners," he said. "We seem to get along very well. Is that not amazing?"

Alero, who was trying to bring out a loaf of bread and some eggs from the refrigerator, turned back to him and looked him in the eye.

"It would have been boring as hell if we did not get along and my project would have been difficult to pursue. Maybe I would have left and returned another time or abandoned everything altogether," explained Tim.

"Maybe when you returned home your family would have helped you out and you would not need to return again."

"That's a possibility. What if what brought me here pulls me back here again. It means I would have to deal with you again and Itse," he said.

"So we are stuck with each other. But you may have a wife or child. Who knows?" she asked.

"If I had, why did they not seek me out? This has been over three months. This is weird. Maybe I don't and that's why I made this trip without any pictures of a child or woman in my bag. No love notes around me."

"But what of your family: parents, siblings? Are there any pictures in your bags?"

"No," he said, contemplating. "Maybe, I have no parents too. Is that why I am here? To find a family? That's absurd. I can't find a family of hundreds of years back. It does not make sense."

"Well," she said, "you've come to a place where nothing makes sense." She paused and added, "If you did not have any pictures of your family in the bag, isn't it strange that the only picture that could be found in your bag has to be that of my mother. Is that not a sign that we have a bond of some kind? And it is a cameo that can change not just my life, but the history of this little place. But even the veteran is not willing to reveal what that history is."

Tim looked at her in the face and said, "We are both drawn to each other, yet I know little about your past and neither you nor I know anything about my past."

He walked toward her and said, "You have to tell me your story and that's one appetite I can testify to right now."

He smiled and put his hand on her shoulder and the arm trembled to the touch but the trepidation eased as he drew her towards him. She obliged only to the extent of resting her head on his shoulder briefly and raising it to declare:

"I'll tell you my entire story, and I'll do everything in my power to help you get back your memory."

Suddenly, her eyes turned moist as those solemn words enveloped both of them. He looked her in the eye and she returned the gesture and both of them lived in the moment as if in a trance. Her gaze soft as dew, his like a huge *iroko* tree, seconds before a fall.

chapter Twenty-Two

A few hours later, the veteran appeared in the house. He had the look of an exhausted toiler. But, as always, his two eyes had the wild vitality that always reminded the world around him of the extraordinary pedigree of this man, the war hero who never blinked at death, the sojourner in the white man's land. He had been to Europe and Asia. Most of the men in the village had not travelled twenty miles away.

But when Tim saw him, he could not decode his looks. Was the man's exhaustion physical or was he weighed down by the message he was about to deliver, or was it just the old man's trick? But as both men looked at each other, a certain generosity illuminated his eyes. He smiled, as his wrinkled face broke into a thousand parts and released an energy that invested him with the look of both an uncle and a teenager.

"How are you my boy, that sort of thing," he said, motioning for Tim to sit. He walked to the refrigerator and shut it as quickly as he opened it.

"Oh, I miss my Itse. In the past, there was always a bottle of beer here."

He walked lazily to a couch beside Tim and sat forward looking both comical and glum. Tim knew he had something to say but, when he started, the direction was far distant from what the American anticipated.

"You know that people always say that a sports star dies twice. Once they fall out of favour athletically, they are gone and live on the glory of their dimmed prowess. But I am going to die many times. I am sure you don't know that I used to be an athlete, a very popular one. I was a soccer player, a sport not appreciated in the country you come from, although it is the best in the world – 'the beautiful game'. I was in my late teens and early twenties and I was called 'submarine'. That name fitted my style of play - of sneaking up on the defence and scoring against them. I enjoyed my glory and it seemed I was going to live forever in the favour of my talent and under the accolade of an adoring world. But, suddenly, everything was cut off.

"One day, while helping our goalie in his practice routine, I over-extended my ankle and the goalie fell on the knee too. No one could explain it. Although the foot seemed to heal and I could walk normally, I could not play football again. Everybody regretted missing the submarine on the field of play and, for a while, I basked in the pity. But months later, the pity became all I had. New stars erupted and I receded from the fans' fancy. It was then I knew that I had died as a man."

Tim paid attention wondering where he was going with his story. He wanted to ask some questions, but decided not to interfere with the flow of the story.

"I started to seek a second life or, if you like, a resurrection. That was one underlying reason I went to the war. I wanted to be alive again. It did not matter if I died there. I was afraid to mean nothing, or to let my life depend only on past exploits. I returned from the war hailed as a hero. Not in this village. But in the city. The villagers knew little about the war. But the heroism has now turned abstract for me. It was not as if anyone saw the Germans and Japanese or knew anything specific about them. The British told us in simplistic terms that Hitler wanted to rule the world and if we did not join in the battle, he would come and take over our lives. That propaganda was fascinating because it provided me with a fruitful lie to overlay the vanquished football icon inside me.

"My return as a hero made sense because of the drama that surrounded it. I came one-handed and the other hand returned by special delivery. They all call me 'Veteran', which is good. The name my father gave me was Nelson. I used to like it because of the way it sounded. But in those tempestuous days of youthful defiance, I wondered why father gave me a name that I could not translate. So, I looked it up in the dictionary, which defined it as son of Nel. I told myself that I was not the son of Nel. From that day I dropped it. My real name, which you should not worry about, was hard to adjust to. It is quite comforting that the name Veteran has stuck. But as you may know, names like that lose their original flavour over time. And at this age, I am beginning to feel the sensation of worthlessness. I feel the need to be reborn.

"That, my son, is the point of all my pointless rambling. This mission of finding the bottom of Alero's mother story is what I am going to live and die by. And it has become tied to your ancestor. There are things I should not say for your protection, but I think the point about the ancestor you are seeking is important. I just had a meeting with the elders and they say they need to fortify both of you against the wild beasts in the forest. The beasts are not just beasts. They are spirits and they have to be appeased, especially for trips like this to succeed. They said both of your must have a ritual bath in goat's blood before you leave. I persuaded them that it was not necessary for you and that I could have the ritual bath on your behalf. It was a long debate and I almost walked out on them. But at long last, they yielded. Tomorrow morning you will go. They are going to give you a map. But I know a better route. Appear to go along with them. This is the most important trip in the history of the world. Take it seriously."

"I really appreciate you doing this for me."

"It has to be done, son."

Strangely, the American was not going to turn down the proposition of a ritual bath. But since they had a replacement arrangement, a ritual bath by proxy, he was not going to offer himself. He told himself it was a waste of time and resources. A goat's blood, the juice of a deadbeat animal had no claws or swords to guarantee any victory over the wilds, and if not drenching himself in the liquid was going to prevent his trip of finality, then he was not going to be a fool.

Tim contemplated the prospect of goat's blood on his skin and shuddered.

"If I'm going to be excused the sacrifice, would it be wrong if I witnessed it? At least, the person is doing it on my behalf."

"If you want, there is nothing stopping you. The powers of occult secrets are not diluted by appearance," said the veteran, impressed.

Not long after, Alero materialised. Tim thought she looked upbeat and touched off a glow like one who carried the sun's best portion on her face.

But the reality was that she had just contemplated the journey they were about to undertake, and what overwhelmed her was not the entrails of the forest but the *iroko* tree that stood on the outskirts of the Forest of Silence.

She was distracted on that stroll, a desultory face and weary legs and sense of a future that might not work. In that bruised spirit, her head quivered with defiance as if she had a cold. She welcomed it. She was going to ride atop any chants of derision or looks of contempt. Let them call her crocodile if that was something new. She was a beast and loved fishes raw and swam furtively. If she had the jaws and malice of a crocodile, how great a feast she would make of her detractors. Of course, some of them would turn from glory to delicacy, and then the village would know what a real crocodile could do. She wanted to smile but a shudder froze her skin pores as they forbade any such sunny tint.

The weather, in all its dreary fog and benign light, still overhung the village. Its enigmatic majesty was no longer a subject of discussion. Alero wondered why no one did anything about this. What happened to the fabled powers of the priests who were known to exorcise the spirits of rains and call the brilliance of sky and sun on green leaves and supple earth? Well, she mused to herself, the villagers had not questioned why the ghosts of a crocodile would not drift out of their lives.

To her utter amazement, Alero had a lonely stroll, which looked oddly comforting. In her spirit, the vision of children and elders walking past her without taunts, or smirks or mock horror was boring enough to portend evil. What was waiting? Not that she had not had boring moments before, but this foreboding was a peculiar routine on the rare occasions when the streets ignored her.

She walked to the area of the river and a whiplash tore through her, so she winced and retreated and made to return and that was when her eyes fell on the *iroko* tree, a mighty tree which soared into the fog as if in a divine halo.

She took a stroll to the tree's precinct and looked at it with all the awe in her soul. There was a huge mystery around the tree. She was not sure if she was insane or happy or inspired, but she felt like talking to the tree whose top was lost in the shroud that rose from its trunk to the belly of the heavens.

Iroko tree, she said, trying to commune with it without stirring her lips. All kinds of things have been said about you. Each night, we hear all kinds of sounds emanating from your bowels. Is it a sigh, a moan, a shriek, a rumble or a belch? They say all the witches of the land dwell and duel inside you. Did you invite them or are you a hostage? Do they nurture your barks and your many leaves like fingertips? I hear many people have died after your nightly cries? Are they really your doing? I wonder how God made you. Nobody sees your bottom and your top laps the sky. What is the divinity in you and what part of you is barks and boughs and leaves and which birds are in your shadows and which ones carry the omens of the spirits.

If only you could talk with me. By this time tomorrow, I would have passed by you into the forest known only for its silence and history of which I don't know enough. My mother's soul is inside. Can you tell me something of it? Did you have a hand in it? Did the witches conspire with the wicked men in the land to turn me into a half orphan? And who is my father? Do you know him? Has he been kind to me or is he dead?

Tell me about the crocodile stuff? What happened to the crocodile? I know I was told that when I was a little girl and I sometimes believed that I emanated from the reptile. Sometimes, I see scales on my skin. I know it's just dryness but some of my school mates thought that was all the evidence they needed. Talk to me. I would love to hear you, if only a whisper. I will really feel relieved. Hey, was that you?

At that point, Alero felt weird and decided to leave. She was not sure if she heard anything. She walked away with both awe and defiance. She wondered why she wasted her time before a tree that had no voice or flesh or conscience. If she was going to find the bottom of the story that perplexed her life, she was not going to rely on a tree even if the tree was that *iroko* tree and stood in the mist of legends.

It was that look that Tim took for an exquisite glow. But as she arrived, the veteran said he was leaving and asked both of them to be ready early in the morning. They should go to bed early, he emphasised, because they would need a lot of energy for the next day.

The veteran looked pensive as he walked away. From the reaction in Alero's face, Tim thought she wanted the old man to leave. After the door creaked shut, a certain light streaked across the woman's face and she sat down on one of the sofas and the American instinctively sat down across her.

"So, I'm going to be smelling of blood tomorrow. Isn't that weird," she said with humour. "The good part is that I can wash it off before the trip."

"So, what is the use of the sacrifice if the blood won't follow you through the hike," Tim was curious and wanted an elaboration.

"That's the point," she stressed, "I don't believe their stuff."

"Neither do I. But the old man is going to do it for me. So the whole thing will be lopsided unless the veteran has a bath too. I don't believe this either. But for the sake of equilibrium, you should avoid the bath. I will endure the smell."

She smiled as though it was a matter to be left for later. She was eager to do something else.

"I thought you should know the rest of my story as I know it before we embark on the trip. It will make no sense if you don't know all the background before we unearth my mother," she said.

"Right on," said Tim and he sat back and stared into the pretty face on the verge of reeling out a tale.

"My name Alero," she said, "has a meaning."

"I noticed you Africans attach special meanings to names. I have been waiting for you to tell me," cut in Tim. "But," he continued, "it is spelt a little different from a street name I have seen in America. That is spelt A-L-E-J-O."

"Oh," she said thoughtfully, "that means a stranger or visitor in our language. I don't know if that has a meaning there."

"So, I will be Alejo," said Tim. "Here again we have something in common."

"Come to think of it," Alero said, "that meaning would also suit me. I am as much a stranger in my place of birth as you. At least, you they treat with respect."

Tim was silent and waited for the lady to unveil her story.

"Alero was not the name my mother first gave me. It was Toritseju, which was Toju for short, meaning God's surpasses all. My present name was given to me one day when my school shoes were dragged off my feet because they resembled those of one of the chief's son. Not chief Tietie. That chief is now dead. The boy organised other boys and they pulled the shoes from my feet and threw them away. I didn't know where, and the teachers did nothing about it. My mom who noticed that I walked home on my bare feet and tears all over my eyes, consoled me and said the God who gave me the feet also made the earth on which they walked. That God, she explained, would not let me walk on hard or painful ground and she gave me the name Alero, which means soft earth.

"My mother gave me that name because she loved me, but all through my life I had wondered if the name was given to me just to fulfil its irony, to tantalise me. My mother once told me she had feared for me since I was born. I was very lightweight and tiny and several pounds less than other children. Any time people visited us

– and it was often for trouble - mama would hide me under the bed or inside the room. She said she did not want anyone to spread the word that I was not really human. Of course, it backfired. What you Americans call catch twenty-two.

"The rumour, as she told me, spread that she hid me because I had developed the features of a beast. That I did not have eyelids and I had webbed feet and talons. Others said I had hoofs. I grew fast and my mother decided not to hide me anymore. When my full features were exposed to their full glare, they said we had, in our wily necromantic genius, covered the features of the beast beneath my skin. But they said they knew better. Things began to look up for me when I finished primary school and I was admitted to a high school in Warri on a scholarship."

"Scholarship? How did that happen?" asked Tim.

"Yes," replied Alero, "it was supposed to happen. But I won it through a Bible contest organised by the Church of the Sword, a big church given to charity. They didn't know me, of course, and I had to live in a boarding house, which was a marvel to me. I could not wait to leave the village. The villagers thought I was leaving for good.

"I have to make a point about the scholarship. It was the village pastor, Mr. Ben Timeyin, who told me about it, and even recommended me to the judges of the scholarship. His English is funny, but he wrote a letter to the judges that I stood a chance because of my circumstances. So, he persuaded them I would benefit from the scholarship. I was tremendously grateful to him that it worked out.

"But the veteran does not look at it that way. He said it was the man's guilty conscience that compelled him to recommend me. The pastor gave validity to the witch claim, he said, because he wanted to remain the village pastor. The pastor had said the Holy Spirit confirmed that demons possessed us in the family. You see, the village has a divided worldview. They all say they believe in Jesus Christ and go to church on Sunday. But when they encounter mysteries, like diseases and other challenges they can't explain, they go to the witch doctor. Pastor Timeyin wants that sort of conflict to continue.

"The veteran may not appreciate what the man did. But I forgive him. He has not associated with me since I returned. He probably is afraid of me. He does not want my trouble. He wants to pastor in peace. I have not bothered to go to church as well. I am not sure though that I would have even attended the church. I think the man is not a false prophet, just a survivor. He did not have to recommend me. No one can take from me what I benefitted from that opportunity.

"As I was about to say, I wished I would not return to this village. But I had not seen much good in my life and I had not learned how to hold on to happiness even if I had it. I did not have any self-esteem. I did not have a father and my mother was taken from me and people did not compare me except to something lower than themselves."

"You were a bright student, obviously. That should have boosted your ego," said Tim.

"Academics alone cannot make you wise, or enrich your life. I performed well because it was an avenue of escape rather than a measure of self-worth. I loved books because they did not judge me. I loved language because it could unveil the special riddle of evil and mock the temper of conspiracy. I also was fascinated by its magic of healing. I would have loved to be a writer about medicine and healing. My teachers told me they didn't offer combined degrees in nursing and literature. I first went to the school of nursing and later proceeded to the university to study literature. I did not have to pay for any degree."

She shifted on her seat and continued her narration. "So, to go to the real story, I left this village at the age of twelve as an escape but with little self-worth. Life could only get better, not that I really asked for it. I faced a new and exquisite routine. Got up in the morning to the toll of a bell, did my assigned chore, brushed my teeth, had my bath with other girls in the dormitory in the same lavatory. That was strange because that was the first time I stripped in front of anybody. My social skills were primitive and attracted little sniggers and contempt here and there but it did not go beyond that. No one called me crocodile girl. No one knew me and all of us were in a new world. I honed my social skills fast, and it was easy since we all were in a new environment that required a new way to look at the world.

"I was made to wear a new set of uniforms and the classes were fine. That was boring and luxurious and I felt real discomfort because I thought it would not last. As I told you earlier, happiness was a strange concept. Not that I did not laugh or play or joke, even in Orogun village but they were peculiar. My smiles were like drooping flowers. My plays were either too wild or too tame, or that undefined cross between the butterfly and the pig. In one word; soulless. My humour had no air. I knew these limitations and kept to myself, so inaction preserved me from worse ridicule than I was set up to bear.

"Well, barely a month into the school term, something was to startle me into normalcy. A male student, one year ahead of me, began to look at me with a certain sternness that was mean. He seemed to have many devils in those stares. He was skinny, with a seamed and sullen face. He walked with little bounce about him and was without much company. When he had company, they showed a little deference to him. He had a K-leg."

"What does that mean?" he asked confused.

"Oh, a knocked knee," she explained.

"He did not speak much," Alero continued with her tale, "but when he smiled he looked like a baby. The smile came like once a day, I guess. I only saw his smile like once a week. I was really afraid. I could not report him to the teachers because he never spoke to me and was never within a foot of me. I wondered if he had been in Orogun, but I had never seen anyone like him. Did he know of me? Was he going to unveil my history to all these people? Even his stares alone were like tumours on my life already. He did not look like a dummy, because his bold eyes of a frog beamed intelligence and that was the scarier thing. What was this boy's design? I looked back at him only to probe for answers and the more I did it, the more mystified I was and the more scared.

"I wanted him to come to me and tell me whatever he thought. But he did nothing. He became my constant scourge when he was around and when he was not. In quiet moments in the hostel, I would contemplate him. I dreaded him. Once, during break, he stared at me so intensely and, just about then, a teacher, who was known for being a good disciplinarian, walked by. He walked toward the teacher and spoke to him, his eyes looking at me half the time. The teacher looked in my direction and I knew he had said something about me because the teacher looked in my direction once while he was with him, my quiet inquisitor. And when they finished, the teacher walked toward me even as something of a shadow of smile broke the boy's dour visage.

While the teacher approached me, I froze, and all my life seemed to be coming to an end at the time. The teacher, who had not spoken to me, gazed at me with intensity as he came near. Out of nervousness, I greeted him, and his face broke into a very avuncular smile, he said hello, and asked if I was enjoying my break and, as I said yes, he smiled perfunctorily and strode away as if I was nowhere near his project.

"He said nothing more and he never even looked back. But this boy still gazed at me. He became a curious Nemesis and I wanted to investigate but I could not. I wanted to know what he told the teacher and why the teacher did nothing about it. Or was the teacher going to investigate the story and go to Orogun? If they knew the crocodile story, would I be treated like the lone and cursed tree again? Or would the church withdraw my scholarship? I became really scared and, one night, I told myself I would walk up to him and beg him to let me live in the school in peace. I was only twelve years old. I did not want to go back to the village and be the target of more chants and taunts. I resolved one Monday to go straight to him. The resolve subsided all my worries. I said I would tell him I would do anything to prevent him from spilling the beans."

"Sorry to cut in," said Tim, "but did you not confide in anybody, any friend?"

She replied, "No, I thought that was too much risk. I had not had a real friend in my life, save Itse. I did not know what female friends were like. I did not want to risk my most intimate secrets. So, that Monday, I did not hesitate. As I walked out of my classroom with all the students who went to play or stroll, I looked out for him and, within minutes, he was out and he saw me. I looked straight at him. I did not feel scared and made straight toward him. He stood a little surprised, which was a good sign. I got closer to him, he retreated, at first tentatively and later emphatically as he moved away into the class and never looked back at me. He joined a group of friends who were playing in the class. I developed cold feet and retreated. I knew this boy didn't wish me well.

"But the following day and several days later, he did not stop staring. He became a perennial pain. I prayed that, if all he did was staring, let him stare so long as he kept my secrets. If he wanted to play the wild animal, who viewed people from its zoo cage, that was fine so long as I was not the red meat.

"Meanwhile, I was doing well in academics and athletics. I was the second best sprinter in the junior category and best long jumper in that category. A certain amount of fame was coming to me. One morning, I walked to the classroom from the refectory after breakfast; one older male student walked up to me and asked me point blank why I did not have a boyfriend. I was embarrassed. I knew about boyfriends and a few of my friends spoke about it, but I was never drawn to the conversation. I loved the concept, and it was only a concept, because the idea of a male friend was not meant for people like me. I didn't think of myself enough to deserve that kind attention from another human being. And if a boy came and wanted it of me, I wasn't going to trust him. The expression of such a sentiment was bound to be a smokescreen. So, when he asked the question, I did not answer him. My face congealed into a scowl and the boy turned away. But one good I need to confess was that I had met a number of boys on the campus who were simply kind to me and they generally loved to talk with me. But no one asked to be my boyfriend and no such thought crossed my mind until then.

"The attention multiplied and I wondered why. All I received from boys in Orogun was hostility, except for Itse who was an unconditional friend in a friendship where any definition of romance would be out of place. As an athlete, they wanted me to win. They rooted for me on the tracks. It was an indescribable feeling. I began to feel good about myself but that mingled with the sense that all of this was going to go wrong because of this sullen stalker of mine who would not talk and who was tearing my skin by holding off the day of revelation. Once he squealed, he would put an end to all the attention that was coming my way. He was in the second year in school. I learned later that he was one of the bright students and represented his hostel in annual debating contests. When I heard that I was more intimidated and knew the teachers would like him and consequently trust him. So, I knew that the teacher he spoke to was probably in on some of my secrets and, one day, the dam would break.

"The term ended and nothing happened. I did not have to return to Orogun because the church often gave us an option of religious picnic which lasted the two-week duration of the holidays. They bought us new clothes and gave us stipends, which was also a surprise since the idea of a stipend was always a concept meant for other people. During one of the Sunday services, I noticed a man in his early thirties staring at me, but he hardly looked vicious. I suspected that he had a sexual design on me. I was scared because I knew he would come after me at the end of the service and all the church guardians were around and they might think I had started messing around at that young age and with a man more than twice my age.

"Once the service ended, I quickly made for the bus that conveyed us to the church hostel. But one of the elder women called me back and said her son wanted to see me and that he heard I was a very bright student and wanted to commend me. He was one of the sons of a prominent church elder. Before I could utter a word, the man alighted from behind her and the woman innocently left us together in the aisle.

"The man smiled and asked what my name was and I told him. He said he was not going to waste my time. I was almost shivering and he saw that I was not comfortable standing with him. He looked at me closely and said he was a photographer among other things and the reason he wanted to see me was to tell me that I was an exceptionally beautiful girl and that he could make money for me while I was at school by taking pictures of me to advertise commercial products. He said I did not have to give him an answer right away, but I should know that God gave me a lot of gifts and beauty was certainly one of them. He promised to see me soon, and asked me to have a good holiday.

"I was almost keeled over. This could not be true. How could anyone believe I was beautiful? That was insane. Nobody apart from my mother had said that to me and mothers said that to all their children, even if they looked like a chimpanzee's neighbours. I did not think anything after he left but stood as if transfixed to the spot on the aisle. I am not too sure that I believed him at that time. But I also told myself that if he did not believe I had good looks he would not want to sell my pictures to companies to market products.

"I had seen several magazines and newspapers with pretty girls and I did not know that was how they got there. It all just suddenly made sense. God bless my mother. God bless Marmalade. She did not lie about my being pretty. But I recall her saying that beauty was not always an asset for a woman. She had to pray for luck. Less attractive women could attract better fortunes, and beauty always brought uncanny attention and it was not always a good thing. I came upon a poem at school from W. B Yeats,"

She called it "Yeets." Tim helped her with how to say the name, and he did it without patronising. When she said thank you, his voice soothed with the exaggerated satisfaction of a rescuer.

"I can recite some lines from the poem:

May she be granted beauty and yet not
Beauty to make a stranger's eye distraught
Or hers before a looking glass
For such, being made beautiful overmuch

Consider beauty a sufficient end,
Lose natural kindness and maybe
The heart-revealing intimacy that chooses right
And never find a friend"

Tim raised his two hands with a flourish and clapped. Caught by some vanity, she took a bow. They smiled full and hearty as though that was the finale to the whole drama she was telling. But she quickly recovered her sobriety with the words, "Maybe we shall have other happy interludes later."

She then continued her story: "When I got to the hostel, the first place I reached for was the bathroom mirror. I tried to believe what the man – whose name I hardly remembered – just suggested and, even though I looked at myself in the mirror, I was not quite sure I was pretty. I just didn't see it. I tried to look at all the features on my face and body. I thought I was bland. I could not be that beautiful. Or was I blind? I expected the man to come around the next day or the day after. He did not show up. Each day any of the guardians came to me I would think the man had come. No one suggested it or even referred to the subject. After a week or two, I didn't see him. My mind eased to other things.

"The next term began fairly well. The first term report was released and I topped my class. My strengths were in the sciences mostly and in English. All was well, of course, except for my quiet and brooding stalker. When we returned, he had grown taller and, each time I saw him, he looked like a long, relentless shadow. This semester, he seemed to come closer but not near enough to utter a word. But that's why his shadowy image tortured me to distraction. I began to sneer at him, twitch my face, and turn up my nose, all to anger him into breaking his silence. The first time, I seemed to crack him up. A certain curious glee, at once shy and vicious, would drape his face, and he would disappear with the contentment of one who had fulfilled a mission. But after I did it three or four times, that look of a hyena turned into the old sullen desperation, and he also disappeared so that I did not see him again, except in the distance where he did not know I was watching.

"I was scared again but only for a short while. I thought he had resolved to do what I hoped he would not do. But that expectation brought back to me a sense of normalcy. I felt a little anxiety, and by my own standard I glowed. People said I glowed when my eyes darkened; my face was vulnerable and dreamy. I wondered what they meant by that. Sometimes, gloom is my safest place. Security for me is like a quicksand. Something is going to go wrong. You just have to wait. I waited for the boy for over a week but nothing happened.

"Gradually, the whole anxiety and thoughts about the boy dropped out of my horizon. I faced my studies, debates and athletics where I did very well. I had a rival in social studies, a scrawny and taciturn boy who barely looked at me. Even when I topped the class, I always had a sense that he was my equal or he could beat me if I relented in my work.

"One day, our social studies teacher told us to prepare for a test. I had forgotten to take my social studies notebook to the dormitory to read the night before the test. After 7pm, we were forbidden to leave the female hostel. But I knew I was going to pass even if I did not prepare for the test. But there was no way I could top the class. Joseph would have the better of me, and I believed he would gloat in his quiet, enigmatic way.

"I took a risk and sneaked out of the dormitory at about 10pm and passed through the lone boulevard, between the hostel and the classroom, where my locker was. It was slightly windy and cold. I heard birds chirp and frogs groan and the night collapse under their curious harmony. The birds nestled in guava trees lost in the ink of dark and the frogs reigned in sewers that smelled like rotten beans. The ground was alternately gravel and sand and my little sandals did little to keep them calm.

"I was not sure if I was scared or not, but I knew halfway that, if I was caught here, I was really going to suffer for it. I reached the classroom and refrained from turning on the light. When I had taken the book, which I recognised from the place where I had put it, I heard a voice and then a flashlight blinded me instantly.

'What are you doing here,' was the deep voice of the security man.

"I explained to him and he said he would let me go because I was one of the few students he liked around there. I was amazed he said that because I hardly saw him and I wondered why he noticed me.

"But I was relieved and retreated fast towards the hostel, praying that I did not encounter any teacher. If a teacher saw me, it wouldn't be funny. I summoned my athletic skills this time and ran through the boulevard. I turned a corner onto a long row of shrubs. Suddenly, I tripped and fell on one of them. Before I knew what is was, a large hand had held my mouth and whispered: 'I'll kill you if you say anything or shout.'

"I was not able to shout and the person, whom I could not recognise, knew the hold he had on me immediately and let go his hand from my mouth. I breathed hard and was nonplussed. He put me on the grass beside the shrub and then I heard his breathing, which was hard and ominous, like a wild beast in between growls. The first thing he did was lie straight over me with his massive body and, for the first time, I felt a man through his pants. I think he was not sure what to do next. The world was coming to an end, I might have told myself. I did not have witnesses apart from the bedewed leaves around me, the agitated chants of insects, the distant moan of frogs and conspiratorial silence of the world. I had not had sex before. How cruel would it feel from the lashings of a brute? I felt cold. Would he kill me? Should I scream? Could I scream, if I wanted to? He was so big and his power so final that I cursed the moment I decided to leave the dormitory. In a few seconds, he was still before his fingers started running through the helm of my skirt. The fingers crawled like a praying mantis on my skin. Then I heard a thud. A stick had fallen on the man's back. He shrieked to his feet and a human form dropped from a nearby tree like a ghostly fruit. In an instant, I thought I was in the land of night fairies. The night had bred a monster and the tree had delivered a ghost.

"My assailant was scared and ran away. The tree man stood, a little hunched. I recognised my saviour immediately, even before he uttered a word. He was my stalker. In the kindest words I had ever heard, he said 'run to your hostel before anyone knows.' That was the first time he had spoken to me and the only time.

"I could not sleep that night. I wondered what he meant by that act of honour. I looked forward to meeting him the next day. I did not see him in school. I nosed around a little desperately in his class and asked one of his few buddies. He wondered why I wanted to see him. He was more feisty than I expected, given what he told me about his friend. He was a huge contrast to his friend. He had a happy tongue and his eyes seemed to repeat or anticipate whatever came out of his mouth.

"'He's in the sick bay. I guess he will really like to receive a visitor like you,' a twinkle elevated his face, but I could not tell if he was being sarcastic or simply happy that his friend was in a dreary solitude in his sick bed. I quickly darted out of his presence, unsure how else to react to what he had just done.

"When I returned to my seat in class, I wondered what had happened to him. Was it connected to his heroism the other night? Was he wounded when he dropped from the tree, a victim of a surreptitious concussion that erupted after he returned to his hostel? Did he go after my assailant after he let me go and did the bastard inflict any injuries on him? I hoped that he did not get into any trouble? I felt really guilty and I knew I had to go to visit him, and maybe, once and for all, we would talk to each other. I knew now that he probably did not wish me any evil. If he did, he would have wanted me raped.

"When classes were over, I planned to excuse myself from any sport that afternoon and faked a little fever, so I could pay a visit to the sick bay. It worked. I was never one to miss sporting activity and the sports' master was favourably disposed towards me.

"As I approached the sick bay, I began to wonder if it was not a bad idea after all. I wondered why he was up that night and why he followed me at a time when he knew I was not supposed to be outside my dormitory. That mystery was outweighed by the act of a good shepherd that crowned the night. I began to wonder too what would have become of me if that man had succeeded in defiling me. What would have happened to my self-esteem which was only beginning to bud? It was a good sign, I told myself, a sign I might not end up like my mother.

"I reminded myself that I was a fruit of a similar circumstance and, in my own case, where would I have hidden if it all led to pregnancy. The missionaries who sponsored my education would have been disappointed and withdrawn their scholarship. The result would have been a disgraceful return to my village and turned me into a funeral pyre for the rest of my life. If this boy did not know what he had done for me, I believed God knew and would reward him.

"The sick bay was a little house, about a mile away from the classroom blocks. It sat alone, surrounded by mango trees, whose lush fruits and leaves wove a balmy blanket over fevered bodies, wounded flesh and desolate hearts.

"When I entered the place, the nurse was not around. He was an old man who had had that job since before I was born. He was a kind man, with a big body and a slight stoop, which I assumed he had acquired from bending over his numerous and frequent patients whom he called children. I wondered if he had gone to one of the two bedrooms. I waited for about five minutes, while trying to put up an act of fever. But I suddenly realised as I waited that the man would know that I did not have any fever. The best idea, I told myself, would be to fake a severe headache.

After ten minutes, the man did not appear. I tried to walk to the rooms. The first one was open but there was no one inside. The second and adjacent room was only slightly closed so I could look in. My heart leapt as I saw my former stalker. His eyes were shut but I retreated and looked in the main office. The silence prodded me back to the boy. I stood by the door and looked at him for upwards of twenty minutes. I wanted him to wake up and see my face. How would he respond to me? As he smiled, so he feared: like a baby. I felt like nurturing him even as I was scared of him. He had done this great thing for me but I still perceived a cruel shadow around him. Once he opened his eyes and saw me, would he charge at me? Now he would have no place to which to retreat as he had the last time.

"After a while as nothing had happened, I braved my way into the room and, my heart leaping, stood by him and spoke. I can't recall what I said but it was something like thank you for saving my life. No introductions. I think I kept repeating about the same words but he did not stir. By impulse, I decided to touch him, so he could wake up. He merely stirred and turned. I spoke while his body moved but he never responded. I wanted to touch him again, when I heard something like a foot shuffle and a door creak. I darted out of the room and the sick bay nurse was already seated at his table, rummaging in his drawers for something. He did not hear me walk in and I stood in front of his table for over fifteen seconds before he sensed my presence. I did not have to explain anything. I just told him that I had a slight headache and he gave me some aspirin tablets.

"I was unhappy and looked for another excuse the next day but his friend came to me during class hours and told me they had "taken my friend home and his parents thought he was allergic to something in the school so he wouldn't be returning. They are taking him to another school in another town.

"He looked less feisty this time. He missed his friend. I missed him too. I miss him still. I have never seen or heard from him since. The one little thing I heard about him was that some people called him *Arocky Joe Joe and Ajimmy Loka.* I don't know what that means."

chapter Twenty-Three

im wanted to break off the tale temporarily. He noticed that the pitch of her voice was dropping off a little, even if her energy level had not flagged. Dusk was weighing in, too, a thing that was difficult to perceive, because of the unchanging temper of the fog outside.

Everyone seemed content with the weather. Children romped about with their drivel and in bare feet. But what really bothered the American was a delicious envy of the woman before him. He marvelled at her command of details and keen sense of perspective.

"You're doing very well," he said, rising to his feet and offering to make them both a cup of tea. He observed that the woman appreciated it and she too rose up.

Beneath his gesture, a thought roiled in Tim's heart. He wondered why he had not progressed from his earlier recollections. He only recalled the funeral and he wanted to know what it was all about. But luck was not coming his way. However, a certain superstitious element crept in. Why did he have to recall a funeral? Was that an omen? He could not go far with the thought. Alero had noticed his distraction. He, too, noticed what Alero had noticed and he quickly responded by talking about the wild that loomed in less than twenty-four hours.

"Do any of those pigs stray to town? Why have I not seen any of them?" he asked.

"That's a good question. Maybe the veteran can answer it, but when I was young a huge snake as long as fifteen feet and very fat was killed in one of the elders' homes. It was waiting when both he and the wife arrived from the bush," she said, a little residual horror evident in her voice.

"They had to rally all the young men around to kill it. It was a huge spectacle. I had to look from far away. Then I wondered whether, if such a thing happened in our house, we'd ever find any volunteers to help us. Thank God for small mercies. On the pigs, I heard of sightings, but I don't know of any incident."

She looked at him, as if to probe any tincture of anxiety about the wild but the man lit up, his face returning to the mercurial spirit that often delighted and puzzled her. And just suddenly, his mien was subdued again, with a shadow that meant he had something to say.

"Why have the recollections that I've had done so little to shed light on the meaning of my life?"

"You mean the funeral and the boy playing basketball?" she asked, recalling their various conversations on the matter.

"The problem with that," he explained, "is that I only recall disjointed parts and sad parts."

"Sad parts can come together and the sum could be triumph. Believe me," she said.

"Are you implying the forest, the hike?"

"Yeah."

"Right now, it's just the drama of it all that fascinates me. The hike, the trees, the beasts and our innate power to probe the mystery and navigate the wild."

"That's not what fascinates me. I'm interested in how it all ends.

How, with our single acts of selflessness, we're going to put an end to the barbarous history and enthrone a new time in this village," she said, glowing while her eyes also squinted like one dreaming.

"The selfless part of it fascinates me. I like to think that, if it were not selfless, I wouldn't have travelled this far in the first place. I like to think that. I like to think that a certain heroic element plays into my whole story, just like yours," he said.

"I'm sure it can't be any other way," she said, the voice level now beginning to drop off into some kind of dreamy borderline. Her eyes looked into his, his into hers and Tim's face turned a little moist as he moved toward her. She stood as if frozen when he put his hands around her waist and pulled her forward. Both their lips found traction in each other after two miscues. It did not last. She withdrew like a stricken bird and he let her go. Silence.

"That was good," he said, with a little nervous fortitude, a happy unease. His fingers shook as if stricken by a gymnastic fever. "In fact," he continued, "it was great."

He handed her a cup of tea, his fingers holding together in all their nervous glory. She accepted it with a sort of flirtatious triumph, as if gloating at the man's worshipful mien. The man who was strong and athletic and to whom she gave something of her soul. He put his hands around her shoulder with deeper confidence in himself, and she yielded with less coyness. Body heat fed on body heat while dusk thickened. The chatter outside of playful children tailed off. The choir of birds upgraded the evening with symphony. And the world outside yielded to the ritual shadows of a closing day.

They sat down again, Tim anxious not to steal the momentum of her story with worries over his blank memory. She took a sip and commented on its right sugar taste and took another sip before setting the cup on the table.

"I'll make the story a little shorter this time, although this is a long story. All humans tend to believe that our lives make great stories. You are making me feel so," said Alero as she rested her head on his shoulder, which heaved slightly to the rise and fall of his chest.

"Well," he said, "I've not been bored just yet."

"Okay," she said, "let's go to my athletic times again. One afternoon we were practising for a regional competition, and I was to represent my school in the junior category. It was the right therapy for the blues I felt from the sudden disappearance of my stalker. I was in my sports gear and making the rounds on the one hundred meters track. I was having fun, because many people relied on me to win the trophy that had eluded the school for upwards of six years. One of the other high schools had captured it consistently because of their coach who knew how to convince the school authorities to put up with academic failures so long as the athletes brought sports' laurels to the institution. My school was content with winning the quizzes and debates and the top grades in the finalists' examinations.

"The boys always watched as the sports master instructed me. On the eve of the competition, I was in the dressing room when somebody came to me and said I was wanted by a visitor. I was nervous. I thought my inquisitor had finally decided to break the ice. But the student who delivered the message described someone that I could not recapture in my memory. My mind went to Orogun, and wondered what had gone wrong again.

"When I left from the room, I saw the young man who had wanted me to pose for a magazine. I was even more shocked. I don't know why. The idea of appearing on a magazine cover delighted me more as a fantasy, as something I wished for, rather than as an actual accomplishment.

"He was a charming kind of man. He had a great smile and chameleon spirit: the right mood for every occasion. This time he was not alone. A man with a huge camera stood by him and embarrassed me with his unflinching gaze.

"You look different in just a few months," he said, instantly introducing the man he brought as his agency's photographer. For one moment, I thought he meant that I had lost the lustre that attracted him to me, but his smile reassured me and he even told me that I probably looked better.

"Do you still remember my name?' he asked. I did. I called him Mister Ofor. His photographer was John Oluwambe. He told me he had been in touch with the school principal and had taken a special permission to feature me in a number of magazines marketing a slew of body creams for young women. He said the principal had approved, on condition that I was not nude and that I was portrayed as a student with a sterling academic performance. He added that the principal asked about my academic records before issuing the approval.

"The photographer said I looked perfect in my sports gear for the concept they had in mind. If, that is, I wanted to do it. He said they were going to pay me about ten thousand naira for the deal, which was hard for me to conceive. I had never owned more than fifty naira in my life. He asked me if I would take the picture then and sign the papers after I was done with practice. The photo session would not outlast thirty minutes.

"I saw the principal's approval papers just when the sports master walked up to us and asked us to be quick about it. It was then I knew the principal had consulted him on the matter. The photographer took shots of me in a variety of positions and poses on the field, and all the students around surrounded the scene and feasted their eyes until the sports master rebuked them and they scattered around like goats with hot yams in their mouths.

"At the end of the practice session, the photographer took more pictures, capturing the beads and rivulets of sweat on my body as well as some activated muscles on my thighs and face. He said they made me "more natural." But I knew he had an eye for the erotic registers. I tell you, within a few hours, I had a sense of sexual energy waking up inside me. I knew, as the camera flashed and eyes danced all over me, that I was not just human, not just a girl who ate and played and slept at night. I knew I was not just a biological specimen from a village or even a village tar brush of taboo, but one whose skin and eyes and thighs and body movement drew the senses to forbidden terrorists, evoked the energies of sin, made eyes droop and twinkled notions of vanity. I became aware of it not just for myself, but also for young women everywhere. I did not, unlike most girls; rouse to that awareness when my breasts sprouted or from pubic debuts, but from the relentless clicks and flashes of a marketer's camera.

"I am not too sure that I loved it at that time. I did not hate it either. But it served for me as a form of escape, in hindsight, from the notoriety foisted on me all my life in Orogun. I was attracting an attention that drew smiles and envy and money without the ink of disgrace or cacophony of jeers. That was a good thing. My about thirteen year-old mind could not articulate it but I accepted it.

"Perhaps, the most telling consequence was my sense of my own beauty. I began to see myself as a special breed incarnated to please the senses. The people of Orogun had never seen it or even acknowledged it all these years steeped in their ill will. They did not see in my eyes, hips or voice any trace of an enchantress.

"They did not love my skin; they just loved their philistine aversion to the belle around town. They loved to hate me because that's what they wanted for their daughters or sisters or future brides. But because of whatever historical baggage, I was better a crocodile than human. Well the beauty was bound to the spotlight now, immune from the evil eye and foul tongue and feline schemes.

"I was in school with people who loved me and teachers who wanted a new path for me. I was sheltered by the people of God. I had only recently been saved from a sexual predator by a boy who would not talk to me. I began to feel he was a Godsend, a cosmic statement of protection and nurture.

"I began to concentrate hard on my books, and my first love was literature. I read books like *Things Fall Apart, Jane Eyre* and *David Copperfield*. I loved the books because they spoke to my wounded parts. My teacher was taken by my adventure in literature and he paid special attention to my progress. I had a special love for word coinages and poems opened my eyes to the depths and cunning of phrases and I loosed myself in memorising long poems and whole paragraphs in novels.

"I was chosen several times to represent my school in recitations. I chose several poems, but my favourites were a poem called *Abiku* by Wole Soyinka, one of our poets and dramatists, and *Ulysses* by Alfred Lord Tennyson. *Abiku* is a child who constantly returns to life after premature death. He or she returns to the mother's womb and keeps being born again. I loved the poem. I especially love the opening verse:

In vain your bangles cast
Charmed circles at my feet
I am Abiku, calling for the first
And repeated time.
No flourish this time.

"That is deep," Tim responded. "I love that beat about "charmed circles at my feet".

"Yes. I agree. So," continuing her story, "one morning, on my way to class, a mail man on a bicycle pulled up in front of me and said, "You're the girl. I've been looking for you all morning,"

He slid his hands into a big bag of mail and handed me six magazines. He said, "Who do you resemble, your father or mother?"

"I don't know my father" I replied, a little surprised. No one had asked me that question before.

"He looked at me, smiled and rode off. He had brought the magazines with my pictures in them. All six magazines had different pictures and the theme was that only smart girls combined physical prowess with beauty. I was told that the magazines would run the advertisements for six months. I was thrilled to see myself in the magazines. I barely paid attention in class that day, although I tried to rein in my excitement.

"By break time, the whole school knew of it. Lots of students crowded around me and wanted to know how much I was paid and whether I was still going to remain in school. One student shouted out "*ashawo*", from the crowd around me. And I was angry. The word means whore. I wanted to shout back at him, but the other students did the job for me. Another asked if the men who arranged the contract slept with me and how many times.

"In the refectory, a senior picked up one of the magazines while I was eating and acted as though she wanted to admire the pictures. Rather she dropped the page with my picture into a bowl of leftover soup. She apologised, saying I could always order new ones. With a smile, she added "Maybe you can pose nude next time," and she walked away. I knew I was naïve to suppose that everyone was happy that I had soared into the spotlight.

"The contracts were renewed over and over until I was sixteen and, in my fourth year in high school. Mister Ofor asked to be my agent. He said he had a number of arrangements lined up for me. He said he was eyeing television and home video which, in our country, is like the movie industry. He maintained I could make lots of money and earn lots of respect.

"He knew little about my past. I told him my mother was dead and I did not know my father. The stuff about crocodile was fading fast from my kin, although it lay hidden inside me like a stealthy beast gearing up for an ambush. I did not return to the village and Auntie Mogha, who constantly wrote me letters and forbade me to return to Orogun for whatever reason, saw my success as the family counterfoil against generations of prejudice.

"You are better," she wrote in one letter," than those men in the family who escaped the village and changed their names and cut off their roots. We are proud of who we are, even if the world treats us as sub-human."

"But before Ofor came up with any concrete deals of his own, the school was going tell me to participate in a fashion show organised by Clear Mobile, a big oil corporation for schools around. They wanted to pick the winner as the spokesperson for their scholarship programme for indigent students in the oil-producing areas. It was a public relations' foray to befriend villages whose environments were degraded by rigs and oil spills. They made tons of money while the people who sat over the wealth had no schools, no good roads, no potable water or electricity. Their farms spread out among creeks and bushes like soot of oil unflattered by wind but baked fallow by a habitual sun. The rivers were, in their violation, dark soups of poison, glistening into the horizon. On the farms, crop stalks stooped. The rivers dripped with dead fish. The people hardly farmed or fished.

"In my naïve sixteen-year old mind, I saw the fashion show as another opportunity to win, to assert my mettle over a childhood of failures. That show deprived me of all my privacy; that was when I hit the spotlight. I won easily and what defined it was a newspaper story the next day that described my skin as having the 'the glory of chocolate'."

"The public relations' department of one of the chocolate companies thought they could take advantage of that to market their product. That was the first job I did for television and Ofor jumped at it as my first agent. It appeared on the local television at first. I was in a bathtub of chocolate in the first scene and, later ,I was in a short skirt and t-shirt playing tennis, the camera highlighting the tint of my skin. It ended with a deep, enraptured voice saying, "the glory of chocolate" as I reached for a chocolate bar, after I took a wild shot."

"Wild shot?" he asked.

Yes, wild shot, but it was kind of sexy, if you know what I mean

It was waxing darker outside and the birds thrilled to the night with deep, resonant trills.

"The birds are in the mood for love," remarked Tim, trying to peer through the curtain of darkness between them. But Alero said nothing and that mystified the man who rose to his feet to turn on the generator.

"The sound of the engine could skew the romantic rhythm of the birds," he said with a lift in his voice and his bounce as he walked outside. Alero was still from the neck up.

When he returned to the benefit of a lighted room, what raced through his mind had little to do with how the blast of the engine overthrew the throaty joys of the canaries outside. As his eyes fell on Alero, he knew why the woman's tongue had not stirred in the past half hour. Beads of tears coursed down both her cheeks and the upper part of her dress around her bosom glistened. Her eyes were bold and distracted as though she saw and did not see. Her bosom heaved as though her breasts would pop out. To Tim, she seemed to crave help.

"Hey, what's the matter? Was it what I said?"

She seemed impervious to the words. Tim did not know what to do except sit beside her and slide his arms over her shoulder and say "It will be all right."

She had reached a part of her story that was hard to tell, where her so-called fairy tale tumbled on the crest of royalty and fame.

"I met a prince," she said, "and that signified the end of my story. He made me think of love and love it. I was in my last year of college and had just been crowned the most beautiful girl in the country. He seemed to know how to treat me and shelter me and show me off. He was not just a prince, he was a prince of one of the major kingdoms the European colonialists knocked down and integrated into a bigger country. But the magnificence of that kingdom, Abiomu, is not lost. The royal family is still rich and wields a lot of influence today and to be the king or prince is to be a sky eagle.

"Many people did not know my name. I was sweet chocolate or the chocolate girl and that was enough for them. You see, beauty ravishes itself. Beauty is suicide. I guess I was caught in this celebrity dazzle, how the media fawned with their generous ink and rolls of TV camera film. I loved the spotlight and sometimes craved it as a potent denial. It was an antidote to the world that pre-dated this, and God's reward for my years of disfavour.

"The natural thing for me was to date a prince who was also in awe. I was lucky to have escaped a life of male predators. A certain Christian allegiance had chastened me from any kind of scandal. I was lucky I did not date any of the legions of married men swarming around me, beasts in suits and *agbada*.

"The prince was a pharmacist, and owned Olu Pharmacy, the

biggest in the land. He loved his work, was unsullied by scandal as well and was not as impressed by attention as I was. I thought that was really good.

The plan was to get married after I left the university. I was going to help start a public relations' firm. Contracts were guaranteed. The family connections were not only rooted in history but also in the big, multinational corporations.

"The family received me well, especially the king, his father. The mother was a little worried that I did not have a family. I told them I lost my dad and mom and had only an aunt. She is a glamour woman who craves the spotlight and presides over the cringing of men. Fat, short and big headed with lips that seemed towards her elaborate nose, Olu's mother lives more by the clothes she wears than the air she breathes. Her walk reminds you of a duck in a hurry. Her voice is like a wasp before the sting. Her ego is massaged in parties by minstrels who serenade her for her money. She loves her son, I thought. I don't think so anymore. I think she shows her son she loves him because, as a man, he guarantees the king's lineage on the throne. So, once the king passes, the successor will not de-jewel her, to rid her of her trappings of glory.

"When she speaks English, her syntax is Humpty Dumpty, like a stack of books knocked down from the middle. She seems to swear when she speaks. She did not like me and it was not just me. She never liked anyone nudging her, if by only an inch, from her special son. But outwardly she seemed to accept me.

"The king never spoke much. He was genial, enlightened but maintained a distance from everyone. This passed for regal superiority. But it may be his security from the venomous eye of the potential enemy.

"Olu and I were told that we were perfect together. A fashion columnist once described us as two groundnuts in one shell. You guys call it two peas in a pod. I loved the metaphor, but our story could force any girl to be cynical of romantic love. I say this because our parting had nothing to do with any lack of love. He loved me and I knew it. He virtually lived for me. Although the world did not know my story, I told him everything. He knows as much detail as anyone could know. We were together for almost a year. He almost followed me to the village but I restrained and told him we could do it after he had told his family about my family's travails. He was looking for an appropriate time.

"As I unveiled the family story, he showed no resentment towards me but he was full of compassion and, in his naivety, asked me to take the matter to the media and expose the inanities of my people. He said the media would be my 'cudgel to the intestines of Orogun hypocrisy.' We would have laughed at that metaphor if the matter had not been so serious.

"Meanwhile, each time I burst on the streets or was seen in a car or shopping centre, I was almost mobbed. I felt the love of the world. Eyes ogled, men blew kisses in the air, kids angled to touch my dress, and sellers cut prices in half and even gave me wares for free. On one occasion, I met a bunch of teenagers cleaning my car as I stepped out of a shop, and they gave me an affectionately delinquent smile as they dabbed away.

"I'm not sure if the media is to blame for all that happened to me. I mean the bad things. Maybe I would have been all right if I had not become a beauty queen, or never been betrothed to a prince or got tethered to a world of voyeurs. I probably will find answers to this someday.

"But it all happened this way. Olu had decided to talk to both his parents on a specific day. He would tell them I did not need to bring any members of my family to the wedding and explain the sordid details of the crocodile lies and alienation. If the media wondered why my family was not represented on the great day, the family would exploit its royal muscles to expose the Orogun village. They would ask the press to go find out the truth. That way the village would be on the defensive and I would emerge a victimised heroine. That was a liberation recipe, he insisted, and planned to tell both his parents. But the king had to travel on urgent business to the capital city and he was away for three weeks.

"One morning, Olu's mother drove to her son's store with a preview copy of *National Life*, which was scheduled to be published on the following Sunday. It was clear she was in disarray. Her blouse was ruffled, famished for the dignity of a pressing iron. The make-up on her face was uneven; an anarchy of sheen, dull spots and contours. The face seemed to puff with simmering rage and an edge grazed her voice as she spoke to her son acting as though I was not there. She passed the paper to her son and I saw the title of the story as Olu raised it to his eye level. It read, Sweet Chocolate is Crocodile Girl.

"At the sight of the title, I thought I was going to faint. But what I felt was worse. It was close to a trance. I daydreamed, lost oxygen, sweated, hated, loved and craved suicide all within a minute. I had reached the end of the world but it also was the beginning. The woman squinted at me and, in her waspish accent, asked me whether I was planning to eat up her son and why I didn't tell her when I planned to do so. She never asked me what I had to say for myself.

"She was livid. You could tell from the sparks that took turns tumbling out of her eyes. If you did not know what happened, you would think I had already eaten up her son. Of course, some people implied that later. Olu's first response was that his mother should use her influence to stop the publication of the story and ask the newspaper reporter to do more investigation. I read the story. She had the devious good sense to let me read it. She savoured my misery as I moved from word to word. My eyes stumbled through the page. I could not read. I just made sense out of key words. The reporter had visited the village and spoken with several villagers, and he took a series of photos, dramatising the isolation of our family.

"The woman always claimed that she was civilised; read books and was steeped in all the glories of cultured people. But she was not even prepared to hear me out. I tried to speak through tremulous lips and a body that quaked with nervous fever. For her, my body language convicted me."

"I won't talk you," she proclaimed, not even wasting her sight on me. "*I blame myself who make my pikin be your friend.*"

"What is *pikin*?" asked Tim.

"A child," explained Alero.

"Her son asked her not to blame me and that he was going to discuss the matter with her. '*Oh, so you know since and no tell me, eh?*' she asked. '*Or she don bewitch you already?*' She turned to me and said, '*So which food you cook for my pikin to take all his sense away.*"

After that, she looked up at the ceiling and put her two hands on her head with sighs of surrender. "*I'm finished. I'm finished. Anything happen to my shild I will bury you in this town,*" she threatened.

"Mama," cut in her son who was nonplussed. "She is not like that."

"What do you know about this world? This is wicked world. *I tell you beware before. You think every beautiful girl good. I know since. You see what I tell you before.*"

"She walked away and got into her car and the driver sped off.

"As she left, I came to my senses and collapsed. The next time I became aware of myself was in the hospital, alone. I did not see Olu for almost three days. Suddenly, the world of my childhood throbbed back in surges.

"The next day the news story was published and the tabloids alone feasted on it. Even when the so-called serious publications reported it, it was clear that, in spite of their veneer of fairness and disdain for superstition, they paid attention to what the majority of people were inclined to believe: that I was not really human.

"A follow-up report in one of the tabloids said the family was worried about things: that I might have destroyed Olu's chances of being a father after having sex with him, and I might have eaten up the prince. He was no more than a human façade. I had eaten his soul. He could drop dead someday mysteriously and the doctors, in their naivety would chalk it up to heart attack or some other so-called medical reasons.

"Apart from the doctor, I felt an insidious hostility from among the hospital staff. They just did their jobs with me and no more. But what bothered me was Olu's absence. I learned what the love of my life was doing from the newspaper, although not much. They said he had not showed up in the pharmacy since the publication, that he had called off the wedding and was in no mood to see me and his mother had convinced him that I was indeed a crocodile. His mother was quoted as having said 'We don't want the prince to make a crocodile heir to the throne someday.' That was what the press quoted her as saying. I don't believe she put it in those words. The press always refined her quotes. She always gave the reporters money. So, they made her look good."

"Do you think the guy was a coward, or was he under some kind of oath as a prince," asked Tim.

"I think he dreads the mother and did not know how to confront the mother in public. The mother had an incredible hold on him. I pity him", she said. "I did not have to stay in the hospital for three days," she continued, "but I did not know where to go. I wanted Olu to come see me and tell me what was going on. I was frightened. I was sick inside. I might have cursed God many times. I was full of rage. I was tired. Gray clouds were about to unhinge over me. I was dying. I tried to call him on phone, but he would not pick it up. I knew he was home. Two days later, I told the doctor I wanted to leave, and he let me.

"He didn't care if I stayed longer. The palace was picking up the tab. I went to the palace and it was as if I was enacting a television show when I alighted from taxicab. Everyone was silent, all the court jesters and hangers-on and routine workers. The king was not at home. Neither were the queen and Olu. When I reached Olu's living quarters, an old woman walked up to me. 'My daughter,' she said. 'Next time don't come here again.' I looked at her quizzically. She already accepted the defiance that brought me there. I peered at her threadbare skin; the proud network of veins around her neck interlocked, loosened and temporarily disappeared under her skin's fragile umbrella. When the veins reappeared, she seemed reborn, a new energy roared in her tongue. Her eyes were almost not there, hidden between two lids that hung on both sides of her nose bridge like foliage fattened by the extravagance of the years.

"You are not what they say you are. But you can't change what they say. If you were I would know. But the gods will be with you until you win the battle. You are the plate the priest of sacrifice gives to the gods. Just go, my daughter. You can't change what they think about you. Olu is a prince."

chapter Twenty-Four

Tara knew it was time. Anxiety was mounting on expectation. The time Tim promised to return home had been exceeded by more than two months. Calls to the embassy had yielded no definite information. The State Department said they had no record of him. In one of the calls, she received nothing but rude replies from one of the embassy officials, who almost implied that she was mad.

"*I had told him not to go,*" she wrote in her diary, which had become her tower of refuge as she battled the omen of her nephew's absence. "*What was the point,*" she wrote on: "*Nothing was guaranteed in the tenebrous thick of those woods and forests, in the belly of beasts and native tongues and exotic accents. I had always known him to do the impossible. But he was always in the ferment of his own impulses.*

What kind of atonement could he have secured with the search? The man who piloted him there, I don't know how much of him he knew. How could he just place his confidence in a foreigner so completely, and follow him to his country just because he was the best person with the clue to our great Forester. Even he would have wanted to have been left in peace.

You don't solve the mystery of over a hundred years by hopping on the plane and flying through the reaches of the American sky, over the Atlantic

Ocean, to some far-flung entrails in Africa and hope you can ferret out some truth about the turbulence and narrow-mindedness of a family. How can I live with my conscience now? After several attempts at dissuasion, it was I who finally gave him my blessing. He was going to go anyway. But I did give him my blessing. He abandoned all the prospects of his life here in the United States and said his life would never hold any meaning until he found out that single material about the man that died in the forest. It happened there too long ago to matter to me.

If he felt his blood was contaminated, well, mine isn't. I blame his father for this. He always believed in special people and struggled with it when it was almost too late. But somehow his son caught the infection and now I have to account for it.

Since he left for Africa, I've not heard from him, not gotten a letter from him. I know he can't reach a computer in the village. I can't write what I imagine may have happened. I don't know if I can bear the thought of it. Three tragedies in one calendar year? That cannot happen. I have to do something. I can't just stay here and fold my arms…"

She stopped writing and stared at the wall in her study in Boston, Massachusetts.

In another part of the country in Atlanta, Georgia, Jim Fallows was about to complete the nuts and bolts of the book he was writing, and seemed to have arrived at an unexpected conclusion about the young man and his family. It was not the way writers of his gifts hope to end any book. It looked less romantic, lacking some of the theatrics of the grand narrative he had envisioned.

It was good to tell the tale anyway, he thought. Not that there was not much to celebrate. Other persons in the family were caught in the story's web. It does not matter, he thought, that they were not contemporaries, even if they were prominent in their time. One or two dramatic personalities were enough condiments. But the tale still had loose ends and, to tie it together, he had to make a little journey himself, out of the depths of Georgia. Who knew what will puff out of it.

Suddenly, he saw himself as an actor, a part of an elaborate tale and he had to play a role in bringing the story, in all its anti-climactic dreariness, to an end.

But first he must meet Tara Forester, Tim's aunt. She was the only one in the family who would even offer any cooperation or recognise any wisdom in writing the book.

Cindy and her mother decided at lunch two and a half months after they had not heard from Itse that something had to be done about it. Her mother suggested they contact the embassy.

Unknown to her parents, she had planned a week earlier to fly to Colorado. She knew something had gone wrong. The last message was a letter in which he had told her about the drama of the village Chiefs before they finally allowed them to go into the forest.

"You know, love, my people still believe in some myths about gnomes and spirits and we may be in danger and all that. I understand their point of view and concern for us. I lived there for most of my life. But that's why I don't try to judge. It makes sense to most of them. You cannot argue with that. I am just happy they are letting us into the Forest of Silence.

We shall not be there for too long. One week at the most. I am bonding with this Tim guy. He still has to overcome some stuff. He is quite fascinated by the environment. He cracked me up when he said the village was quieter than he anticipated. He cracked me up at first. Then I understood what he meant.

And it made me kind of sad. Hope all is well with mom and dad. I should return in about a mouth. After we are through with Tim's search, I will spend a few days in Lagos and come over to Chicago. I miss you badly.

Love,

Itse.

That was about two months before. So, what was the matter? Cindy decided to begin her search by visiting Itse's town house. That was the last option, she decided. None of his Nigerian friends could really explain what happened. Bimbo told Cindy that he was worried himself, and he feared he might be hurt. He said he wanted to contact Nigeria and send one of his relatives in search of the village. Cindy wanted to know how long that would take. Bimbo said a few weeks. That was a month ago. Two days before the lunch with her mother, Bimbo had told her that the relative had still not gone as he was trying to secure leave from work before embarking on the journey. Cindy could not wait.

Her goal was to rummage through his town house for any valuable clue. She found nothing. Now, she decided to call the American Embassy in Nigeria.

The man at the embassy was surprised at the call.

"I have had two other people call over this same guy. Then there must be something to the story," said Brian Alderman.

"Do you know who they are? Can I have their contact information?" she was given the details of a Tara Forester who was eager to get in touch with anyone who could help.

Cindy contacted Tara immediately and her story made Cindy even more nervous. Not long after that, they decided to travel together with Fallows.

Chapter Twenty-Five

Only in such dark hues could it happen, the place of the blood of rituals. To step into the Forest of Silence, what else could keep mute the omen of the gods? One white man, an elder who had seen the savage orgies of battle, and a girl of abomination. They were like birds in a cumulus cloud, no feather or beak to boast shelter.

So, that evening as night encroached, only the blood of the goat could supply nutrients for the forest's greed. The road was narrow and the journey deep. The quest of three people was a weak triangular affront to a million trees, leaves, snakes, pigs, monkeys, cheetahs all ferociously zoned in a divine halo.

The three of them stood before the priest, just barely a mile from the forest and at what was regarded as the most sacred portal to the forest. The priest was clad in a flame-red attire that exposed his back, his legs and part of his chest. He tied a band around his head with a feather stuck on the right side. The old man had a look that was at once serene and frazzled, the kind of concentration the villagers attributed to the presence of the ancestor. Tim thought he looked frightened. To Alero and the veteran, that was no surprise at all. The man was in a sort of trance.

The ritual did not take much time. The goat had been slaughtered and the blood extracted for the purpose. Tim was taken aback by the smell of the place. Obviously, that was the setting of several rituals in the past. He thought the air was heavy with putrescence and strange perfumes and an assortment of things that he could not fathom. The ritual ground had relics of parts of dead fowls and animals; a feather or a blood clot here; broken bottles there.

He thought sacrifices abhorred hygiene. Maybe you don't clean up for the gods. He made the observation later and the veteran was impressed by the comment. That was when he heard for the first time that the veteran was an atheist. After the blood bath was administered for each of the three of them from separate buckets and the head of the goat lay on the portal, they left with the rest of the animal. The goat's head would not be removed.

Nobody ate the goat's head. It would just disappear. The veteran explained to Tim that the gods were expected to eat the goat's head but not in the physical sense in which a human munches a piece of meat. That was not the veteran's belief, but the villagers'. The gods gorged on the spirits, so when the two of them went to the forest, the gods would recognise the spirits in the blood both of them carried on their bodies.

The ritual was done with only four of them present. Everyone else was forbidden to see the ceremony or even hear the incantations of the priest. Not all sacrifices required this rule, but the priest insisted that this sacrifice demanded it. It lasted about an hour.

The fog presided and provided enough pall to keep peering eyes at bay. Sometimes it thickened to such an extent that it seemed the heavens lowered their positions to hug the earth.

Tim had decided, at the last moment, that he would take part in the sacrifice but the veteran said he still had to do it as well for the goodwill. His goodwill would open their journey to the treasures, the veteran said. Both men had to pull off their clothes, save their shorts, so the man could sprinkle the blood on their bare bodies. Alero wore only a skirt and bra. It was called a blood bath, but it was no more than half a quart of blood that each of them had.

They were not supposed to have their baths until they returned. Tim complained about the blood, saying it made him feel miserable.

"This whole exercise had better be worth it," he said, as they sat on the sofa, once they returned home. "I'll kill myself if it turns into a fiasco."

"You won't have to," remarked the veteran.

Alero was a little irritable and so preferred to retreat into her shell. Later, when she got over it, she explained to Tim that she thought the priest was a lecherous old man.

"I'm sure he would have preferred me completely naked," she said.

"I noticed his hands lingered a little longer on you than on us," Tim replied, justifying her position.

The veteran did not follow them home. He just uttered a prayer for them, wishing them God's speed.

chapter Twenty-Six

With the prospect of the journey looming like a ghost in a nightmare, none of them expected to have much sleep.

But the anxiety was different for both personalities. Tim thought he had been pushed to this precipice by sheer male pride and a mysterious bond with a woman who continued to enchant him with the myths of Africa. He wondered whether he had control over himself any more.

His amnesia turned into another tangled chronicle of a continent he had to probe first by not knowing who he was. If only he could figure out what pranks fate had played with his soul, why he had travelled thousands of miles from America and ended up in the belly of forests and lost the only tool he needed to survive: his memory.

As if to emphasise his new state, he got caught in the drama of crocodiles and mermaids and murders, woven together by a woman he truly could not let go of. He wondered how things might have shaped up if he and Itse had been all right, if all of this could have happened. Maybe he would not have had trouble with the villagers and all things would have worked out well. He probably would not have needed Alero. At that prospect, his thoughts froze.

He could not push the sequence any further. So his thoughts had to find vigour elsewhere. He wondered again why his recollections made no progress, just the disjointed parts that deepened the puzzle. Even there, he met a wall and surrendered himself to wakeful misery, just like Alero in the next room.

The only thought that veered off the whirlwind in his mind was when he wondered if she was sleeping, or if he could tell her he wanted a lullaby. The thought of a lullaby soothed him further, making him feel like a little kid. He told himself that must be a good sign.

What he wanted to avoid all night was to focus on Alero's body, which he did not see completely. But he saw enough to stir demons. He had held her, savoured kisses, inhaled something of her innate sexual scent. But he had not prepared himself to see her skin and full outline of her body in its willowy glory concealed only by her brassiere and a short skirt. She had never looked at him. She had never looked at anyone. She was toned by the fog-draped, evening light, which made her look like a sort of sculpted halo. It was as though she was dreaming, he thought, a character in a dream and every part of her body, a part of the illusion.

Rather than focus on that thought, he rose from his bed and walked to the living room. Alero was there, defined by a faint light from an oil lamp.

"Why are you still up," he asked.

Alero was taken aback by the question and shifted on the sofa. She did not say anything until she reached for the oil lamp on a nearby stool with intent to turn up the light.

"No," he said. "That's enough light." Alero returned to her seat while the man stood looking at her, wondering what was going on in her mind. She finally broke the silence.

"I'm very happy. That's why I can't sleep," she said. She asked him to quit standing over her like some squad leader. So, he sat down on the sofa next to her.

"I wish I could be happy like you," he said, holding the woman. "The last time I went there I almost lost my life and my friend has been in a coma."

"Look at it this way," she said, "you did not lose your life but your past and you will get a new one from this trip."

"I'm not so sure. I am going there because of a past," he said, pulling her toward him and she yielded.

"So am I."

They were silent. Alero was distracted for a moment while the man held her close. It was clear that both of them had something today. The silence in that dye-cast night, sprinkled with chirps from trees outside, resounded between them.

"The oil in the lamp is running out," he remarked. "What oil runs the light between you and me?" she asked, breaking gently from his hold and looking at him, through the room's dying light, like one blindfolded.

"The oil that sticks two together as one," he said.

She was quiet and wanted the man to look straight into her eyes.

"But all oil can't last forever. The light will go out some day. Lights often go out in my life as I'm sure you can tell."

"We can always refuel," he said. "The oil of the soul is better than the soul of the oil. No one can separate us again, not now and not ever. This light is guaranteed to last a lifetime. Trust me."

"You left once and you might have been at home by now," she said.

"But here I am with you," he said. He paused after those words and broke with something he felt the woman should know.

"I don't care for taboos," he said earnestly. "Love has no eyes and ears. It sees within and listens to its own voices."

"Well, maybe because you are not like us and don't have to answer to anybody. I've heard and read of problems between blacks and whites in America."

He was quiet and puzzled, but couldn't understand why those words startled him. But he drew from strengths within.

"All I can say is that if you want to prove it, you have only to follow me there. You'll know whether or not I am a coward," he cleared his throat. "When all of this is over, you can come with me to the United States and you won't have eyes looking at you as though you are God's reject."

"Maybe they won't see me at all there. I read *The Invisible Man* by Ellison. That will be the exact opposite of people seeing too much of me," she intoned.

"I don't know that book," he admitted.

"Maybe you do or did. When you get back your memory, maybe it will come to you, too," she said.

"Maybe," he said.

"One thing I know is that you are as sincere as you can be. And you are no coward. If you were, you wouldn't have taken the journey to this place at all," she said, a little tired and she asked him to hold her.

"Maybe I was desperate," he replied.

This was a subject they had not fully addressed.

"Who was it you had, a wife, or a very close girl friend or something?" the question seemed to be plucked out of the darkness of the forest.

"She would have come here. She should have known about my whereabouts and come here looking for me. Or don't you think so?"

Alero nodded. But the affirmative gesture of head was to fend off further discussion. She also told herself the man could not be married. He wore no rings and there was no mark on his finger indicating he had ever worn one.

There was a brief silence, and then a timorous knock on the window.

It frightened Alero. But a feminine voice followed the knock. "It's me Tuoyo." Her voice trembled to their ears.

Another silence.

"Come in," said Tim. He walked to the door and opened it. The girl's nervous smile barely shone through the expiring lamplight. She fidgeted as she stepped across the threshold into the living room.

"Why are you here this late? Does your father know?" Alero inquired.

Tuoyo shook her head. Her fidgeting became more obvious.

"I learnt you are going to the bush tomorrow. I came to tell you to beware of the pigs. My parents said the pigs will kill you."

Tim smiled and placed his hands on her left shoulder, which was bare. She only had a cloth which was tied above her small breasts.

"Nothing will happen to us," Alero replied.

Tim reached for the lamp and placed it in front of his face.

"Can you see blood on my face? It's the same with Alero. It will scare the pigs or any bad animal for that matter. We will look too ugly and dangerous for them."

Emboldened by the warmth around her, she asked, "Do you believe that?"

"Our village believes it. So why won't it work?" said Alero. The little girl smiled, and there was silence.

Alero thought she would leave then.

"I learned that you used to wear beautiful clothes in the city. Is that true?" she asked Alero.

"Yes," answered Alero cheerfully.

"Why are you not wearing them anymore?" the girl asked.

"When I come back from the forest, I will wear them and you will see how beautiful they are," Alero promised.

"Are they in this house?" she asked as though she wanted to see them at that instant.

"No, but don't worry. The time will come for me to wear them and I will bring them from where they are."

Tuoyo held her two hands together in a gesture of happiness. Suddenly she reached for the door, and said "Goodbye. Don't stay long in the forest. Come back after one night."

"Okay," Tim said. The girl stepped out of the house and Tim and Alero saw the charming vision disappear with her quick feet into the fog-bound night.

"There is something about the girl's features that make me think of you. Her face especially."

"She likes me," Alero said, rather uneasily.

He held her close like one trying not to let something slip away.

They woke up in the morning cradled in each other's arms, heart to heart, blood to blood, head on shoulder.

chapter Twenty-Seven

Before they left that morning, Tim and Alero wanted to communicate something to Itse. He was getting better, they told themselves. The doctor was taciturn, and his body language did not reassure Alero. All that was left for Itse was to rebound, Alero told herself. He was still basically weak. His eyes looked but could not see. His breathing was increasingly laboured.

"Let's hope he'll be fine," the doctor said; that was all he would say. He was not going to give any time-line. Alero's eyes moistened. The two people who were headed to the woods could not say anything to the man, so they left the room with a prayer, asking God to keep him alive and speed up his recovery. Both of them asked their maker to bless their trip to history. The veteran would be the only person to monitor and care for the young man.

Alero and Tim were in the right gear for the adventure. They wore jeans and denim jackets over tennis shoes. They stuffed Tim's backpack with some foodstuff, mainly loaves of bread and sardines. They also armed themselves with a machete, two daggers tucked into a quiver-like bag and a gun Tim had brought from the United States. Alero had not known of the gun until she was helping Tim pack his things for the adventure. Tim had no memory of the weapon either.

The only other person in the house with them was the veteran, who was at once nervous for and proud of the young people. The doctor had left. But the veteran's mien was subdued and he could scarcely look them in the eye. He wanted to pray for them.

"Both of you should come and kneel," he said. They understood what he wanted to do and obliged. He placed his only hand on each of their heads in turn and unloaded.

"O God, we know that we need you at this moment more than we ever did in this village. These two people are about to embark on a dangerous mission. They want to unveil the lie of years and plunder the hypocrisy of the mighty. No weapons shall pierce their bones and flesh but the courage of belief and the uncertain shaft of hope. This young man has lost the glue to his past and this society has vowed to abandon this young woman to a sterile past. In the sanctuary of this forest lies redemption. In that redemption also lurks tragedy. O God, we pray you turn this omen into vindication. Vindication will bring healing and a new day."

They all said amen, and the old man burst into tears as his wiry body vibrated as if bowled over by some electric shock. It infected Alero whose face glistened as she tried to console the man with the assurance that they were determined and all would be well.

"Don't worry, that sort of thing. I'll be all right. My spirit will be with you. Get ready."

He stood on his feet and, without looking at them, the veteran walked out of the house. Tim would remark later in the forest that this was the closest hint he had of this man's military pedigree. Between the veteran's tears and his decision to leave, Tim said he saw both warmth and warrior.

Once the man left, Tim and Alero suddenly realised that they were alone. The mission dawned as if thunder suddenly clapped at them from under their feet. A cruel epiphany.

"It's time," Tim said looking Alero in the eye with a cross between defiance and surrender.

"When you plan for things like this," she said, "something inside you denies it will ever happen until it does. And suddenly you seem unprepared."

They hugged each other and Tim slung the backpack over his shoulder to its proper position and walked out of the house.

Tim knew the marker of his own destination was surer than his partner's. He had been told that his ancestor was buried in a clearing bordered by ten coconut trees. It was a clearing up. Who knows what the place had become. He should not expect an epitaph or any form of grand grave in a modern sense.

The whole village seemed waiting to see them go. Many people were outside, as if their journey was the first rite of a grander ceremony scheduled to follow later in the day. They looked at them as though they were two compulsive suicides who already knew their lives were over and only wanted to make a great drama of the parting. Suicides anointed by community, they thought. They also pitied the white man for not having the good sense and spiritual antidote to this wicked crocodile-in-human-form who would turn the man's life into the sewer that was her life.

They knew all the stories about the Forest of Silence. They knew of the fertility goddess who danced every night, with innumerable virgins. She was responsible for any child born in Orogun. No one saw her and lived. She was beautiful and looked like a nubile teen until you moved closer. If you looked her in the eye, you were gone. All the virgins would pounce on you. Seeing her was like deflowering the great goddess. No one deflowered the fertility goddess and lived. No one, however, had claimed to see her. You had to see her virgins first. She was the most vicious wraith of the Forest of

Silence. And if you were a male and saw a virgin, the first virgin you set your eyes on would lose her virgin status and would be killed by the other virgins. But that would be after they had slaughtered the intruding eye.

Other than the fertility goddess, there were gnomes who clung to tree boughs. They were all over the place. They were the custodians of the fruits and legumes and seeds. They preserved the arboreal integrity of the forest. Only the natural inhabitants of the forest had a right to the wild fruits and leaves and flowers. Humans were forbidden. Snakes were the spies of the forest. They usually were the first to know of an intruder, and felt instantly the vibration of a foreign foot. At night, the owls were the witches from Orogun village and flew about with bats to keep watch at night. The wild pigs were the soldiers, the enforcers of forest purity. With the purification bath, they were supposed to be immune to the attack of pigs. The fertility goddess would see them. So would all the other beings of the spirit world. But Tim and Alero would be blind to them.

The first time Tim heard this story, he was impressed.

"I think we need this kind of forest all over the world," he told Itse before their first trip to the place.

"Why?" Itse asked.

"That would preserve all the forests and bushes in the world," Tim said.

For their part, Tim and Alero were hardly surprised that the crowd was waiting outside. It rankled them all the same that the world would postpone all their morning activities just to see them leave. They walked fast; focused on the task ahead, trembling inside but making a show of a brave front.

As they approached the portal to the Forest of Silence, Tim took out the map drawn out by the veteran. This was different from the one given by the elders. As they entered the forest, they were overcome by a serene glow. This was helped by the absence of the fog that befuddled the village. Both seemed to have lost their worries all of a sudden, but would be perturbed by that lack of fear later on.

The path looked straightforward as they followed the map. Alero saw a small dove after they covered about a quarter of a mile. She asked him to stop and tried to befriend the bird. Tim obliged.

"But how can you reach it? It will be frightened."

Alero asked Tim to cut out a little chunk of bread, which he did. She broke the chunk into little crumbs and lined them on the trail to entice the creature. The bird responded and pecked at the crumbs until it reached where they were and Alero picked up the vision. She lifted it to her face and a tear streaked down her left cheek.

"This is memory right here," she said as she gave the remainder of the bread to the dove. She recalled a bird that she owned as a pet when she was little, not long before her mother disappeared. It was her only friend. It was always there as a shield from the buffeting of life. One day, she returned from school and did not see it. She searched all over the place for days on end until she concluded that the village had spoiled another joy that she thought was untouchable.

"About a week later," she said, "when my mother was sick and could not provide for me, I got home and discovered that she had cooked a meal with the bird. She told me the bird returned and it was better we ate it before it disappeared again and this gave me another heartache. I did not understand why she should have done that. I did not eat the meal but preferred to starve all day. My mother was mad at me. I was mad at her, although I didn't show it aggressively. But I was sullen, unable to comprehend how the wing of the darling creature could wallow in my stew."

She looked at the bird with moist eyes and said, "This is a good sign. My mother must be here." She let the bird go into the forest air.

The first thing Alero noticed in the forest was that it smelled of tangerine, but she could not understand why. Was tangerine the abomination smell? Or was the smell in her mind? She saw no tangerine tree at first. What appeared before them were the guava tree, the *iroko* tree, the mango tree, the palm tree, a concourse of the arboreal elite. Each tree abided in its own light, it seemed to these visitors. Fruits hung lush on the sometimes-nodding boughs, as though they exploded into being, showcases for the gods who never ate them, except the birds and animals. Its plenty was sure to shame any gluttony. The fruits also frightened her with their virginal fullness.

But all that denial evaporated in a second when they saw a python coiled on a bough. It was large and long. If it stood on its tail, would be taller than a guava tree. It seemed to them that the beast saw them but lay there a mute and sullen omen, large with spots.

"It just swallowed something," remarked Tim. He was right. The snake was still in the process of digesting what it just conquered. It bulged in the middle. Both of them walked away and did not say anything for about an hour. Even when they said things, the words came out in spurts beneath the Babel of the forest.

The chill in Alero reflected a wistful moment. Was this beast the python the villagers narrated in their stories?

Not long after, they saw what looked like a red tree bough broken from one of the trees. It dazzled Alero.

"What's that?" she asked, slowing her pace, and instinctively holding Tim's right hand. But Tim saw it clearly.

Once he recognised it was blood-strewn, he saw something else. At the foot of an *iroko* tree was the head of an animal, two slices of uncooked yam, a red piece of cloth and several cowries.

"What's that?" he asked. He knew it was a shrine. They moved to the bloodied wood first, and as Tim tried to pick it up, Alero urged caution.

"Don't touch it," she said.

"Why? Tim was astonished. He saw it as a piece of curiosity. Who could have brought this here? Who defied the holy orders of this hallowed place, he wondered.

Alero had no answer to his question. She just felt it was out of place. But in her inaudible hysteria was a feverish awareness of all the stories about the place, the fiery presences of gods and demons, the possibility of a sudden nightmare of gnomes and witches in that walk of indeterminate dips and turns. Which of the animal clamours were animal? Which of them mocked terrestrial throats?

"Do you want to pick it up yourself?" he asked Alero.

She shuddered.

"Let's examine it without touching it," she suggested.

That option seemed all right to Tim, a compromise. So, he picked up a twig, and both of them walked gingerly to the broken bough. The air was still around them. But a hollow sound, like muffled thunder, wrapped up the forest. The sound served as backdrop for the incessant choir of birds and distant hoots and occasional growls from four-legged creatures. Even the sounds seemed abstract for the moment. The bough gave off a fresh odour. The wood glistened unevenly. Wet clay and sand and dust smudged parts of the blood curtain to dullness, like the signature of an intuitive artist.

"This thing happened not long ago," remarked Tim.

Alero said nothing. With the twig as leverage, Tim rolled the bough on the forest ground. They confirmed some person or persons had come to the forest not longer than two days earlier. Tim insisted it must have been earlier.

They did not want to speculate why, or who would do that, or whether it had any bearing on their own adventure in that sacred place.

They moved near the shrine, and saw that it was not the head of a goat. It looked like an antelope. The rest of the animal was not around. Parts of the slices of yam had been eaten into by some animals, maybe squirrels or rabbits.

They decided to move on after what felt like half an hour. They tried to follow the map as the veteran instructed. They passed trees, crawling beasts, flying beasts. Part of the tension arose as they delved deep into the forest and saw monkeys leap from tree to tree and heard squeaks, squawks, squeals, bellows and sighs. An assortment of birds flapped and flitted about in quarrels and play, cavorting in their roles as choristers whose mellifluous and raucous songs met the more martial tone of the primates.

"I hope they just ignore us," said Alero, breaking a long and frightened silence. The man responded by rubbing her back.

They tripped over jutting weeds, evaded rock outcroppings, scaled buttes, and waddled through muds. Now, it was dark; now, it was bright. As always, they felt besieged; the wild was upon them in its riotous omen and vitality.

Hours tiptoed into dusk and suddenly they realised that something was wrong. They did not seem to have made any progress yet. They rested beside a pawpaw tree and tried to evaluate their journey.

"We are about four trails to the left of where we should be," said Alero, pointing to a hillock about half a mile back as a marker of where they should have turned right. Tim agreed and they turned back. But it looked darker. Tim sighted a four-legged beast cross a trail in front of them, and asked Alero to stop. They didn't see it properly, but its shadow streaked fast before their eyes.

"It saw us. It's an antelope," she said, explaining to Tim that she knew from the general outline of the animal and the way it moved. Tim brought out his flashlight and flipped it on. Its light stabbed through the heart of the forest and set off a cacophony from the beasts. The two eventually located a hillock and moved right. The trail they now walked was smothered in leaves and flowers. They preferred it for its texture, which eased their tired feet. Tim observed that Alero was getting exhausted. They had been in the forest all day, and they had not come near what they were looking for.

"They expect us back tonight," intoned Tim. "Do you think they will come looking for us?"

"It will depend on the chief priest. If he tells them that we are in danger or need to be rescued, he'll ask them to come," she said, contemplating. "But you can never predict what's going on in their narrow circle and what they are thinking. They are such wicked people."

"Not to worry," glowed Tim. "We are going to fix them."

"Amen," she said.

Tim's torch swept the forest as his eyes tried to pick up as much detail as he could. Most of the forest heaved as if breathing. Most of the beasts were quiet; it seemed a good number of them were asleep, and this highlighted the few sounds that defined each moment that night.

"What's that?" asked Alero, pointing to a glade. The clearing also was covered in many layers of leaves. "Can't we rest there for a while?" she asked, in a tone of surrender. Tim obliged.

The glade was a few yards away, and it looked like a bower of comfort after a long day. Tim eased himself of the weight of the backpack as Alero sank into the carpet of leaves.

"This is as cosy a bed as you can get out here," she said, a little spark in her tired voice. She lay on her back and her eyes looked straight into the sky, at all the verse of the stars and the big eye of the moon. Tim also lay down, but squeaked as his back reached down.

"What's that," she asked, as Tim reached for the thing that pierced his back. It was a little rock. He vaguely saw it and felt his fingers around its sharp edge. It did not cut his skin, but the pain lingered, he said. He handed Alero the flashlight, so she could see the extent of the harm. He pulled his shirt up, and stood on his feet.

"It's a little swollen," she said, "but I think it will be fine." She offered to massage it a little as they stood.

"That felt good," he said, once she was done.

Both of them did not find much to say as they lay down. The flashlight was off and the forest maintained a constant whir that lulled them to sleep. But before they lapsed, they agreed that Tim should hold his machete and Alero the gun. They probably would not sleep at all. Neither wanted to sleep.

They felt their souls merging with the entrails of the forest. The chorus of birds, the quiver of the leaves, the hiss of the boughs, the subdued clamour of animals, the tinted shimmer of the moon, the lullaby of the breeze. This romance of the wild seemed to lift them out of the glade, leaves and all, into a feast of dreams as they lay, body and heart calling to the other, skin yielding to skin, and after what seemed like an eternity of waiting, they quelled the anxiety of all flesh.

He looked up into the skies. The stars seemed to bustle in the night.

"This night must be the most important in all my life," he said.

"You can't tell," she said. "How many nights of your life can you remember?"

"The point exactly. All those nights I can't recall do not matter because they don't weigh on my mind." He looked at her and said, "This night we just became one indeed."

They were close again the second time, and woke up in the morning having hardly slept.

Their first discovery was that they had lost the map. Second, it was clear they had missed their way, and had followed the wrong trail to the glade. Alero said that misstep was the sum of her fears.

"We can go back, and retrace our movement. I have a fair idea of the route."

They concluded that they missed their way after the shrine.

"If they hear the story back in the village, they would say the shrine worked," said Alero.

"Was that why they set it up?"

"I don't know. Just a guess. I suppose somebody or a group of people did not set up the shrine for fun. The animal was hunted in this place and used for sacrifice," she said. She also noted that the map disappeared.

"Well, that probably was the wind. If we search hard enough we will find it. But that could complicate our journey," he said.

"Yes," agreed Alero. "We may not be able to locate where we are from the spot the map may be hiding…"

It took about two hours for them to locate the shrine, and one of the yam slices had disappeared. The cowries were scattered.

"The shrine is coming undone," Tim said.

They decided to trek according to their mental recall of the map. In about twenty-five minutes, they walked into a pond.

"There was no pond in the map," Alero observed.

"Hmm, we are on our own," Tim said.

They smiled.

"I am hungry," Alero said. They decided to have breakfast. The bread had begun to harden. But they enjoyed the meal. It had all the feeling of furtive fun to them.

When they were done, Tim stared at the water.

"This is a great pond," he said.

They could see through its limpid surface, frolics of fishes enticing them.

Tim stood up, pulled up his shirt and took down his trousers and leapt into the water. The splash contradicted what sounded like a quiet threnody about the place. It frightened Alero. The forest responded with hoots from the lower tiers and twitters of birds from the tree branches and tops. But Tim did not seem to care. He tumbled with abandon. He was in his element. This was his fish moment. He defied the forest mainstays not with his muscular prowess alone but also by his antics in the pond whose water, tranquil forever, flew off his back and head. It sometimes bobbed in imperfect exclamation marks. At other times, the water arched like a tremulous drawing in the air. Alero wondered if Tim had come to liberate the pond, bond with it or violate it. If people went there in hypocritical flouting of its sacred law, not many would contemplate swimming there like he was doing.

His head popped above the water, his two hands went high into the forest air and he pleaded: "Come and join me. It's a wonderful feeling."

Alero resisted at first. But the young man tossed himself about like he belonged in the water.

Alero joined him, without taking off any of her clothes.

Itse died while they were in the water. The veteran had come to see him, in what he thought was a routine visit. Tears coursed down his cheeks with abandon. He walked out of the house with his drenched face. It did not take any questioning to know what had happened. The villagers knew that their son had passed on.

He asked one of the young boys around to call the doctor for his final verdict. When the doctor came, he asked them to make burial arrangements. He had known that this was going to happen. The veteran knew. Tim knew. So did Alero. No one wanted to accept the moment was coming. Itse had been too alive for them to accept the possibility.

"This is what the white man has brought on us," remarked Chief Tietie, after they had interred the young man.

They needed the bath in the pond, the ecstasy of wild water and play of limbs. The rest of the journey was not going to offer them any rest. The trails stunned them with the motif of death and corpses.

The first were skeletons that lay beside a mango tree. They were stark and blanched.

The sight gave Alero a fever. She did not want to look at them and yet she would not walk away. How was she going to handle her mother's if the remains of the anonymous dead petrified her so completely?

What bothered Tim was different. What could have made the villagers drop the body of a fellow villager? No dignity of burial. Could there have been a funeral? What sort, Tim asked. Alero explained that the person might have committed some sort of taboo, such as incest.

"Did they kill the person?" Tim pursued his curiosity.

"No but when they die, no one allows them to be buried in the town like others."

That answer sent a train of thoughts through the mind of the young man. But he would not say anything. Alero understood. "You're thinking if I die, I would end up here. My mother would have ended up here anyway, right? Well, often such people leave the village to a different place before they die. Their relatives take care of their remains and bury them with the dignity they deserve. I am never going to die here. If Marmalade was not cut short, I would not have allowed her to grow old here."

"So," observed Tim, "those here died either prematurely or without the support of relatives."

"Exactly."

His mind went to the woman they called the white witch. She probably would end up there.

"I am not sure of that," she explained. "People like that have quiet supporters, known only to them. Don't be surprised that if she falls terminally ill somebody would arrange to take her out of town."

"What if she dies suddenly?" Tim inquired.

"Well, if she dies now, we will have to hope that the wrong people don't know first. If the right people know first they will secretly bury her in town, or whisk her out to somewhere else she might have arranged with them."

Tim looked at the bones closely, they were scattered within a narrow radius, and he played in his mind how he could rearrange them like a jigsaw puzzle. The clavicles, the feet, the thighbones and so on. Then he remembered that this had once been a real person.

"That means they allow animals, possibly vultures to pick the person clean?"

Alero did not say a word. They eventually left. By nightfall, their bread had turned dry and crusty and too hard to eat. The real challenge was that they had lost their way in the jungle.

They were now living at the mercy of the wild. They could not return yet and, even if they did, they had to accept the mockery of a wasted effort. They had to trudge along, to comb about for a place they could see a skeleton with the feet of her mother, feet with six toes.

Meanwhile, the veteran had begun to worry. The young people were supposed to have returned. Locating the bones and the grave of the young man's ancestor should not be that difficult. It should be done in less than five hours. The veteran promptly gathered some young men and asked them to accompany him to the forest. They were asked to go through the pre-visit ritual just like Tim and Alero. But the priest procrastinated. The veteran was livid. He went to the king, and demanded that they be allowed to go and that meant a prompt response from the priest.

"I am the king, not the priest," the king asserted with a little impatience. The veteran's eyeballs rolled in their sockets. But he kept mum.

Later the veteran learnt that the delay was a ploy to frustrate their mission. The veteran was not going to let the elders harrumph in secret. He was going to get things done his own way. He called some of the young men to his home and asked them to follow him to the village without the normal rites.

"It's all nonsense anyway," he said defiantly. The young men did not object. The veteran was not the sort of man they could disobey. The veteran knew that. So, when he finished, he told them that those who wanted to go with him had to follow him immediately that afternoon to the Forest of Silence. Most of them obliged. Itie and Omoni said they could not stake their lives among gnomes and witches. They begged to be excused. A few walked with confident strides with the veteran. But most of the boys dreaded the forest. The mission was a leap of faith for a few others. A good number of them could not face the taunt of cowardice from the rest.

As they followed the man into the forbidden place, Chief Boyo materialised. He was the person who knew about the story of Alero's mother from the beginning. He was a quiet objector. But he would not be the monkey among hens, so he played along. This was his chance to show chivalry to Alero, the woman he had stalked in the forest, the woman who did not trust the libido of his aged body. So, he met with the veteran and told him the whole story. It was their secret. He took the veteran to the forest secretly, and showed him the spot where Alero's mother's bones were laid. He also took him to the place where Tim's ancestor was buried. Palm trees formed a circle around the grave. It was unmistakable, on the outskirts of the forest. The chief and the veteran had wanted Tim and Itse to fulfil all righteousness by identifying the bones themselves.

That night neither Tim nor Alero slept. The sighting of a wild pig conquered sleep. Tim was now very hungry. They had to live on fruits. With the gun in one hand and torch in the other, he looked around for fruits or something edible. Alero had secured a long stick Tim would apply to pluck down fruits or any other edible thing from the trees. As for Alero, she would make do with the last tin of sardines. She did not want to touch the fruits. She did not want to eat anything. She was relieved that the swim in the pond ended without incident.

Tim asked her to walk with him as they scoured for dinner. The torchlight woke up the forest, and they heard movements, some of them quick and nervous, others sounded like sly slithering. They saw plantains on trees. But they were too high. Alero said, they were not ripe, and it made no sense to try. Tim was not familiar with them and he was not going to pluck them down. Why were there so few edibles where they were now? When they had not been hungry, many low-hanging edibles had teased them.

"What is that?" he asked, pointing the torch.

"That's pawpaw," replied Alero. "It may not be ripe."

Tim took the stick from Alero and handed the torch and gun to her. He stood on high ground so that he could push the pawpaw against the branch. The first time he missed and he kept missing it; only nudging it weakly a few times. He was getting frustrated when the thing fell down.

"How did that happen?" he asked.

Alero suggested it might have been a target of some of the primates that jumped around. They might have weakened the tree's hold on it.

It was only half ripe. He took out a knife and cut it open. It crunched in his mouth. He ate half of it. All this while, Alero was quietly anxious about the animal that made a cameo appearance to them.

chapter Twenty-Eight

The two lay wounded when the young men reached there. They had been attacked and wounded, but they had enough consciousness to know where they were and what had just happened to them.

Tim was more conscious than Alero and he tried to latch on to his woman in the place of peril and sanctuary of their vows. The veteran was the only person over thirty years old in the team.

Alero held on to her mother's scattered bones. They had dug them up when they were attacked by three wild pigs. The beasts knocked them down and roughed up the woman more than the man. The machete was alienated from them during the foray as they lay on the ground. Tim mustered the presence of mind to lift up his hand to reach his gun. He could not draw it out of the pocket, so he shot one of his assailants through his pocket. The bullet cruised right into its neck. The sound frightened the other two and they scampered away into the forest.

It all began about three miles away from where they had made love and where, as two forest strangers, they had basked in the afterglow as they searched for what they knew as the emblems of their lives.

"Look," Alero had said, as she pointed at what looked like a skeleton of a toe peeping out of the ground. All around the jutting bone were clay and tufts of grass and an army of ants making their way through a nearby guava tree in an interminable line.

Tim and Alero stood, as if held in a trance. But just as they saw the mysterious skeleton, a light stabbed Tim in the eye as he tried to avert his face.

"It must be the route to the village of Ovwor," exclaimed Alero, who was under a shade and saw through the narrow path of trees from where the light came.

"What should we do now?" asked Tim, who was now nervous; his mind calculating a thousand thoughts and possibilities and scenarios at a time.

"I think we should cool down and not be excited," he said in answer to his own question, his voice as nervous as his two trembling hands. "I'm sure this is what you're looking for, thank God. Let's dig it up." He bent down and crept quietly to the bone and touched it like one venturing into a hallowed place. Alero did not move. She, too, was nervous. She said nothing and just watched her friend touch what she was sure was the substance of her life.

"You know what?" he said, as Alero hung on every word that dropped from his lips. "This is it. Your mother. We shall begin here."

Alero nodded, nervously. He tried to dig in when Alero said, "Why don't we find out where the sun is shining from and see if we can find the tomb. It seems Ovwor is just a few yards away."

Alero, who was frozen in space and time, could not comprehend what she had just seen. She was anxious to see the bones but she felt she had to deny that it was really happening. The mystery of all her life could not come to an end that easily.

Tim agreed and they walked quickly through the path of trees and alighted in Ovwor. But as they walked away, she kept looking at it as if asking the bones to remain there awaiting their return. Tim's heart palpitated and he was not sure whether it was for happiness or fear of a wasted journey. But both of them wondered if this was not just a dream. She had found her mother and he his ancestor? What if it all ended in a fiasco and the thing he wanted was not there. Was he also curious? What could it be? Could it all be a lie, a wasted journey for the American?

They also thought about her mother and what impact that would have on the village and Alero's life and all those newspaper reports and all the tar brush. What kind of life would be open to her? Where would they live? Would they go to the United States, or would her life be revived there at home. Both of them would make a decision. But how could she really tolerate the hypocrisies of all those who tormented her and live among them? Why not go with Tim to the United States instead? But that would mean starting life anew. Any life here or in America would mean to begin anew. One in a new culture, the other like a new culture.

They didn't think aloud but their thoughts were the same. Tim concluded that they would sort this problem out in due course. That was exactly what was going through the mind of the young woman beside him, as they walked through the relics of history. But both kept looking into each the other's eyes that communicated what they were thinking but were too nervous to say anything.

"This village must have been abandoned hundreds of years ago," wondered Tim, who saw that Alero was a little scared.

They moved past huts, some of them standing with pride but buried in weeds. Most of them showed evidence of a conqueror's blisters. Where the roofs had not disappeared, where the walls were not broken, the remains were usually cracked in shapes like an innumerable series of web-feet designs on the walls; also indicating the depredations of time.

Most of the open ground showed signs of crawling things and that was what scared the young woman. But they saw no animals as yet, except lizards, rats and squirrels making the only sounds; apart from the essential hollowness of the place.

As they moved toward the interior they heard the waves of the ocean and isolated shrieks of birds. The place smelled like a rotten tree, Alero observed. Once they reached what might have been the centre of the defunct village, they felt lost, until Tim saw what both of them recognised as the main building of the place, the palace. It was just five minutes away but, just before they reached it, an elevated butte emerged before their sights and Tim saw a tomb, surrounded by wild palm trees. In a flash, tears rolled down Tim's eyes. The tomb was made of clay.

"My God!" he cried as he read the word Forester on it. "My God!" he repeated, his face, that was pink with anxiety, was now awash with glee. Rather than walk up to the tomb, he embraced Alero, who was quaking with excitement.

"This whole trip is not in vain," declared Alero, also teary-eyed.

He preceded Alero up in between two palm trees to the butte where the tomb sat. Age had diminished the grandeur of his ancestor's resting place. It was all built with mud of the enduring kind. From the tomb, they could see all the ends of the village. The words on the tombstone were carved with an eye to eternity. They said nothing for a while, Alero watching whether her friend would say anything about regaining his memory.

"Itse is really a special guy," he said, his tears not relenting. "I know how I got here. I am healing gradually."

"You remember everything?" asked Alero, her voice in a fever.

"Enough for now. I remember enough for now," he said. Then he looked Alero in the face, and said, "This is a miracle. I can't believe what I have done." He held the young woman around the shoulder and lifted her high with great gusto. "This is a miracle. Is this me?" he exhaled and said, "God sent me here for a reason and not just because of this tomb. He brought me here to set me free."

"I don't understand," remarked Alero.

"I will tell you the full story," he said. "But we must dig up your mother first. Without that, all of this is meaningless."

They moved fast to the place of the jutting toes, and once there both of them were agitated. What if no one accepted the remains as her mother's? What would become of this whole expedition? The people had never believed anything she did or said.

The thought paralysed her as they made to dig up the skeleton.

"What's the matter," asked Tim.

She said nothing.

It was not yet full day in the forest as it was outside. The fat bark and dense foliage still conspired against the encroaching sun, except for a few furtive discharges of light into the Forest of Silence just like the one that had lured the couple to the defunct village.

In a whiplash of energy, Alero shook off her distraction and took the machete and started digging. Her heart beat in time with the animal chants and wails in the forest. As they made progress, the darkness of the forest faded, opening their eyes to the bones. On occasion, Tim would pat the young woman on the back as if to say, "It will be over soon."

"These people did not even dig this deep enough, how clever," remarked Tim.

"Well," said Alero, breaking her silence. "They didn't expect anyone to come into the Forest of Silence."

Both of the seemed really excited suddenly and also a little tired.

Alero felt an odd feeling of intimacy with the bones, as they uncovered them. She touched them fervently. Was this the root bone of my bones, the toes I saw every morning? The same that walked to the stream that morning? Was this the bone that held the flesh that most people knew as beautiful and yet condemned as abominable, as crocodile? It rattled once and again, and she said to herself, this bone did not rattle when I last saw it and I didn't see it. I didn't know it. What sounded was human voice, the sweet, comforting, affectionate tone of a mother. The sound that wailed and laughed, begged and sobbed, commanded and sighed, and careened away in madness. It was not it; it was she, a woman. The bones walked and swung and kicked and had blood and marrow surging. The bones were not apart; they were held by muscles and coordinated her. These same bones cannot say a word, cannot bite or protest or sigh or get her food or boast about how beautiful her daughter was, or bemoan the treachery and insidiousness of the world. She could not hear the confidence of her daughter, or triumphs of the day. She could not go mad.

Suddenly, she blurted out, "Marmalade, O Marmalade! Talk to me." She broke into sobs and that was when the three pigs attacked. The wild beasts attacked from different directions. They kicked up clouds of wild dust and made ferocious noises, setting the whole world in chaos. The other beasts joined the discordant chorus either out of fear or bonding, or both. The victims, caught by surprise almost were helpless but their instinctive cry set back the animals for a moment, enough time for Alero to scramble for the machete and Tim to slide his hand into his pocket for the gun.

They had prepared for the attack but lost a sense of the moment when it happened. Tim held the pistol at the ready for a while. But he wanted to help Alero gather the bones together. He too was too excited to repossess himself. For leverage, he needed to use both hands and he temporarily put his gun in the pocket. Shortly he would retrieve it from his pocket. But when the beasts came for plunder, he did not recover his presence of mind in time. Alero had had the machete, but it was a little too far from her when she needed it.

Neither Alero nor Tim was sure they would survive, but they fought the beasts through their fears and with the sense that their lives depended on the little weapons they held. Fear coursed through their veins, energising them until Tim pulled the trigger.

His head was draped with caked blood and he could hardly see when the veteran and his team arrived. He had little energy left and so looked at the rescue team with something akin to surrender. Alero's skin had suffered several lacerations and deep wounds, especially on her torso and forehead. She, too, was covered in congealed blood. The bloated remains of the dead, wild pig lay beside the spot where the bones were buried.

The veteran was happy with what he saw. The first thing he noticed was the sixth toe. Alero's mother was supposed to be the only person with six toes on both feet.

"Who can doubt this?" he almost hollered.

Chief Boyo smiled. "That was the reason you had to have me here. Do you remember Edomi whose wife had leprosy?" he asked.

Edomi was a very sprightly and conscientious farmer whose wife, Temi, had leprosy. He married her from another village. No one except her husband knew of her sixth toe. Unlike Alero's mother, Edomi's wife had a sixth toe only on one foot, her right foot. She developed leprosy not quite two years after their wedding, and Edomi hid his wife at home all day.

"When she died, he was forced to bring her here," he narrated.

"But unlike others, he sneaked back to give her a proper burial in this place. On his way, an animal struck him. Nobody knows what animal, and he died quietly in his home."

What both elderly men wanted to tell the stricken couple, who had just been lifted off the forest ground, was that the bones they first saw did not belong to Alero's mother. Hers were somewhere else.

In her febrile and debilitated state, Alero wanted to disbelieve them. In a short time, she had bonded with the bones. She had invested too much in these bones to want others, if she could help it. Her miracle was being taken from her.

Tim and Alero recognised Chief Boyo, and they could still see in his eyes, in the sobriety of the hour, an old man's lecherous light. But he was business-like nonetheless, full of the benevolent spirit of a rescuer.

The young men who had come there to fulfil the mission of the elders suddenly realised that the world was wearing a new hat.

The veteran noticed a trail leading out of the forest to an open area outside. It was Tim who had crawled out of the forest and back in. They had been there before they found the couple. The veteran and Chief Boyo had searched the area and it was also an education for the young men who followed them. The boys followed them on the trails to the open area.

It was not a glade. It was a big open country, abandoned over a century ago. They saw scores of huts overgrown with weeds and trees, and play grounds and what might have been a market place. It was desolate and prostrate.

"What is this place?" asked a young man.

The veteran answered, "This is Ovwor. This village was a bastion of slave wars in those days. The white man came here to buy and raid for slaves and our people sold them out to the white men. Orogun delighted in, and profited from, this business long ago, but this village had a king who wanted to stop the trafficking. But Orogun lived and died by the business. This created a war between the two villages. Orogun had more weapons and was helped by arms supplied by the white man to defeat Ovwor. The village was routed and all the inhabitants scattered everywhere. Not only that, the king was killed and the royal family captured."

They tried to trace Tim's trail, so they walked through the abandoned relic of history and, suddenly, they saw a crocodile glide gently into the Atlantic Ocean and the water splashed in its wake. They continued on the zigzag pattern of Tim's movement in the abandoned place until they finally turned a corner and saw the end of the white man's trail. The trail also was smeared with blood. It stopped at a tomb, which had suffered much ruin but was clearly special when it was built. The quaint grandeur was not lost on the veteran.

It read, "Lord Forester, special emissary of the King of England."

Tim's father often boasted that the family history was rooted in English royalty. The circumstances in which the family had moved to the United States were still foggy. Some records hinted at a rift between the Foresters and other members of the nobility around the period when the Church of England prised loose of the Catholic Church.

"Who is this?" asked one of the boys.

The veteran provided the answer again, "This is the person the young *oyibo* came all the way here to find. He was a very special man in the history of this place. He was a missionary, just before the slave trade came here and he persuaded our people to abolish the killing of twins. The issue of twins was a special taboo in those days. Twins were an abomination.

"He died here of malaria which, at that time, had no cure. It killed a lot of white men then. This place was called the white man's grave. But he did not just die. He had a child by one of the king's daughters. Alero descends from that line. This grave was built by him. He also wrote the epitaph and it was carved in clay as though he knew this day would come. In those days, people merely dug graves with no special epitaphs."

Tim said that both he and Alero had been to the tomb.

"The story of the sixth toe always shows a cardinal thing about our village: things are not always what they seem," the veteran observed.

They took the wounded people back to the village for medical help. But, before then, they had to see the bones of Alero's mother.

Chief Boyo had suggested that they did not touch the bones, so the daughter could see them in their state of chaotic innocence in the forest. When they got there, the bones were half buried. A grave had been dug, but it was not deep, probably two and half feet. It was probably done that way so the village aristocracy could keep track of it, explained Chief Boyo.

Alero was carried by two young men, one of them held her by the torso and the other by the legs. At the spot of the bones, Alero's eyes melted. In her sick state, she was desolated. She said nothing, could say nothing.

The young men scooped Alero's mother's scattered bones into a special bag brought by the veteran, and he insisted on carrying it himself. The others carried the couple back to the village.

chapter Twenty-Nine

Nothing within the powers of the Orogun villagers prepared them for the set of visitors they received that afternoon. The young men brought the couple and Alero's mother's remains just as Tim's aunt Tara, Cindy and author Jim Fallows arrived the village. It was as if both ears were simultaneously jammed with bad news. The heart of the village was cut right down the middle.

Tara, Cindy and Jim went to the king's palace directly, knowing no one to communicate with. They were driven there in a chartered van and, once they reached the palace and alighted from the vehicle, the villagers knew that the white man's people had worried enough about their son to pay a visit. It sent some jitters around the ordinary people. Was this the prelude to the invasion? They saw worry in the faces of Tara and Cindy. These must be the young man's parents and sister or wife, they concluded. Some of the villagers opined that the parents were probably the understanding types. That's why they decided to come first, rather than send a military force here. Maybe it was no act of charity. They probably brought their birds of prey but they could not penetrate the fog, a few others thought.

The king was notified of their arrival, and sat on his throne as the white people stepped into his royal chamber. All the Chiefs who had been hanging around in anticipation of the news from the Forest of Silence were on hand to welcome the unlikely visitors.

The visitors declined an offer of water to drink. There was a huge silence in the chamber, as the elders hung on the lips of the white visitors.

"We are here to find my nephew, Tim. He left the United States months ago. He's supposed to have long returned."

Cindy then adjusted nervously and said: "I came here to see my Itse."

The Chiefs were impressed with her pronunciation of the name of their favourite son. They were instantly curious.

"What kind friend was Itse to you?" Chief Tietie asked, he was again acting as interpreter.

She observed the past tense but, of course the whole syntax was jumbled, so she assumed a flaw of expression rather than indicating some real fact.

"He is my partner. We plan to get married."

Every chief understood what she said. But they said nothing. The visitors were not comfortable with the body language of the Chiefs, especially Chief Tietie, whose face softened from that of a hostile inquisitor.

The king cleared his throat and said, "It's so kind of you to come find your nephew and friend. When I saw you I thought you were his mother and his father."

He paused as Jim said he was not Tim's father nor was he a relative. Some of the elders concluded, without inquiring, that he must be an emissary of the United States government. "Well," the king said. "Tim is in the forest with a young lady from this village. Both of them wanted to go there to search for Tim's ancestor and we granted their wish. They've been there for more than two days. We, too, have been worried and asked our young men to find out why they have not returned. We hope they will be here soon. The team left early this morning."

Cindy was impatient.

"Where is Itse?"

It was then the king knew what was at stake. He regained his imperial look and lofty sobriety.

"I am sorry to say, young woman, that our son, Itse, has joined our ancestors," the king said.

Cindy froze. She had heard that phrase from Itse before. But never did she think she would hear it in reference to him. Jim understood the phrase but not Tara.

Tara put her arms around Cindy and the young woman collapsed in tears. Her tears infected Tara. The village Chiefs and king watched, not knowing what to say. Jim's face fell.

In a tremulous voice, Cindy asked what had killed Itse and the king told her. She wanted to know when and whether he had been buried. She wondered why he did not let her know of his condition. She could have done something to help, to save him. She was told of the conditions that surrounded his death; the attack and coma.

She asked again where he was buried and the Chiefs told her. She wanted to go there. He had been buried in his sitting room.

Once they walked out of the palace portal, they saw several people in clusters looking at them and talking in hushed tones. The white people wondered what was going on with the crowd. Tara was now too frightened to gather her thoughts together. Cindy's tentative steps embarrassed her but she could not help it.

The sitting room had changed. The furniture had been dumped in the bedroom to make room for the young men who dug a grave in the concrete floor. Itse was buried but the floor was covered with sand. The borderland between concrete and sand was hard to see. The villagers did not have, as yet, the resources to buy cement to make concrete with which to seal the floor. The room was a little moist and dark and the window had to be flung open before they could see. The first thing that struck Itse's fiancée was his picture on the wall. It was an old picture, evidently taken before his American sojourn. She stared at it almost as though unaware of anyone else in the room. This was the Itse of the vivacious face. He looked darker and leaner and sweetly naïve, she thought. She wanted to touch the face on the picture. That was when she was torn out of her reverie. Even at that, her face lit up with a nervous smile as she ran her fingers over the picture. She shivered at the sight. Then she turned to everybody. She did not need anyone to tell her Itse was buried in that place. She knelt on the grave but said nothing. Tears just wet her face and she ran hands on the sand as though it had a corporeal quality. This lasted for about fifteen minutes. Most of the Chiefs were outside. The three visitors and two Chiefs were in the house. Once they left Itse's house, Tara did not know how to face the possibility of her nephew's death and having to take his remains home. That was not why she had come; although that was the fear that she could not admit to herself. She hoped that it never happened.

Suddenly, they heard excited voices around them and saw the villagers looking in one direction. The young men who carried both Tim and Alero showed signs of exhaustion as they walked back to the village. No less tired was the veteran. The villagers stirred with murmurs; there were no clear tears and no celebrations. A curtain of wonder was drawn over their faces to compound the eternal presence of the fog.

They milled around the couple as they were taken to the veteran's house. Were they dead? What had happened to them? What was all that blood about? How long had they been like that before the rescue team found them? So, the gods still pounced on them in spite of the charms of the chief priests? Wasn't there a limit to the mortal powers of an intercessor? Were they not warned of the consequences? What would happen next? If this white man died, what would become of the village? Was it a coincidence that the white people arrived just when the tragedy struck? Why didn't they come earlier to avert the trip?

They also wondered what the ex-soldier had on his shoulder. The weight of Alero's mother's remains seemed destined to shatter his shoulders but he declined the offers of the villagers to rid him of his burden. Some wondered if he carried the remains of the beast that attacked the couple. Was he holding on to it because it was a sacred animal? If it was, why was he taking it to his home?

"Hello," said Tara to the veteran, trying to mask her anxiety.

"Good afternoon, that sort of thing," he replied through his tired voice and motioned them to follow him to his house. Just then he saw the van that the Americans had brought.

"Let's use your vehicle to take the children to the hospital immediately," he said to Tara, who was just about to say the same thing. The young men took the wounded couple to the van. Meanwhile, Tara, Cindy and Jim had looked at the two of them and showed a little self-control, which impressed the villagers. They expected the Americans to burst into rage. The villagers still expected that to happen. If it was not rage, they expected the visitors to burst into something. Into tears. Or both.

Two of the young men accompanied the couple, Jim, Cindy and Tara to the local private hospital just outside Orogun. The veteran remained behind and latched onto the bones of evidence and the sixth toes. Tara collapsed into sobs. Tim and Alero stirred and they opened eyes and stared at them, they opened their mouths to speak but no sounds came out.

There was, however, on both faces a curious ease, as if they were not aware that they were on the brink of oblivion. Tim's face, which always had a languor, seemed innocent of all human worries. It took barely half an hour to reach the hospital, it was the same hospital Itse's doctor worked at. But he was not on duty as were the other doctors. So, the nursing staff took the couple to the emergency room and began treatment while they placed an urgent request for one of the doctors to come in.

Cindy asked if they had been bleeding a lot. One of the young men that came along with them nodded without looking at her.

"Let's wait for the doctor," the head nurse said coming out of the emergency room. "I think they are in a stable condition right now. But they still can't talk."

Jim was amazed at the strange languor on the young man's face; he seemed more at peace than anyone he had ever seen. The last time he had seen him, he had had an easy languor, which translated into the most perturbed visage on earth. Now, the turmoil had dissolved into the peace of God. Moments later, the nurse asked Jim and Tara to leave, as they had fallen asleep again and reassured them that the worst was possibly over.

A little relieved, the three Americans headed back to the village. They wanted to see the old man. They wanted to know the story behind the accident, and the right person to meet was the old man. Jim was also impressed by his English. He seemed more articulate than any person they had met in the village.

"What kind of weather do they have there with all the fog and clouds?" remarked Tara, who was fascinated with the setting, although she did not have enough presence of mind. Inside, her heart was about to rip open. She found anchor in Jim's grip on the moment. Jim was not related to Tim. He was considered the family adversary by a good number of the Foresters, Tim included, who thought he had no business pursuing the subject of his book. The only person who accommodated him was Tara.

Tara knew that the day's events enriched the narrative of his book and Jim could not be too emotional or the nuances would be lost on him.

"The old man must be very interested to have followed them to the forest," remarked Jim.

"That's why I would like to speak with him."

What amazed her most of all was that Tim might have been cosy with this African woman. The Tim, she knew, would not to yield to such tangles. What really happened? Or was her imagination a little over excited?

Jim had come to know Tim, as he pursued the project and he also wondered what was going on. It was, however, a subject which neither of them felt comfortable talking about at the time.

When Jim and Tara arrived in the village, the buzz of people had subsided. Tara imagined that the villagers had gone about their businesses. She was fascinated by children frolicking half naked in the sand; some chased hens and cocks with dust-laden feet; some loosed themselves in chants and dances. One or two displayed poise and just watched their mates as they exuded visceral peace. Bare feet, nimble birds, skimpy clothes, feisty waists, throaty rhythms, flying sand, presiding fog. Whatever she saw or heard were like sequences of a Hollywood movie, without the flawed hands of a director.

Their return seemed to have caught the attention of the villagers as the grown-ups began to look out through the window. Tara asked the driver to drive straight to the house of the old man, which he did not know. The driver stopped the car to ask a young man where the old man that went to the forest lived. Tara noticed that the young man's eyes focused on the three of them as he gave directions to the driver.

Once the car pulled up in front of the veteran's house, two of the elders they had met earlier opened the door and walked away, acting as though they did not see the van or the people inside.

"Are they mad at something," asked Jim. Tara remarked that she hoped it had no negative meaning for Tim or their coming. The door was left open by the two men, so the Americans were a little uncomfortable going right in. But as they stepped up to the doorway, they heard moans and the voice of the same person talking as though he was swearing. Tara was careful not to misunderstand what was going on. Cindy was still distracted. She had been distracted since she heard of Itse's passing. Jim stepped forward and saw the old man. The old man saw them and quickly asked them to come in.

"How are my children, that sort of thing," he asked, his tearful face quite a contrast to the glow in his eyes and the bounce of energy in his ancient skin.

Jim saw the man's pictures on the wall and knew this man had some military pedigree. He confirmed that with the epaulettes hung in another part of the room.

"Are you the war hero?" Cindy asked.

The veteran was surprised.

"I fought in the war but I don't call myself a hero. Itse must have told you about me," he said.

Cindy said nothing, but the epaulettes reminded her of the impressive old man Itse had told her about.

"Itse told me about you. He said only good things about you. I am sorry about what happened. He was like a son to me," the veteran said.

Cindy was relieved to hear somebody say something about Itse. She was also pleasantly surprised that the veteran knew about her. In the same way, Tara would not live down the veteran's reference to the couple as children. She understood that he may have bonded with them. Was the girl his daughter or grand-daughter?

"They are sleeping," she said. "No doctors were there but the nurses assured us they'll be okay."

He was quiet for a moment and the two visitors wondered as he looked at them straight in the eye. They saw both menace and a cry for help.

"You see," he said, clearing his throat. "This is the happiest day of my life, that sort of thing. Tomorrow will be even happier. You see the elders of this town, including those men that just left here? They are scared to death. I hold all their secrets in my hand."

The visitors had no clue what he was talking about. He was not ready to belabour the details of the story of Alero's mother or the romance between Alero and Tim and the amnesia. All he told them was that Tim had lost his memory and it was probably a good thing. Without that fact, the underbelly of the royal brass would not have been unearthed.

"For the first time in my life, this village is going to be free," he declared.

Tara would not yield to his reticence. She wanted details, at least about her nephew's condition. She had heard it from the king but there was a palpable barrier between her and the elders that made probing a little uncomfortable, although she planned to ask questions in the long run. She wanted to know how much he had forgotten and how it affected the way he acquitted himself.

"I can't answer that. He forgot, that sort of thing."

He paused and stared hard at her, which made her blink.

"Are you afraid he will forget you?" he asked.

"I don't know. I hope not."

Jim cut in and asked him what he meant by the village being free. The veteran said it was a long story, and they should not bother about it. It was his battle and they were foreigners.

"If Tim was involved in the story, why shouldn't we? It seems to me the story affects us," remarked Jim.

The veteran thought quietly for a while; his mind was in a whirl and no course of action was, as yet, cast in stone, so he was open to suggestion. He thought that he would need the outside world to know the story anyway and spreading the information abroad would only help to expose the leadership as being at the sewer, where it had been forever. Only nobody saw it. He suddenly felt compelled to tell the story, tracing the origin of the discrimination against Alero's family. What stuck Jim was a cursory reference to Queen Oyowa, as one of the slaves caught and transported to the Americas.

"So, she was a queen. That figures," remarked Jim. The veteran and the two American women were surprised by his comment.

"She is one of the characters that fascinated me in my research," he said.

"What research?" asked the old man.

"I am writing a book on Tim's family and I went way back to the plantation days, and Princess Oyowa was actually one of the Forester slaves." Both listeners were quiet.

"She carried her charisma with her to the plantation and the other slaves bowed to her and treated her like royalty when the slave masters were not around. She was a very young queen when she was captured. One of the Foresters took a special interest in her and she eventually was removed from the rigours of the plantation and became a domestic in the big family mansion. She got pregnant for one of the Foresters but it was concealed. The baby grew up and looked very white.

His name was David. He was made to marry into the family through a cousin." He paused.

"What have you just said?" asked the veteran.

"I am saying I just cleared a fog of over a century."

The women got it. So did the veteran.

"This is interesting," said the veteran. "There was a reason he came here. Now we know it. He came here to unloose a knot of history."

"History has come home to roost," said Tara.

No word stirred the quiet evening air for as long as one minute. Tara and Cindy grew curious. How did the village come to discriminate against the royal family?

The veteran provided the explanation: "Once slavery ended and trade in other items replaced it, they cast the family as the champions of human trafficking because one of the men of the family traded in it with as much fervour as anyone. He did not want the trade to end. Neither did most of the chieftains in this village. After all, they sacked Alero's village because it stood against the institution. Other villages and even some of the white missionaries wanted to boycott Orogun from any commercial activity. So, they picked out a man who was called Ofori and branded him as a leader of a family of slave dealers. They needed to tar that family to save the face of the village. The others in the family never interacted with Ofori who almost traded away one of them in the heated days of slave raids. The family was gradually ostracised. Stigmas turned into myths and legends; over decades and now centuries, the village has found a convenient carrier of their burdens. Tim's family must be very important in the U.S., or why are you doing a research on it? Is the family paying you to do it?"

"It's a long story," said Jim. "But suffice it to say, his father was a prominent politician and statesman and that prompted a look at some of the highlights of the family history, which stretches back in time to the plantation era and back here in Africa."

They had been there for a little over an hour and the evening shadows were drifting through the immutable fog. The Americans had to travel back to their hotel rooms in Warri, about a couple of hours away. But not before the veteran told them about Alero's mother and the sixth toe.

"That's her unmistakable signature," he said after telling them that the elders wanted to see the remains. He would not show the bones to them and their noses were out of joint in desperation.

"Whoever ate the forbidden fruit has to come forward and Alero's family has to be set free from the bondage of ages," said the veteran.

"How's this going to happen?" asked Cindy.

"I don't know yet. My mind is a little confused. It's like a pinned-down soldier who just discovered the enemy army's weak point and is careful not to blow it," he said. "I am fighting against spiritual wickedness in high places."

He let the visitors know that he had no weapons, except the guilt of a hundred years, while admitting that it lacked the finality of a bazooka.

"It's all I have. It's all I will use."

chapter Thirty

After the Americans left for the night, the veteran contemplated what he would do the next day. He wanted to go and see the couple in the hospital, but he knew he had to latch onto the bones of Alero's mother. The elders already knew he had them. And they wanted him to hand the bones over to them.

He teased them that it was not right for him to violate the Chiefs with the remains of abomination, promising that he would handle them himself without fuss or stir. He would bury them in Alero's compound once the daughter returned from her sick bed. The elders were not satisfied, but both parties parted on the perfidy of words.

He was fascinated with the Americans. He thought these were good ones, or looked like good ones. He thought there was just mutual respect between the man and woman. The man was more careful about phrasing his reason for writing the book and his face twitched a little when he had asked him if the Forester family were paying him to do the book. He believed once Tim came to, he would get to the bottom of it. If their answer to his questions about the book was on the sly, Tim should be able to help unveil the truth. If, that is, he regained his memory. He thought if his family did not help retrieve his past, then any prayer was like a bird without wings.

He also wanted to ask why they, and not either of his parents, came and why the only reference to his father was in the past tense. So, they were deceased? Or was it just the father? He was a little too distracted by all that was going on to ask enough questions. Tim had become part of him and he was becoming so curious about the young man with the partial attachment of an uncle.

After the toil and drain of the day, the old man knew that rest was of the essence. He did not have the bounce and resilience of his soldierly days and to collapse was the worst thing he could do to the cause he considered a hair's breadth from fruition. Two people were adequate for the hospital. Three, if he added Itse. He was the last latch holding the unfolding tale, he told himself.

It was now dark and he needed to eat the two ripe plantains his wife had roasted while he was with the Americans. It was as delicious as only a labouring man could attest to. He told himself it was no credit to his wife's artistry but merely to his taste buds, which were about the only parts of him that could boast quickness and life at that point.

It took him longer than necessary to finish the meal. He then shuffled to the kitchen and reached for the key to one of the cupboards he had built there for special quarries in his hunting days. Although he still made for the bush for prey, it was only on occasion. The key was on the kitchen-door lintel inside a disused and tinted aspirin bottle.

The bag was still inside the cupboard, he reassured himself as he unlocked the cupboard door to see for himself. It had a certain smell; not the stench of decay or rottenness, but a stench all the same. It was, however, a smell that did not nauseate. It jarred a sterile memory. It made him want to recall how she smelled when she was the belle of the region, when her perfume wafted through the world around her. That was what rankled him at that moment. He could not recall that particular scent. If he could, it would offer a clear and present danger to the smell oozing out of her bones.

The smell notwithstanding, he loved having the bones with him. It was like taking a bitter pill for a nagging illness. He did not sense the bitterness. He saw the restorative, he told himself. He tried to lock up the bag of bones when it occurred to him that it would make sense to sleep close to the bones, so as to invoke and enjoy the favour of her spirit. She may endow him with wisdom to pursue this mission. He had not decided yet what to do the next day. He knew he wanted the villagers to hear that the woman's bones were indeed hers, and show them the sixth toe, and let the whole world come in and see a whole generation of hypocrisy lie belly up.

He also thought her spirit would not appreciate her being slid into a dark place for dead animals, as if she were some meal in the making. So, the veteran pulled the bag, now too heavy for him to lift, on the floor to his bedroom. He did not put it on his bed, settling for the right hand side of where he lay, away from the window. He lay on his bed, not even undressing. Before he lapsed, he thought of near intimate moments in the past with this woman, his secret fascination with the person who was now only bones. No one knew of this except him and the spirit that breathed in the skull and scapulars now rattling in the bag. She was so beautiful, he said to himself. But she was afraid of him. That day in the forest when he had hugged her was like the beginning of a glow. They extinguished her and also what would have been the love of his life. The bones hit his nose with a whiff of smell, and it awakened curious images of Alero's mother beside the stream bending over to pick up a pail of water. He recalled the woman looking straight into his eyes when she stood up and noticed the unapologetic leer in his eyes. The veteran winced at first at being caught but then he was defiant, which he demonstrated with a boyish wink. The woman seemed to scowl back; although he swore he saw an impish glow peeping out of her face.

His wife was not home that night. She said she wanted to be with her mother, who had been sick for a couple of days. His exhausted body did not give him much time to contemplate more before he dozed off.

Less than two hours later, his body stirred to what sounded like a shriek. When he opened his eyes, he was not sure whether he had imagined the sound or not. His eyes shut again and opened a moment later. They reacted to the light from the lantern which he had forgot to put out. Just as he decided to shut his eyes again, his vision corrected itself and he saw two human shadows flit past the front of his closed door, across to his kitchen. His heart surged with fear and defiance.

His first impulse was to reach for his rifle. It was always cocked to fire. He wanted to yell at first, then he restrained himself and lay in a recumbent pose facing the door with the pointed gun. He heard two cracking sounds and simultaneously saw a body reach towards the door, shadow first. The shadow that emerged looked like a weapon, so he fired a shot and a body went down with a thud. The gun blast pierced through the night and set off an assortment of cries and screams and shouts of wonder all around.

The other person ran away and the victim of the shot was in deep pain, writhing and pleading to be allowed to live. The bullet had hit him in the left thigh.

chapter Thirty-One

Once the first light of day broke, the Americans made for the hospital to see the couple. The hospital was privately owned and had a limited number of patients and the Americans were told that this was an elite hospital even if they thought that it appeared pretty low-brow by their standards. Their son was getting the best treatment in the circumstances. The Americans gleaned these facts from the taxi driver who had become at once a chatterbox and mine of information. The puzzle, though, was how to winnow substance from his prattle.

The hospital staff was on hand to meet the Americans, who were getting used to being stared at by virtually everyone.

"Good morning," said a man in a white coat.

The Americans returned the courtesy and tried to walk on, when the man continued.

"My name is Doctor Kelly. I am the one handling the patients you are here to see."

"Oh, how are they?" asked Tara as the doctor motioned them to follow him to a nearby room in the hallway, which turned out to be his office. The office was compact, with a small bed by the wall and two chairs that smelt of disinfectant.

"It's nice to have you here," the doctor said, adding that one of his professors in medical school was an American, a Professor Kyle Macatee. That was over a decade ago, he said. He learned the man had passed away from some kind of degenerative disease.

Jim asked if there was any such disease in his hospital, which was a back route to making the doctor address why they were there. Tara cast a baleful glance at her fellow countryman. Her eyes narrowed into a squint. Her face looked like a prelude to a storm. He did not seem bothered by her objection to the humour but respected her feelings. Although this happened in a fleeting moment, it did not escape the doctor's attention, who might have missed the sarcastic sting. But the woman's body language was so explicit. The doctor thought that must be an American brand of humour. Cindy looked on quietly.

"Their condition suddenly relapsed. Both their conditions changed within about two hours of each other. I trust that they are going to make it. We are going to do our best. Both of them sustained serious injuries. Tim in his thorax, and Alero around her liver. The good news, though, is that they are young and healing can happen quickly enough if we get the right treatment. They can also manage to communicate through the condition," he explained.

"Can we see them," asked Tara.

"Yes," agreed the doctor.

All three rose to their feet and proceeded to the couple's hospital room.

"Aunt Tara," Tim said with a smile and a weak voice, which was full of joy. "I can remember everything now. Everything. I know they might have told you I lost my memory. That's history. Everything came to me as I woke up this morning." The boyish glee infected even the nurses. Aunt Tara walked straight to him on his bed and tried to hug his weak body as she quaked and shed tears.

"Mr. Fallows," he said when his aunt disengaged from him. "It's good to see you. Thank you for coming here."

"I'm glad you are very cheerful, Tim," said Jim, who was forcing himself to be genial to a man who would not walk with him on their last encounter.

Tim turned to his left, and asked all of them to meet his wife. It was a shock to his aunt, who did not know that they were married. No one, not even the veteran, had mentioned that, she thought.

She walked over to Alero, who was also weak, although she thought the black lady had a face full of peace.

"You're so pretty," she said, trying to disguise her surprise. Alero appreciated the comment with a nod. Cindy who had heard much about her smiled at her.

"My name is Cindy," and Alero smiled back knowingly, and Cindy did not feel it necessary to say more. Itse had told her about Cindy.

"You are a really attractive woman," Cindy said. Alero's face broke into a smile. But more than anything else, she was just happy she could see a member of Tim's family. Jim introduced himself and Alero immediately smiled and said Tim had told her about him.

Tim then turned to Tara. "I know you're baffled, Aunt Tara, about the wife thing. We are not married formally but I've asked the hospital staff to organise a priest for us. The doctor has told us what he already told you. We have a good chance. We have a lot to live for. But we have two major things to do first: Get married and ensure that Alero's mother's remains are buried with dignity. We hope the whole world will hear about it."

Jim had questions that he thought the young man should answer. He began by saying that he had some things Tim should know about. Before he could begin, Tim gave his blessing with regards to the book.

"Before you leave Africa," suggested Tim, "try and see where my great, great, great grandfather was buried. It was awesome what he meant to this place and I'm proud of him."

In spite of his weak, often tremulous voice, he was determined to talk. Tara's face was dry but mournful. The doctor tried to persuade him to put off any conversations till later, but the patient would not.

"I'm glad I came and had this experience. I'm now healed. I told her, my wife, everything."

Tim referred to how his father, one of the major senators in the United States, had unconsciously made him hate other people, especially blacks because of the positions he took in the United States Congress.

Although his father's position had mellowed before his death and his public speeches had become conciliatory, he had not known how his father's bigoted years in the rough-and-tumble of law-making had affected him growing up until Jim Fallows tried to dig up the family history and how the great senator may have descended from a black slave who had had a liaison with one of the masters.

"I came here to find a way to prove him wrong. Or, if I couldn't, I thought I could find a story in Peter Forester's life here to dilute whatever the book said. I thought it would be hard for me to live with the sense that I had black blood in me. But it's all good. I actually came here to find my blind spot and that's the woman on the other bed. My vision was severely poor and prone to accidents. If any swastikas had dissolved in my blood, they have already has lost their fangs. The negro blood in me must have seen to that any way. More than anything else, it has ennobled me," Tim said, noticing that Jim wanted eagerly to chip in.

"The point exactly," Jim began, "our research shows that the line of the Foresters your father comes from does not really have negro blood."

He paused and a silence fell in the room. Jim reeled out a delicate yarn of the Forester family tree. All listened with awe until it almost veered into pedantic display. Tim, however, loved it like a little child titillated by a bedside story. Jim, however, recoiled from continuing his story after observing his telling was losing taste with his audience. It wounded his spirit.

"I won't say your trip was in vain," Jim said, facing Tim. His voice dropped a few decibels and lacked the triumphal tone of the raconteur of the family tree. "We use illusions to help us kill our demons. Lies are not always bad for us if they propel us to the right place."

Tara was surprised and wondered why he had not told her, knowing full well that she was the only one in the family who had cooperated with him on the project.

"I'm sorry. I just wanted to be in control of the information," said Jim.

"You're right," said Tim, not referring to Jim's reply to his aunt but his research findings. "That news now has value not for me but for your project. I am now at peace with myself and my God. Except one thing, though. Have they executed Terrell Washington yet?"

"No," said Jim. "That will not happen until another month.

"Why?"

"Remember I had said I was not sure if he killed the cop? Well, I need to save his life. I know he didn't kill the cop. He was an onlooker, like myself, during the drug raid. He was just too naïve to leave. He ran when the other cops asked him to stop. Withdrawing my former statement in court and issuing a new one in his defence should lead to his release. I don't have the strength to write but put it on tape and the witnesses of all of you here will validate it and could change things for him. I look forward to meeting him and making peace with him."

"We'll get you a tape recorder. I have one at home," remarked one of the nurses. Quietly, Alero and Tara noticed a spark in Tim's vault of recall and they hoped it was a sign of the past to come.

Just before they left, Tara asked him to tell both Tim and Alero what he had told the veteran about Alero's slave-ancestor who gave birth to a Forester. The story sent a chill through Alero's bones and tears rolled down her cheeks. Tim didn't shed tears, but his face fell.

Tara walked to Alero's bed, leaned over her and said, "My long lost cousin," in between tears. The distance between her lips and eyes and Alero's cancelled the chasm of centuries - centuries of race, doubt and fear that burned between them.

"Please," remarked an emboldened Alero. "It's important that we know what's going on in the village as regards my mother's remains. And how the village is taking it."

"We'll be back this evening to tell you the full story. That's why the veteran is not here. He's taking care of business," said Jim, who was especially happy.

Tim had woken up that morning to his memory, but his excitement almost caused a stir in the hospital as he tried to cut off the IV lines connected to him. He woke Alero, who just looked at him with wondering eyes. He thought she did not believe him. So, he put together a narrative of his life and how he had met Itse through an Internet website when he was searching for who knew where the obscure village of Orogun was in Africa. And Itse responded through another friend. He clarified the hazy memory about the neighbour who couldn't play basketball anymore. He was his childhood friend who was black and both his own parents and the boy's parents had not agreed on something and that cost them their friendship. His parents did not say what the rift was about.

His parents died barely two years ago when their private aircraft crashed. The autopsy said his father had lost control after a heart attack. That was one of the reasons he hated other people, he said. The doctor that gave his father a clean bill of health to fly was black. He had filled in for his regular doctor, who was on vacation in Europe.

Alero was pleased, but she was more terrified than optimistic at the speed and clarity of his recall.

Chapter Thirty-Two

The gunshot extinguished anybody's chances of sleeping that night. While the veteran was trying to identify the intruder, most of the villagers had gathered in front of his house. Most of the villagers thought he had shot his wife. They thought the assailant, who was seen streaking through the night by a few people, dropped the tragedy on that rustic night.

The crowd buzzed that the young woman was too pretty to live with the old man and this was bound to happen someday. Beneath the buzz was a distinct knowledge: the delicate tint of her black skin, the arcs of her waistline over her throbbing buttocks as well as the wild curiosity of her eyes. These easily drew and entrapped the red-blooded vigour and cravings of Orogun youths. She was not Alero but she was a "compass of desire," to translate what a young man called her from a crowd just a few months earlier. No one identified the lusty tongue.

"Why did he sneak into a soldier's den?" remarked somebody in the crowd. "Now the poor woman has paid with her life."

"How do you know she's dead?" asked another one.

"Well," remarked an old woman. "That is not the question. Once you are married, you are married. These boys don't know that.

They just keep daring with that foolish thing between their legs."

As the crowd focused on the discussion, Chief Tietie materialised with two others and everybody yielded room for them to walk through to the man's home. Just as they stepped on his porch, the veteran opened his door with a lantern in his hand, as he kicked the intruder out. He dropped the lantern so it could illuminate the sitting room where his quarry lay. He picked up his gun again.

The young man kept muttering, "Please don't let me die. Please don't shoot me."

"Tell me what you came here for," he asked, as the crowd was surprised to see the intruder, instead of the veteran's wife. His wife brought up the rear.

"What did you come here for," asked Tietie. A hush descended on the village.

"We came to meet Lola," he said, "And he caught us. John Bull ran away." The crowd hissed and sighed. But the veteran's wife yelled, "Liar, liar. They came to steal the bones of Alero's mother," and she collapsed into sobs.

"What bones?" asked the crowd.

Tietie cut in and asked the crowd to go and the matter would be settled.

"No," said the veteran. "Let's settle it here. Let me tell you all today," he continued facing the crowd in the dark. A flash of lightning slashed through the night revealing dozens of heads.

"When I got to the bush yesterday, I uncovered the remains of Alero's mother, Ovie. I was not alone. All the young men that followed me saw the bones."

"How can you prove it? How come the crocodile turned up in the bush in human bones?" Tietie asked.

Not the walking stick, his hat with its colourful feather, nor his light blue lace top gave him his swagger that night. His shoulders sagged while he tried to assert authority and he gave off a ruffled and awkward dignity. So embarrassed was he that he wanted the crowd not to pay attention and that the elders would handle the matter. One voice responded with a roar, "Why did the boys not say anything about it?"

"Ask John Bull who ran away. He was one of those who went with us."

Someone in the crowd wondered if John Bull could recognise a woman who died when he was barely one year old. Someone else countered with a note of sarcasm: "I'm sure John Bull knew of the sixth toe, too." The crowd responded with a biting laughter. The veteran sent a chill into the night by replying that, if they wanted to see her remains, he would show them with the sixth toe.

Thunder roared in the distance. Tietie would not say anything after that. He tried to strike a respectable pose but his hand trembled on his walking stick. His stoop defied his attempt to maintain a regal carriage.

The crowd was fascinated and hung on the old man's every word.

"Look," said the veteran. "I plead with you all to wait here and I will go in and bring the bones and everyone can stand in line while I put Ovie's remains on this porch with the sixth toe. You all can take turns to see it. If you don't believe it, after you see it, then there is one thing we can do. The white man has a machine that can show who a person is long after death. I am prepared to go that way. We know they are around and they can go away with parts of the bones for testing. The truth must be told. Ovie was not a crocodile. She was a human being, just like you and me. How she ended up in the forest and was buried is yet to be known. If you wondered why

Alero wanted to follow the white man to the forest, it was because she already knew how her mother got there. A lot of people know a lot of things in this village, but they will not say anything for fear of fouling the air."

An old man in the crowd was not impressed with his speech and asked him to bring the bag of bones and show them the sixth toe. The crowd said nothing, as another roar of thunder followed a flash of lightning.

"I will bring the bag out right now," said the veteran, with a note of defiance.

"Wait, Papa," said a young voice. "I was one of the men that went to the forest yesterday. We saw the white man and Alero and we also saw the half grave where her mother's bones lay. I saw the sixth toe. That man is not lying. When we arrived, one of the elders quickly called us and said we should not say a word of what we saw to anybody. He said the elders would handle the matter peacefully. But I just can't keep quiet any more. I am sure John Bull and Toritse came to steal the bones. They should confess."

There was at first silence, followed by a sustained murmur. One by one, the people started to disperse. No one asked any questions. No one insisted on anything. They just left. Everybody seemed to know what to think but they did not know what to say and to whom to say it. Words can be very heavy, especially when they are words you have not said before and ideas you had only contemplated as abomination.

They were struck by the young man's boldness. Omatsola was only seventeen and he was taking destiny in his hands. The crowd did not think it necessary to ask if the wounded man was lying. As they said in the village, you don't see lightning and hear thunder roar and ask why the heavens did not show you signs of the coming rain.

chapter Thirty-Three

When the Americans entered the village that morning, it was not the decline of the fog that struck them most, but the various straggles of people with "eyes full of shadows," as Tara described them. She also remarked that the people were "quiet," a thing she thought was out of character. If anything, the Orogun people were a buzz of happy people whose tongues rolled with Itsekiri phrases and pidgin English for as long as 'God supplied oxygen to the living.'

The driver knew there was something strange about the atmosphere of reticence and offered to stop and ask one of the villagers and the Americans had no objections.

"*One man kill his self dis morning,*" announced the driver to the visitors, after inquiring from a group of murmuring boys. Cindy, Tara and Jim said nothing for a second and hoped the driver would put flesh to the skeleton of the story the bystanders had just told him. But he did not say more than that. Tara was agitated for a second and wondered whether the veteran had not been killed and that it have been made to look like suicide. "So, how's the veteran," Tara asked uneasily.

"*We go reach him house soon.*"

As they drove through the village, everyone cast eyes on them and Tara did not think it a good sign. The air seemed light and light was gorging up the fog quickly and bringing a climatic normality to a village that had seemed foreign to the sun.

When they reached the veteran's home, the old man sat on his porch with a few boys. Tara sighed and wondered a second later whether the recent death was not a ploy to inflict the already tangled tale with another puzzle. The veteran, she told herself, would clear the air.

Once the veteran saw the car approach, he stood and put his arm around the shoulders of one of the young men. His eyes had a shadow and vigour and he was eager to meet with the white people who had come to see him.

"Good morning," he said to Jim, who was the first to get out of the van. But Tara was the first to acknowledge the greeting. "So, why is there so much chill this morning," asked Jim, whose curiosity was as deep as that of his travelling companions.

"We just solved the riddle this morning," remarked the veteran. He dismissed the youth while he and the visitors went into his sitting room.

"Alero's father killed himself this morning. He sent some boys to steal the bones from my house but they failed."

The man's name was Atake and he was one of the influential Chiefs in the village who hardly said a word in public but inspired fear in most people around him.

"Did he confess?" asked Jim.

"Yes," said the veteran. "Not with his tongue but with his silence. The elders said he would be buried in an unmarked grave and the whole village would organise a special burial for Alero's mother. In that ceremony, the king will announce a plan to rebuild the home of Alero's family."

"I think Alero needs to know about this," remarked Tara.

"Yes," said the veteran. "That was the matter I was discussing with the young men. He presided over the carcass of lies in this village. His hands are full of blood. He has no right to build Alero's new home. It is a terrible absolution. He wants to mourn the person he slayed with his two hands. You cannot murder a person and be the funeral priest. His son should do it. It is only on that condition that I will hand over the bag of Alero's mother's bones to the palace. As it is presently constituted, the bones are purer than the palace."

"Does that not sound subversive? You want to provoke an insurrection?" asked Tara, with affectionate mischief. She seemed to enjoy the squint of defiance in the soldier's eyes.

"Not now. Alero and Tim will have to be well first," he replied in a deadpan tone.

"Don't you think you will be playing the God of the Old Testament...?" asked Tara with a roguish tint on her cheeks.

"No," he protested, without allowing her to complete her thought. "I don't believe in your Bible."

"I don't think Tara is a Bible-loving person," intervened Jim, who loved the tension between them. He had looked forward to seeing the old soldier in the raw.

"I grew up in a Christian household," Tara said when she won back the attention of both men, "what I wanted to say had nothing to do with whether I am Christian or not. I just saw a parallel. David in the Bible was forbidden to build a temple because he had dipped his hands in blood. He had killed too many people. So his son Solomon took charge to build the temple."

The veteran's spirit sparkled at the fortuitous boon of the coincidence between the two stories - that an Old Testament tale could help unspool the mysterious knot of an African crisis.

"You are a sharp girl," he said with a look of condescension, an attempt to conceal gratitude. But he knew the visitors saw through his superior airs, the thought that they knew made him a little uncomfortable. It however generated an understanding between them that many weeks of interaction could not pull off in many other relationships. It encouraged him to work with the visitors on his new scheme. He had to convince them, but it did not take too long before the Americans agreed to take the bag of bones in their car to a mortuary in an undisclosed hospital near Warri.

When they entered the palace, all the elders were there, their eyes ripe with regret. They expected the bag of bones to rattle beside the veteran. But he said he wanted to respect Alero's wish.

"She said she wanted to see her mother's bones go down. If it could wait for this long, why not a few days or months more?"

The elders, including the king, had nothing to say by way of objection. Chief Tietie broke the funereal silence. "Well, we only wanted to help." It was clear that they did not believe the veteran but they had no bulwark against the temerity of the warrior.

As they walked out of the building, the veteran remarked, "I have not seen the elders this quiet before in my life."

Just as they entered the car, a young man emerged from behind them and asked if they were going to the hospital that day, saying he would like to join them.

The veteran turned around and saw him. He was taken aback.

"When did you come here?" he asked. "You are never here."

"Yesterday," replied the young man. "I arrived yesterday."

The young man had an imperious bearing coupled with a certain polish and brash self-confidence.

"This is the prince," remarked the veteran to the Americans. "I have seen this fellow about four or five times in my life time. He is never here."

Tara and Jim looked at him and at the veteran but hid their astonishment behind poker faces.

The young man said he had heard about Alero's condition and also learned she and her man might not make it, so he would like to see her before it was all over.

"You are welcome," replied the veteran, "but these kids have too much spirit to cave in now. Believe me." There was silence.

The Americans knew that this young man's soul did not belong to the village, not to the village of the king and the people around him.

"Thank God," said the young man as they drove through the village. "The sun is finding its place above this village again."

He turned to Tara and asked, "I learned that Alero's man also had a life-transforming experience."

"Yes," she said, "Africa has purged his heart."

"From all I heard, he helped to purge ours, too," said the prince. "It seems everyone is born again."

The veteran cut in: "As they say, you can't clap with one hand." The irony was not lost on all around him.

They entered the hospital room. The patients did not have the strength to get up. The hospital slid their beds close to each other so they could hold hands.

"She is my blind spot," they heard Tim say as they entered the room. "My crocodile girl."

The two shed tears. When Alero's eyes met the prince's she just kept staring.

"What's going on?" asked Tara.

Silence dropped on the room. Tim wanted to know the story behind the absorbed look. How did they know each other and how had they met? She could not say anything. The prince who was unaffected by the anxiety of silence eventually broke the silence, and told everyone that he was Alero's high school mate, who had stalked her. Tim remembered the story.

"So why did you play hero and keep your identity hidden and why are you showing up now?" asked Tim.

"He's the prince," said Tara.

"And he's a great person," remarked the veteran.

Alero chipped in, "I looked for you to say thank you and you were gone."

"I'm sorry," said the prince. "I am here to make my peace with you. Somehow, I felt I was part of your misery and did not know in my teenage mind how to convey it."

"So, was that why you left the school?"

"I tried to escape from you. But one can't do that forever. At twenty-four, I feel strong enough to confront my fears."

"Alero," the veteran began after a brief silence. "A man killed himself this morning, and he was your father. His name was Atake. He let the king and the elders support him all these years. The king planned to rebuild your home and bury your mother in a special ceremony later tonight. But I said no. You will recover and see your favourite bones slide into silence."

Her eyes turned moist half way through the veteran's bulletin. It looked as if words were about tumbling out of her lips and at the same time as though her lips were frozen. Fever caught her eyes. Her cheeks radiated a mock glitter, pallor's shine.

"So, that's the man," she responded, almost like a stutter, fighting back tears. The face, formerly moist, now hosted a dam.

"He was always kind each time he saw me. I wondered why. Why didn't he tell me? Why didn't he tell me? I could have kept a secret."

"He also was a slave of an age-old tradition of prejudice," said the prince.

"Prejudice makes a coward of decent people," said the veteran. "I also want to say something. We have taken your mother's bones away until you leave this place, you and your man."

Alero's face broke into a furtive smile. "Yes, they are mama's bones."

Tim said with a feeble voice, "We have something to look forward to. It will be a big party."

The room fell silent, Tim and Alero had grown tired from the talk. The doctor came in and hinted that they had lost a lot of energy and needed rest.

Sobs answered sobs and the room succumbed to a fear of the unknown.

The doctor cautioned them.

"I am not pronouncing a death sentence here," he said solemnly, if his voice also betrayed certain impatience. We have ordered a few drugs that will keep them away from danger. Those who pray are encouraged to appeal to heaven. We cannot give up hope. The drugs have worked on some people. They have a good chance."

A vehicle had left a few hours earlier to the city of Benin. They hoped Zetics, a new set of antibiotics would arrest their drift and beckon their vitals back to life. But all the visitors had to leave, so IV could pump new vigour into the couple's veins while they rested.

Just before they left, a little girl was let into the room. Tuoyo had been at the hospital gate but denied entrance. She came the previous day, too. A nurse yielded out of compassion for the little girl whose father had just committed suicide. She was not just going to see Alero, unknown to her; she was paying a sibling visit. She did not know that Chief Atake, her father, had also sired Alero, her role model.

Once she entered, Alero and Tim spotted her. A whiplash paralysed Alero. It seemed to have flashed upward from her throat. Suddenly she felt tired and happy. She did not know it but Tuoyo and her were family more than they imagined. Tuoyo ran to Alero and held her hand. Tuoyo could not say anything. The couple was beginning to fade. There was only silence. But they all hoped it was not a deathly quiet but just a biological reprieve. The sedative in the IV was already lulling them to sleep.

They all left the room.

Tuoyo was quiet until the veteran, who held her hand, took her outside and she began to weep.

"She will be okay," said the veteran with a tremulous dignity in his voice. They left the hospital.

The doctor called out to them, his coat's lapel hanging lopsided to the left shoulder. "The vehicle will be here in less than an hour and we will have the medicine. With your prayers, something good may just happen." After those words, he rebounded to his sartorial sanity after adjusting the lapel.

No one knew for certain that Alero would be in good enough health to see her mother's bones rattle down to mother earth in final repose soon. But all the visitors and locals could not wait to see the couple walk into the crisp, fogless air of Orogun; into an Orogun where mothers stoked breakfast fires to the crackle of dawn, and lullabies and candle light tales embalmed every disappearing night.

When they were leaving, the prince called his cab driver. The car had returned to Warri after dropping him off in Orogun. Now back in Orogun, the prince did not need to hike a ride from anyone.

"Are you not sleeping here tonight?" inquired the veteran.

"No sir. In Warri," he said in the clinical tone of one who baulked at any further questions. The veteran understood and looked as a car drove up and the young man slid into the front seat. In the wake of the disappearing car's dust cloud that blended riotously with the ink of dusk, somebody suggested to the veteran that the young man wanted to avoid a palace ritual that night.

"He does that all the time," remarked a nurse who accompanied the visitors out of the hospital premises.

Tara then said, "Maybe he is the real author of mutiny."

They all walked into the gathering twilight, believing that a final silence had dropped over the exclamation mark in the tangled tale of over a century.

It was too early for such a confused clamour around his door-step. The veteran did not sleep on time the previous night. For his septuagenarian bones and muscles, he needed a few more restful hours. His silver hair entitled him to some silence. But the noise would not abate. Their words scratched the morning with anxiety but, for him, whatever it was should wait. His half-conscious state resisted the growing Babel.

He wanted to open his eyes, but his eyelids were leaden. So he yielded to his languor and turned away from the window, as though that would save him from the frenzy outside and rein in the violators of a serene morning.

Then he heard a phrase, "Why should any of them die?" The voice, masculine but chafed by doubt, seemed to project itself against an anonymous foe.

In the nervous quiet of his room, the veteran asked himself, "Who died?"

He hoped for his own peace it was one of the royals yielding to another suicidal impulse. Then he heard, "It is better that both of them died rather than what we have on our hands. Now, the one will bury the other."

His eyelids lightened, and his eyes opened to the ambiguous light of dawn.

Postscript

It did not take long for the old man, though groggy from the previous night, to reach the hospital. Ahead of a weary throng of funereal faces, he met the doctor at the entrance of the hospital. Flanked by two nurses, the doctor's white coat sat tortoise-shell like over his shoulder. His head and spindly neck craned out as though searching for air. He looked at the crowd with furrows on his forehead, his eyes with the look of exhaustion, like one who laboured all night.

A smile draped his lips as he asked the veteran, "Is anything the matter sir?"

"What happened to my children?" quizzed the old man, in a low, tremulous voice.

"They are in stable condition. I hope they will only get better," he said emphatically. Just as the veteran's lips uttered the first syllable of "but", Doctor Kelly's head, lolling between his lapels, suddenly stiffened, signalling he wanted to make an announcement. The veteran restrained himself.

"I had to wake up early and come all the way here because some people have been saying that Tim died …" said the physician.

Somebody in the crowd interrupted, "Alero was the one who died."

The doctor shook his head. Everyone else sighed. The veteran hissed.

"You can come in and see them. They will be glad to see you now sir," the doctor said, and the old man, his feet light from worry, followed the physician to the ward. Barely half an hour later, the old man walked out of the hospital like a sprightly tortoise, his spirit loose like beach sand.

The crowd saw his enthused face, and one of them yelled, "Ah, so it was all a rumour. Our people, our people!" A low murmur ensued as the crowd milled away.